高考实战训练丛书·英语系列

U0133764

语法与词汇

第二版
含2007年考题

本书编写组

紧扣 考题
真题 回顾
分类 训练
模拟 测试

华东理工大学出版社
EAST CHINA UNIVERSITY OF SCIENCE AND TECHNOLOGY PRESS

本书编写者:刘 弢 吕春昕 朱志玲 吕豪亮 丁妙媛 范引梅

图书在版编目(CIP)数据

语法与词汇/本书编写组 编. —2 版. 上海:
华东理工大学出版社,2005.12(2007.9 重印)
(高考实战训练丛书·英语系列)
ISBN 978 - 7 - 5628 - 1814 - 4

Ⅰ.语... Ⅱ.本... Ⅲ.①英语—语法—高中—
升学参考资料 ② 英语—词汇—高中—升学参考资料
Ⅳ.G634.413

中国版本图书馆 CIP 数据核字(2005)第 137716 号

高考实战训练丛书·英语系列

语法与词汇
(第二版)(含 2007 年考题)

本书编写组 编

策划编辑/郑斯雄
责任编辑/戎 炜
封面设计/王晓迪
责任校对/金慧娟
出版发行/华东理工大学出版社
    地　址/上海市梅陇路 130 号,200237
    电　话/(021)64250306(营销部)
    传　真/(021)64252707
    网　址/www.hdlgpress.com.cn

印　刷/上海展强印刷有限公司
开　本/787mm×1092mm 1/16
印　张/13
字　数/335 千字
版　次/2002 年 6 月第 1 版,2005 年 12 月第 2 版
印　次/2007 年 9 月第 3 次
印　数/44271-49290 册
书　号/ISBN 978 - 7 - 5628 - 1814 - 4/H·511
定　价/18.00 元

前　言

目前市场上的英语高考教辅用书多而又多，而真正出类拔萃的却少之又少。我们正是本着出好书、出精品、为广大应考学子和辅导教师服务的原则，认真编写了这套丛书。本套丛书的特点和优势体现在以下三个方面：

第一，容量得当，涵盖面广。高考英语总复习通常有所谓"三轮"之说：第一轮即单元过关，或称分册过关，即复习高一、高二两年的内容；第二轮即专项训练，包括听力、语法、阅读理解、完型填空和写作；第三轮综合复习即模拟训练。本次我们将陆续推出三轮复习的全部用书，涵盖高中英语的所有内容。考虑到教学的实际情况，本套丛书的总体训练量不超过400个课时，这样的安排，无论用于课堂集体测试或学生自测，都是非常适当的。

第二，体例完备，内容丰富。本套丛书试图从方方面面诠释高考。以"语法与词汇"分册为例，全书共分20章。前19章内容均为历届高考真题，高考题具有无可替代的标尺作用，演练这些题目，可以使学生从方方面面把握高考，而且可以感受"原汁原味"所带来的实战气氛。第20章为综合提高训练，该部分内容难度略高于高考。从2007年的语法与词汇试题来看，总体情况是难度保持平稳，没有出现偏难怪题，这对中学英语教学具有良好的导向作用。但从考查内容上看，仍然充分考虑了语言知识的覆盖面。此外，在考查形式上也出现了新面孔，比如广东省今年就没有采用单项填空这一形式，而是采用了全新的语段填空，这为长期不变的语法教学模式带来了一股春风。

第三，使用方便，经济实惠。本套丛书的绝大多数内容均设计为16开正反面2页一套题，学生可以将书展开，撕下一套题即可作为活页试卷使用。

本丛书在编写过程中，曾先作为内部试卷多次试用，受到了广大师生的欢迎，很多一线教师对本书提出了大量的宝贵意见，对我们最终修订成书起了关键作用。另外，华东理工大学出版社的郑斯雄先生也对本书的出版倾注了极大的关心和帮助，在此一并表示感谢！

编　者

2007.7

目　　录

第二十章　综合提高训练

第一章 冠 词

班级_____姓名_____分数_____

1. [**1999 全国**]

Paper money was in _____ use in China when Marco Polo visited the country in _____ thirteenth century.

A. the;/   B. the;the   C. /;the   D. /;/

2. [**2000 春季 北京/安徽**]

Summers in _____ south of France are for _____ most part dry and sunny.

A. /;a   B. the;/   C. /;/   D. the;the

3. [**2000 春季 上海**]

—Where's _____ nearest bookstore?

—There's one at _____ end of the street.

A. the;an   B. a;the   C. the;the   D. a;an

4. [**2000 全国**]

Most animals have little connection with _____ animals of _____ different kind unless they kill them for food.

A. the;a   B. /;a   C. the;the   D. /;the

5. [**2001 春季 北京/安徽/内蒙古**]

Mr Smith, there's a man at _____ front door who says he has _____ news for you of great importance.

A. the;/   B. the;the   C. /;/   D. /;the

6. [**2001 春季 上海**]

His daughter is always shy in _____ and she never dares to make a speech to _____.

A. the public;the public   B. public;the public

C. the public;public   D. public;public

7. [**2001 全国**]

The warmth of _____ sweater will of course be determined by the sort of _____ wool used.

A. the;the   B. the;/   C. /;the   D. /;/

8. [**2001 上海**]

A bullet hit the soldier and he was wounded in _____ leg.

A. a   B. one   C. the   D. his

9. [**2002 春季 北京/安徽/内蒙古**]

I don't like talking on _____ telephone; I prefer writing _____ letters.

A. a;the   B. the;/   C. the;the   D. a;/

10. [2002 春季 上海]

The cakes are delicious. He'd like to have _____ third one because _____ second one is rather too small.

A. a;a 　　　B. the;the 　　　C. a;the 　　　D. the;a

11. [2002 全国]

Jumping out of _____ airplane at ten thousand feet is quite _____ exciting experience.

A. /;the 　　　B. /;an 　　　C. an;an 　　　D. the;the

12. [2002 上海]

One way to understand thousands of new words is to gain _____ good knowledge of basic word formation.

A. / 　　　B. the 　　　C. a 　　　D. one

13. [2003 春季 安徽]

—Where is my blue shirt?

—It's in the washing machine. You have to wear _____ different one.

A. any 　　　B. the 　　　C. a 　　　D. other

14. [2003 春季 北京]

There's _____ dictionary on _____ desk by your side.

A. a;the 　　　B. a;a 　　　C. the;a 　　　D. the;the

15. [2003 春季 上海]

An accident happened at _____ crossroads a few metres away from _____ bank.

A. a;a 　　　B. /;a 　　　C. /;the 　　　D. the;/

16. [2003 全国]

The sign reads "In case of _____ fire,break the glass and push _____ red button. "

A. /;a 　　　B. /;the 　　　C. the;the 　　　D. a;a

17. [2003 上海]

I earn 10 dollars _____ hour as _____ supermarket cashier on Saturdays.

A. a;an 　　　B. the;a 　　　C. an;a 　　　D. an;the

18. [2004 春季 北京/安徽]

On _____ news today,there were _____ reports of heavy snow in that area.

A. the;the 　　　B. the;/ 　　　C. /;/ 　　　D. /;the

19. [2004 春季 上海]

As a rule,domestic servants doing odd jobs are paid _____.

A. by the hour 　　　B. by hour 　　　C. by an hour 　　　D. by hours

20. [2004 全国 I]

When you come here for your holiday next time,don't go to _____ hotel;I can find you _____ bed in my flat.

A. the;a 　　　B. the;/ 　　　C. a;the 　　　D. a;/

1. [2004 全国Ⅱ]

If you buy more than ten, they knock 20 pence off _____.

A. a price   B. price   C. the price   D. prices

2. [2004 全国Ⅳ]

—John, there is _____ Mr Wilson on the phone for you.

—I'm in _____ bath.

A. a;the   B. the;a   C. a;/   D. the;/

3. [2004 北京]

_____ on-going division between English-speaking Canadians and French-speaking Canadians is _____ major concern of the country.

A. The;/   B. The;a   C. An;the   D. An;/

4. [2004 天津]

When he left _____ college, he got a job as _____ reporter in a newspaper office.

A. /;a   B. /;the   C. a;the   D. the;the

5. [2004 重庆]

The most important thing about cotton in history is _____ part that it played in _____ Industrial Revolution.

A. /;/   B. the;/   C. the;the   D. a;the

6. [2004 辽宁]

When you finish reading the book, you will have _____ better understanding of _____ life.

A. a;the   B. the;a   C. /;the   D. a;/

7. [2004 江苏]

Tom owns _____ larger collection of _____ books than any other student in our class.

A. the;/   B. a;/   C. a;the   D. /;the

8. [2004 浙江]

The Wilsons live in _____ A-shaped house near the coast. It is _____ 17th century cottage.

A. the;/   B. an;the   C. /;the   D. an;a

9. [2004 福建]

It is _____ world of wonders, _____ world where anything can happen.

A. a;the   B. a;a   C. the;a   D. /;/

10. [2004 湖北]

There was _____ time _____ I hated to go to school.

A. a;that   B. a;when   C. the;that   D. the;when

11. [2004 湖南]

For a long time they walked without saying _____ word. Jim was the first to break _____ silence.

    A. the;a   B. a;the   C. a;/   D. the;/

12. [2004 广东]

While he was investigating ways to improve the telescope, Newton made _____ discovery which completely changed _____ man's understanding of colour.

    A. a;/   B. a;the   C. /;the   D. the;a

13. [2005 春季 北京]

_____ recent report stated that the number of Spanish speakers in the U. S. would be higher than the number of English speakers by _____ year 2090.

    A. A;the   B. A;/   C. The;/   D. The;a

14. [2005 全国Ⅲ]

If you go by _____ train, you can have quite a comfortable journey, but make sure you get _____ fast one.

    A. the;the   B. /;a   C. the;a   D. /;/

15. [2005 北京]

It is often said that _____ teachers have _____ very easy life.

    A. /;/   B. /;a   C. the;/   D. the;a

16. [2005 辽宁]

This book tells _____ life story of John Smith, who left _____ school and worked for a newspaper at the age of 16.

    A. the;the   B. a;the   C. the;/   D. a;/

17. [2005 山东]

I knew _____ John Lennon, but not _____ famous one.

    A. /;a   B. a;the   C. /;the   D. the;a

18. [2005 江苏]

On May 5, 2005, at _____ World Table Tennis Championship, Kong Linghui and Wang Hao won the gold medal in men's doubles with _____ score of 4∶1.

    A. a;a   B. /;the   C. a;/   D. the;a

19. [2005 浙江]

Mrs. Taylor has _____ 8-year-old daughter who has _____ gift for painting—she has won two national prizes.

    A. a;a   B. an;the   C. an;a   D. the;a

20. [2005 江西]

If you grow up in _____ large family, you are more likely to develop _____ ability to get on well with _____ others.

    A. /;an;the   B. a;the;/   C. the;an;the   D. a;the;the

1. [2005 安徽]

After dinner he gave Mr. Richardson _____ ride to _____ Capital Airport.

A. the;a   B. a;the   C. /;a   、D. /;the

2. [2005 湖南]

I can't remember when exactly the Robinsons left _____ city. I only remember it was _____ Monday.

A. the;the   B. a;the   C. a;a   D. the;a

3. [2006 全国Ⅰ]

I know you don't like _____ music very much. But what do you think of _____ music in the film we saw yesterday?

A. /;/   B. the;the   C. the;/   D. /;the

4. [2006 全国Ⅱ]

—Hello,could I speak to Mr. Smith?

—Sorry,wrong number. There isn't _____ Mr. Smith here.

A. /   B. a   C. the   D. one

5. [2006 北京]

—I knocked over my coffee cup. It went right over _____ keyboard.

—You shouldn't put drinks near _____ computer.

A. the;/   B. the;a   C. a;/   D. a;a

6. [2006 重庆]

Everywhere man has cut down _____ forests in order to grow crops,or to use _____ wood as fuel or as building material.

A. the;the   B. the;/   C. /;the   D. /;/

7. [2006 辽宁]

Of all _____ reasons for my decision to become a university professor,my father's advice was _____ most important one.

A. the;a   B. /;a   C. /;the   D. the;the

8. [2006 山东]

For him _____ stage is just _____ means of making a living.

A. a;a   B. the;a   C. the;the   D. a;the

9. [2006 浙江]

Don't worry if you can't come to _____ party—I'll save _____ cake for you.

A. the;some   B. a;much   C. the;any   D. a;little

10. [2006 湖南]

In _____ review of 44 studies,American researchers found that men and women who ate six key foods daily cut the risk of _____ heart disease by 76%.

    A. a;the   B. the;a   C. a;/   D. /;a

11. [2006 陕西]

According to _____ World Health Organization, health care plans are needed in all big cities to prevent _____ spread of AIDS.

    A. the;the   B. the;/   C. a;a   D. /;the

12. [2007 全国 II]

—Could you tell me the way to _____ Johnsons, please?

—Sorry, we don't have _____ Johnson here in the village.

    A. the;the   B. the;a   C. /;the   D. the;/

13. [2007 北京]

I looked under _____ bed and found _____ book lost last week.

    A. the;a   B. the;the   C. /;the   D. the;/

14. [2007 天津]

I wanted to catch _____ early train, but could't get _____ ride to the station.

    A. an;the   B. /;the   C. an;/   D. the;a

15. [2007 重庆]

George couldn't remember when he first met Mr Anderson, but he was sure it was _____ Sunday because everybody was at _____ church.

    A. /;the   B. the;/   C. a;/   D. /;a

16. [2007 辽宁]

Christmas is _____ special holiday when _____ whole family are supposed to get together.

    A. the;the   B. a;a   C. the;a   D. a;the

17. [2007 山东]

_____ walk is expected to last all day, so bring _____ packed lunch.

    A. A;a   B. The;/   C. The;a   D. A;/

18. [2007 江苏]

We have every reason to believe that _____ 2008 Beijing Olympic Games will be _____ success.

    A. /;a   B. the;/   C. the;a   D. a;a

19. [2007 浙江]

I like _____ color of your skirt. It is _____ good match for your blouse.

    A. a;the   B. a;a   C. the;a   D. the;the

20. [2007 江西]

Many people have come to realize that they should go on _____ balanced diet and make _____ room in their day for exercise.

    A. a;/   B. the;a   C. the;the   D. /;a

第二章　名词和数词

班级_____ 姓名_____ 分数_____

1. [1993 全国]

He dropped the _____ and broke it.

A. cup of coffee　　B. coffee's cup　　C. cup for coffee　　D. coffee cup

2. [1994 上海]

Mr. Smith _____ me to buy several _____ eggs for the dinner party.

A. asked；dozen

B. suggested；dozens of

C. had；dozen

D. persuaded；dozens

3. [1995 全国]

He gained his _____ by printing _____ of famous writers.

A. wealth；work　　B. wealths；works　　C. wealths；work　　D. wealth；works

4. [1998 上海]

—Who did you spend last weekend with?

—_____.

A. Palmer's　　B. The Palmers'　　C. The Palmers　　D. The Palmer's

5. [1998 上海]

Paper produced every year is _____ the world's production of vehicles.

A. the three times weight of

B. three times the weight of

C. as three times heavy as

D. three times as heavier as

6. [1999 上海]

It is not rare in _____ that people in _____ fifties are going to university for further education.

A. 90s；/　　B. the 90s；/　　C. 90s；their　　D. the 90s；their

7. [2001 春季 上海]

The _____ is just around the corner and you won't miss it.

A. bicycle's shop　　B. bicycle shop　　C. bicycles shop　　D. bicycles' shop

8. [2001 春季 上海]

_____ people in the world are sending information by E-mail every day.

A. Several million　　B. Many millions　　C. Several millions　　D. Many million

9. [2002 春季 上海]

Americans eat _____ vegetables per person today as they did in 1910.

A. more than twice

B. as twice as many

C. twice as many as

D. more than twice as many

10. [2003 春季 上海]

Many students signed up for the _____ race in the sports meeting to be held next week.

A. 800-metre-long
B. 800-metres-long
C. 800 metre length
D. 800 metres length

11. [2003 北京]

He did it _____ it took me.

A. one-third a time
B. one-third time
C. the one-third time
D. one-third the time

12. [2003 上海]

The house rent is expensive. I've got about half the space I had at home and I'm paying _____ here.

A. as three times much
B. as much three times
C. much as three times
D. three times as much

13. [2004 春季 上海]

The village is far away from here indeed. It's _____ walk.

A. a four hour
B. a four hour's
C. a four-hours
D. a four hours'

14. [2004 全国Ⅲ]

It is reported that the United States uses _____ energy as the whole of Europe.

A. as twice
B. twice much
C. twice much as
D. twice as much

15. [2004 重庆]

The husband gave his wife _____ every month in order to please her.

A. all half his income
B. his half all income
C. half his all income
D. all his half income

16. [2005 上海]

At a rough estimate, Nigeria is _____ Great Britain.

A. three times the size as
B. the size three times of
C. three times as the size of
D. three times the size of

17. [2005 福建]

—Would you like _____, sir?

—No, thanks, I have had much.

A. some more oranges
B. any more oranges
C. some more orange
D. any more orange

18. [2007 浙江]

It is reported that the floods have left about _____ people homeless.

A. two thousand
B. two-thousands
C. two thousands
D. two thousands of

第三章　代　词

班级_____姓名_____分数_____

1. [1996 全国]

—When shall we meet again?

—Make it _____ day you like; it's all the same to me.

A. one　　　　　B. any　　　　　C. another　　　　　D. some

2. [1996 全国]

Tom felt that he knew everybody's business better than they knew it _____.

A. themselves　　　B. oneself　　　C. itself　　　D. himself

3. [1996 上海]

Some people would rather ride bicycles as bicycle riding has _____ of the trouble of taking buses.

A. nothing　　　　B. none　　　　C. some　　　　D. neither

4. [1997 全国]

Sarah has read lots of stories by American writers. Now she would like to read _____ stories by writers from _____ countries.

A. some; any　　　B. other; some　　　C. some; other　　　D. other; other

5. [1997 全国]

I agree with most of what you said, but I don't agree with _____.

A. everything　　　B. anything　　　C. something　　　D. nothing

6. [1998 全国]

Dr. Black comes from either Oxford or Cambridge; I can't remember _____.

A. where　　　　B. there　　　　C. which　　　　D. that

7. [1998 全国]

—Can you come on Monday or Tuesday?

—I'm afraid _____ day is possible.

A. either　　　　B. neither　　　　C. some　　　　D. any

8. [1999 全国]

—Are the new rules working?

—Yes. _____ books are stolen.

A. Few　　　　B. More　　　　C. Some　　　　D. None

9. [1999 全国]

Few pleasures can equal _____ of a cool drink on a hot day.

A. some　　　　B. any　　　　C. that　　　　D. those

10. [2000 春季 北京/安徽]

—Do you want tea or coffee?

—_____. I really don't mind.

　A. Both 　　　　　B. None 　　　　　C. Either 　　　　D. Neither

11. [2000 春季 北京/安徽]

One of the sides of the board should be painted yellow, and _____.

　A. the other is white 　　　　　　　　B. another white

　C. the other white 　　　　　　　　　D. another is white

12. [2000 春季 上海]

Mr. Alcott, headmaster of the school, refused to accept _____ of the three suggestions made by the Students' Union.

　A. either 　　　　　B. neither 　　　　C. any 　　　　　D. none

13. [2000 全国]

—Why don't we take a little break?

—Didn't we just have _____?

　A. it 　　　　　　　B. that 　　　　　C. one 　　　　　D. this

14. [2000 全国]

If you want to change for a double room you'll have to pay _____ $15.

　A. another 　　　　B. other 　　　　　C. more 　　　　　D. each

15. [2001 春季 北京/安徽/内蒙古]

If this dictionary is not yours, _____ can it be?

　A. what else 　　　　B. who else 　　　　C. which else's 　　　D. who else's

16. [2001 春季 上海]

Some of the wheat is from Canada. What about _____?

　A. another 　　　　B. the other 　　　　C. others 　　　　D. the rest

17. [2001 上海]

Both teams were in hard training; _____ was willing to lose the game.

　A. either 　　　　　B. neither 　　　　C. another 　　　　D. the other

18. [2002 春季 北京/安徽/内蒙古]

—He was nearly drowned once.

—When was _____?

—_____ was in 1998 when he was in middle school.

　A. that; It 　　　　B. this; This 　　　　C. this; It 　　　　D. that; This

19. [2002 春季 北京/安徽/内蒙古]

—You're always working. Come on, let's go shopping.

—_____ you ever want to do is going shopping.

　A. Anything 　　　　B. Something 　　　　C. All 　　　　　D. That

1. [2002 全国]

The mother didn't know _____ to blame for the broken glass as it happened while she was out.

A. who   B. when   C. how   D. what

2. [2002 全国]

Meeting my uncle after all these years was an unforgettable moment, _____ I will always treasure.

A. that   B. one   C. it   D. what

3. [2003 春季 安徽]

—Your coffee smells great!

—It's from Mexico. Would you like _____ ?

A. it   B. some   C. this   D. little

4. [2003 春季 上海]

Equipped with modern facilities, today's libraries differ greatly from _____ .

A. those of the past   B. the past

C. which of the past   D. these past

5. [2003 全国]

—There's coffee and tea; you can have _____ .

—Thanks.

A. either   B. each   C. one   D. it

6. [2003 全国]

—Susan, go and join your sister cleaning the yard.

—Why _____ ? John is sitting there doing nothing.

A. him   B. he   C. I   D. me

7. [2003 北京]

—I hear they aren't pleased with the house you've chosen for them.

—Well, _____ could they live in such comfort?

A. where else   B. what else   C. how   D. why

8. [2003 上海]

Shanghai is really a fascinating city and we've decided to stay for _____ two weeks.

A. another   B. other   C. the other   D. other's

9. [2004 春季 上海]

Some of the stamps belong to me, while the rest are _____ .

A. him and her   B. his and hers   C. his and her   D. him and hers

10. [2004 全国 II]

That's an unpleasant thing to say about your father after _____ he's done for you.

   A. something   B. anything   C. all   D. that

11. [2004 全国 III]

We needed a new cupboard for the kitchen. So Peter made _____ from some wood we had.

   A. it   B. one   C. himself   D. another

12. [2004 北京]

I invited Joe and Linda to dinner, but _____ of them came.

   A. neither   B. either   C. none   D. both

13. [2004 北京]

There's _____ cooking oil left in the house. Would you go to the corner store and get _____?

   A. little; some   B. little; any   C. a little; some   D. a little; any

14. [2004 上海]

I had to buy _____ these books because I didn't know which one was the best.

   A. both   B. none   C. neither   D. all

15. [2004 天津]

I got the story from Tom and _____ people who had worked with him.

   A. every other   B. many others   C. some other   D. other than

16. [2004 天津]

It is easy to do the repair. _____ you need is a hammer and some nails.

   A. Something   B. All   C. Both   D. Everything

17. [2004 重庆]

I intended to compare notes with a friend, but unfortunately _____ couldn't spare me even one minute.

   A. they   B. one   C. who   D. it

18. [2004 重庆]

—One week's time has been wasted.

—I can't believe we did all that work for _____.

   A. something   B. nothing   C. everything   D. anything

19. [2004 辽宁]

I have done much of the work. Could you please finish _____ in two days?

   A. the rest   B. the other   C. another   D. the others

20. [2004 江苏]

I will never know what was on his mind at the time, nor will _____.

   A. anyone   B. anyone else   C. no one   D. no one else

21. [2004 浙江]

We had three sets of garden tools and we seemed to have no use for _____.

   A. none   B. either   C. any   D. each

班级_____姓名_____分数_____

1. [2004 福建]

—Which of the three ways shall I take to the village?

—_____ way as you please.

A. Each   B. Every   C. Any   D. Either

2. [2004 湖南]

Playing tricks on others is _____ we should never do.

A. anything   B. something   C. everything   D. nothing

3. [2004 广东]

She doesn't know anyone here. She has got _____ to talk to.

A. anyone   B. someone   C. everyone   D. no one

4. [2005 春季 北京]

We asked John and Jerry, but _____ of them could offer a satisfactory explanation.

A. either   B. none   C. both   D. neither

5. [2005 春季 上海]

My daughter often makes a schedule to get _____ reminded of what she is to do in the day.

A. herself   B. her   C. she   D. hers

6. [2005 全国 I / II]

We haven't enough books for _____; some of you will have to share.

A. somebody   B. anybody   C. everybody   D. nobody

7. [2005 上海]

No progress was made in the trade talk as neither side would accept the conditions of _____.

A. others   B. the other   C. either   D. another

8. [2005 天津]

I prefer a flat in Inverness to _____ in Perth, because I want to live near my Mom's.

A. one   B. that   C. it   D. this

9. [2005 重庆]

—Victor certainly cares too much about himself.

—Yes. He's never interested in what _____ is doing.

A. no one else   B. anyone else   C. someone else   D. nobody else

10. [2005 江苏]

I'm moving to the countryside because the air there is much fresher than _____ in the city.

A. ones   B. one   C. that   D. those

11. [2005 浙江]

We've been looking at houses but haven't found _____ we like yet.

A. one   B. ones   C. it   D. them

12. [2005 安徽]

I don't think we've met before. You're taking me for _____.

A. some other   B. someone else   C. other person   D. one other

13. [2005 江西]

Cars do cause us some health problems—in fact far more serious _____ than mobile phones do.

A. one   B. ones   C. it   D. those

14. [2005 福建]

I made a call to my parents yesterday. To my disappointment, _____ of them answered it.

A. either   B. none   C. neither   D. nobody

15. [2005 湖北]

First, it is important to recognize what kind of person you are and which special qualities make you different from _____.

A. everyone else   B. the other   C. someone else   D. the rest

16. [2005 湖南]

You will find as you read this book that you just can't keep some of these stories to _____. You will want to share them with a friend.

A. itself   B. yourself   C. himself   D. themselves

17. [2006 春季 上海]

Both sides have accused _____ of breaking the contract.

A. another   B. the other   C. neither   D. each

18. [2006 北京]

—Which driver was to blame?

—Why _____! It was the child's fault, clear and simple. He suddenly came out between two parked cars.

A. both   B. each   C. either   D. neither

19. [2006 上海]

I made so many changes in my composition that only I could read it. To _____ else, it was hard to make out.

A. none   B. everyone   C. someone   D. anyone

20. [2006 天津]

We had a picnic last term and it was a lot of fun, so let's have _____ one this month.

A. the other   B. some   C. another   D. other

21. [2006 重庆]

My grandma still treats me like a child. She can't imagine _____ grown up.

A. my   B. mine   C. myself   D. me

班级_____姓名_____分数_____

1. [2006 江苏]

My most famous relative of all, _____ who really left his mark on America, was Reb Sussel, my great-grandfather.

A. one   B. the one   C. he   D. someone

2. [2006 浙江]

If you can't decide which of the two books to borrow, why don't you take _____? I won't read them this week.

A. all   B. any   C. either   D. both

3. [2006 安徽]

You may drop in or just give me a call. _____ will do.

A. Either   B. Each   C. Neither   D. All

4. [2006 安徽]

Catherine bought a postcard of the place she was visiting, addressed _____ to _____ and then posted it at the nearby post office.

A. it; her   B. it; herself   C. herself; her   D. herself; herself

5. [2006 福建]

—Who called me this morning when I was out?

—A man calling _____ Robert.

A. him   B. himself   C. his   D. /

6. [2006 四川]

Of all the books on the desk, _____ is of any use for our study.

A. nothing   B. no one   C. neither   D. none

7. [2007 春季 上海]

Treat _____ to a glass of wine to help you relax at the end of the day.

A. one   B. oneself   C. you   D. yourself

8. [2007 北京]

He has made a lot of films, but _____ good ones.

A. any   B. some   C. few   D. many

9. [2007 上海]

The mayor has offered a reward of $5 000 to _____ who can capture the tiger alive or dead.

A. both   B. others   C. anyone   D. another

10. [2007 重庆]

Jim sold most of his things. He has hardly _____ left in the house.

A. anything   B. everything   C. nothing   D. something

11. [2007 辽宁]

The information on the Internet gets around much more rapidly than _____ in the newspaper.

A. it   B. those   C. one   D. that

12. [2007 浙江]

—He got his first book published. It turned out to be a bestseller.

—When was _____?

—_____ was in 2000 when he was still in college.

A. that;This   B. this;It   C. it;This   D. that;It

13. [2007 安徽]

The school's music group will be giving a big show tomorrow night and two _____ on the weekend.

A. more   B. other   C. else   D. another

14. [2007 江西]

—What do you think of the performance today?

—Great! _____ but a musical genius could perform so successfully.

A. All   B. None   C. Anybody   D. Everybody

15. [2007 福建]

The book is of great value. _____ can be enjoyed unless you digest it.

A. Nothing   B. Something   C. Everything   D. Anything

16. [2007 湖南]

To save class time, our teacher has _____ students do half of the exercise in class and complete the other half for our homework.

A. us   B. we   C. our   D. ours

17. [2007 四川]

Little joy can equal _____ of a surprising ending when you read stories.

A. that   B. those   C. any   D. some

18. [2007 陕西]

—There is still a copy of the book in the library. Will you go and borrow _____?

—No, I'd rather buy _____ in the bookstore.

A. it;one   B. one;one   C. one;it   D. it;it

第四章 介 词

班级_____ 姓名_____ 分数_____

1. [**1998 上海**]

I wanted two seats _____ *Madame Curie* for Friday night, so I rang the cinema to see if I could book two tickets.

A. of   B. about   C. to   D. for

2. [**1998 上海**]

_____ most students, she was always well prepared and never came to class late.

A. Like   B. As   C. For   D. To

3. [**1999 上海**]

Washington, a state in the US, was named _____ one of the greatest American presidents.

A. in honour of   B. instead of   C. in favour of   D. by means of

4. [**1999 上海**]

The number of the employees has grown from 1000 to 1200. This means it has risen _____ 20 percent.

A. by   B. at   C. to   D. with

5. [**2000 春季 上海**]

The suit fitted him well _____ the colour was a little brighter.

A. except for   B. except that   C. except when   D. besides

6. [**2000 春季 上海**]

—You seem to show interest in cooking.

—What? _____, I'm getting tired of it.

A. On the contrary   B. To the contrary

C. On the other hand   D. To the other hand

7. [**2000 全国**]

I don't think I'll need any money but I'll bring some _____.

A. at last   B. in case   C. once again   D. in time

8. [**2000 全国**]

_____ production up by 60%, the company has had another excellent year.

A. As   B. For   C. With   D. Through

9. [**2000 上海**]

I know nothing about the young lady _____ she is from Beijing.

A. except   B. except for   C. except that   D. besides

10. [**2001 春季 上海**]

Rose was wild with joy _____ the result of the examination.

A. to   B. at   C. by   D. as

11. [**2001 全国**]

The home improvements have taken what little there is _____ my spare time.

A. from   B. in   C. of   D. at

12. [**2001 上海**]

The sunlight came in _____ the windows in the roof and lit up the whole room.

A. through   B. across   C. on   D. over

13. [**2002 春季 北京／安徽／内蒙古**]

—You are so lucky.

—What do you mean _____ that?

A. for   B. in   C. of   D. by

14. [**2002 春季 上海**]

Marie Curie took little notice _____ the honours that were given to her in her later years.

A. of   B. on   C. about   D. from

15. [**2002 北京**]

—What do you want _____ those old boxes?

—To put things in when I move to the new flat.

A. by   B. for   C. of   D. with

16. [**2002 上海**]

Luckily, the bullet narrowly missed the captain _____ an inch.

A. by   B. at   C. to   D. from

17. [**2003 春季 上海**]

The speech by the mayor of Shanghai before the final voting for EXPO 2010 is strongly impressed _____ my memory.

A. to   B. over   C. by   D. on

18. [**2003 北京**]

They had a pleasant chat _____ a cup of coffee.

A. for   B. with   C. during   D. over

19. [**2003 上海**]

The conference has been held to discuss the effects of tourism _____ the wildlife in the area.

A. in   B. on   C. at   D. with

20. [**2004 春季 北京／安徽**]

There at the door stood a girl about the same height _____.

A. as me   B. as mine   C. with mine   D. with me

21. [**2004 春季 北京／安徽**]

In order to change attitudes _____ employing women, the government is bringing in new laws.

A. about   B. of   C. towards   D. on

班级_____ 姓名_____ 分数_____

1. ［2004 春季 上海］

I am sorry it's _____ my power to make a final decision on the project.

A. over   B. above   C. off   D. beyond

2. ［2004 北京］

_____ two exams to worry about, I have to work really hard this weekend.

A. With   B. Besides   C. As for   D. Because of

3. ［2004 上海］

The accident is reported to have occurred _____ the first Sunday in February.

A. at   B. on   C. in   D. to

4. ［2004 江苏］

He got to the station early, _____ missing his train.

A. in case of   B. instead of   C. for fear of   D. in search of

5. ［2004 福建］

I'd like to buy a house—modern, comfortable, and _____ in a quiet neighborhood.

A. in all   B. above all   C. after all   D. at all

6. ［2004 福建］

It was a pity that the great writer died _____ his works unfinished.

A. for   B. with   C. from   D. of

7. ［2004 湖南］

You can't wear a blue jacket _____ that shirt—it'll look terrible.

A. on   B. above   C. up   D. over

8. ［2004 广东］

I feel that one of my main duties _____ a teacher is to help the students to become better learners.

A. for   B. by   C. as   D. with

9. ［2005 春季 上海］

—Does Lisa have a new hair style?

—Yes. In fact, it is quite similar _____ yours.

A. as   B. like   C. to   D. with

10. ［2005 全国 I／II］

No one helped me. I did it all _____ myself.

A. for   B. by   C. from   D. to

11. ［2005 全国Ⅲ］

We hadn't planned to meet. We met _____ chance.

A. of   B. in   C. for   D. by

12. [2005 上海]

John became a football coach in Sealion Middle School _____ the beginning of March.

A. on   B. for   C. with   D. at

13. [2005 重庆]

—You know, Bob is a little slow _____ understanding, so...

—So I have to be patient _____ him.

A. in; with   B. on; with   C. in; to   D. at; for

14. [2005 江西]

_____ and no way to reduce her pain and suffering from the terrible disease, the patient sought her doctor's help to end her life.

A. Having given up hope of cure   B. With no hope for cure

C. There being hope for cure   D. In the hope of cure

15. [2005 福建]

The classroom is big enough _____, but we'll have to move if we have more students.

A. for the moment   B. on the moment

C. in a moment   D. for a moment

16. [2005 湖南]

He suddenly saw Sue _____ the room. He pushed his way _____ the crowd of people to get to her.

A. across; across   B. over; through   C. over; into   D. across; through

17. [2006 春季 上海]

More and more young people are fond _____ playing tennis nowadays.

A. on   B. to   C. in   D. of

18. [2006 北京]

—When do we need to pay the balance?

—_____ September 30.

A. In   B. By   C. During   D. Within

19. [2006 上海]

—It's a top secret.

—Yes, I see. I will keep the secret _____ you and me.

A. with   B. around   C. among   D. between

20. [2006 重庆]

I saw a woman running toward me in the dark. Before I could recognize who she was, she had run back in the direction _____ which she had come.

A. of   B. by   C. in   D. from

21. [2006 辽宁]

People have always been curious _____ how living things on the earth exactly began.

A. in   B. at   C. of   D. about

1. [2006 山东]

A clean environment can help the city bid for the Olympics, which _____ will promote its economic development.

A. in nature   B. in return   C. in turn   D. in fact

2. [2006 江苏]

This new model of car is so expensive that it is _____ the reach of those with average incomes.

A. over   B. within   C. beyond   D. below

3. [2006 浙江]

I would like a job which pays more, but _____ I enjoy the work I'm doing at the moment.

A. in other words   B. on the other hand

C. for one thing   D. as a matter of fact

4. [2006 安徽]

It's quite _____ me why such things have been allowed to happen.

A. for   B. behind   D. against   D. beyond

5. [2006 福建]

Sorry, Madam. You'd better come tomorrow because it's _____ the visiting hours.

A. during   B. at   C. beyond   D. before

6. [2006 湖南]

Fred, who had expected how it would go with his daughter, had a great worry _____ his mind.

A. on   B. in   C. with   D. at

7. [2006 湖南]

_____ achievement, last week's ministerial meeting of the WTO here earned a low, though not failing, grade.

A. In terms of   B. In case of   C. As a result of   D. In face of

8. [2006 陕西]

My sister was against my suggestion while my brother was _____ it.

A. in honour of   B. in memory of   C. in favour of   D. in search of

9. [2007 春季 上海]

Dolly wants to cycle round the world and she is really keen _____ the idea.

A. on   B. for   C. at   D. with

10. [2007 全国 I]

The manager suggested an earlier date _____ the meeting.

A. on   B. for   C. about   D. with

11. [2007 全国Ⅱ]

Some people choose jobs for other reasons _____ money these days.

A. for   B. except   C. besides   D. with

12. [2007 北京]

This is a junior school. You should go to a senior school _____ girls of your age.

A. for   B. about   C. from   D. to

13. [2007 上海]

Leaves are found on all kinds of trees, but they differ greatly _____ size and shape.

A. on   B. from   C. by   D. in

14. [2007 天津]

_____ fire, all exits must be kept clear.

A. In place of   B. Instead of   C. In case of   D. In spite of

15. [2007 山东]

I have offered to paint the house _____ a week's accommodation.

A. in exchange for   B. with regard to

C. by means of   D. in place of

16. [2007 浙江]

The open-air celebration has been put off _____ the bad weather.

A. in case of   B. in spite of   C. instead of   D. because of

17. [2007 江西]

Scientists are convinced _____ the positive effect of laughter _____ physical and mental health.

A. of; at   B. by; in   C. of; on   D. on; at

18. [2007 江西]

Experts have been warning _____ of the health risks caused by passive smoking.

A. at a time   B. at one time   C. for some time   D. for the time

19. [2007 福建]

Although _____ my opinion, the old professor didn't come up with his own.

A. against   B. on   C. for   D. in

20. [2007 湖北]

People try to avoid public transportation delays by using their own cars, and this _____ creates further problems.

A. in short   B. in case   C. in doubt   D. in turn

21. [2007 湖南]

_____ the silence of the pauses, we could hear each other's breathing and could almost hear our own heartbeats.

A. In   B. For   C. Under   D. Between

22. [2007 四川]

Some students often listen to music _____ classes to refresh themselves.

A. between   B. among   C. over   D. during

第五章　形容词和副词

历届高考题选 1（测试时间 20 分钟）

班级_____姓名_____分数_____

1. [**1998 全国**]

If I had _____,I'd visit Europe,stopping at all the small interesting places.

A. a long enough holiday　　　　B. an enough long holiday

C. a holiday enough long　　　　D. a long holiday enough

2. [**1998 全国**]

Professor White has written some short stories,but he is _____ known for his plays.

A. the best　　　B. more　　　C. better　　　D. the most

3. [**1998 上海**]

We advertised for pupils last autumn,and got _____ 60.

A. more than　　　B. more of　　　C. as much as　　　D. so many as

4. [**1998 上海**]

It is _____ work of art that everyone wants to have a look at it.

A. so unusual　　　　　B. such unusual

C. such an unusual　　　D. so an unusual

5. [**2000 春季 上海**]

Although Linda tried hard in the exam,she did _____ than her brother.

A. more badly　　　B. much better　　　C. much badly　　　D. much worse

6. [**2000 全国**]

_____ to take this adventure course will certainly learn a lot of useful skills.

A. Brave enough students　　　B. Enough brave students

C. Students brave enough　　　D. Students enough brave

7. [**2000 上海**]

You're standing too near the camera. Can you move _____?

A. a bit far　　　B. a little farther　　　C. a bit of farther　　　D. a little far

8. [**2000 上海**]

Greenland,_____ island in the world,covers over two million square kilometres.

A. it is the largest　　　　B. that is the largest

C. is the largest　　　　　D. the largest

9. [**2001 春季 北京/安徽/内蒙古**]

Many people have helped with canned food,however,the food bank needs _____ for the poor.

A. more　　　B. much　　　C. many　　　D. most

10. [2001 春季 北京/安徽/内蒙古]

In that case, there is nothing you can do _____ than wait.

A. more   B. other   C. better   D. any

11. [2001 全国]

It is generally believed that teaching is _____ it is a science.

A. an art much as   B. much an art as

C. as an art much as   D. as much an art as

12. [2001 上海]

In recent years travel companies have succeeded in selling us the idea that the further we go, _____.

A. our holiday will be better   B. our holiday will be the better

C. the better our holiday will be   D. the better will our holiday be

13. [2001 上海]

As I know, there is _____ car in this neighborhood.

A. no such   B. no a   C. not such   D. such no

14. [2002 春季 北京/安徽/内蒙古]

—I'm very _____ with my own cooking. It looks nice and smells delicious.

—Mm, it does have a _____ smell.

A. pleasant; pleased   B. pleased; pleased

C. pleasant; pleasant   D. pleased; pleasant

15. [2002 全国]

Boris has brains. In fact, I doubt whether anyone in the class has _____ IQ.

A. a high   B. a higher   C. the higher   D. the highest

16. [2002 北京]

It was raining heavily. Little Mary felt cold, so she stood _____ to her mother.

A. close   B. closely   C. closed   D. closing

17. [2002 上海]

As far as I am concerned, education is about learning and the more you learn, _____.

A. the more for life are you equipped   B. the more equipped for life you are

C. the more life you are equipped for   D. you are equipped the more for life

18. [2002 上海]

Quite a few people used to believe that disaster _____ if a mirror was broken.

A. was sure of striking   B. was sure of having struck

C. was sure to be struck   D. was sure to strike

19. [2003 春季 安徽]

Four of Robert's children were at the party, including _____, Luke.

A. the oldest   B. an oldest one   C. the old   D. an old one

班级_____ 姓名_____ 分数_____

1. [2003 春季 北京]

—I was riding along the street and all of a sudden, a car cut in and knocked me down.

—You can never be _____ careful in the street.

A. much   B. very   C. so   D. too

2. [2003 春季 上海]

After supper she would sit down by the fire, sometimes for _____ an hour, thinking of her young and happy days.

A. as long as   B. as soon as   C. as much as   D. as many as

3. [2003 全国]

Allen had to call a taxi because the box was _____ to carry all the way home.

A. much too heavy   B. too much heavy

C. heavy too much   D. too heavy much

4. [2003 北京]

Our neighbor has _____ ours.

A. as a big house as   B. as big a house as

C. the same big house as   D. a house the same big as

5. [2003 上海]

The young dancers looked so charming in their beautiful clothes that we took _____ pictures of them.

A. many of   B. masses of

C. the number of   D. a large amount of

6. [2003 上海]

It is believed that if a book is _____, it will surely _____ the reader.

A. interested; interest   B. interesting; be interested

C. interested; be interesting   D. interesting; interest

7. [2003 上海]

We were in _____ when we left that we forgot the airline tickets.

A. a rush so anxious   B. a such anxious rush

C. so an anxious rush   D. such an anxious rush

8. [2004 春季 上海]

I have worked with him for some time and have found that he is _____ than John.

A. more efficiently a worker   B. a more efficient worker

C. more an efficient worker   D. a worker more efficiently

9. [2004 春季 上海]

_____, some famous scientists have the qualities of being both careful and careless.

A. Strangely enough   B. Enough strangely

C. Strange enough   D. Enough strange

10. [2004 全国 I]

Mary kept weighing herself to see how much _____ she was getting.

A. heavier   B. heavy   C. the heavier   D. the heaviest

11. [2004 全国 II]

I must be getting fat—I can _____ do my trousers up.

A. fairly   B. hardly   C. nearly   D. seldom

12. [2004 全国 IV]

Lizzie was _____ to see her friend off at the airport.

A. a little more than sad   B. more than a little sad

C. sad more than a little   D. a little more sad than

13. [2004 全国 IV]

If you can't come tomorrow, we'll _____ have to hold the meeting next week.

A. yet   B. even   C. rather   D. just

14. [2004 上海]

He speaks English well indeed, but of course not _____ a native speaker.

A. as fluent as   B. more fluent than

C. so fluently as   D. much fluently than

15. [2004 辽宁]

John Smith, a successful businessman, has a _____ car.

A. large German white   B. large white German

C. white large German   D. German large white

16. [2004 江苏]

The _____ house smells as if it hasn't been lived in for years.

A. little white wooden   B. little wooden white

C. white wooden little   D. wooden white little

17. [2004 浙江]

_____ students are required to take part in the boat race.

A. Ten strong young Chinese   B. Ten Chinese strong young

C. Chinese ten young strong   D. Young strong ten Chinese

18. [2004 福建]

The number of people present at the concert was _____ than expected. There were many tickets left.

A. much smaller   B. much more   C. much larger   D. many more

19. [2004 湖南]

Everyone was on time for the meeting—_____ Chris, who's usually ten minutes late for everything.

A. but   B. only   C. even   D. yet

班级_____ 姓名_____ 分数_____

1. [2004 广东]

It is _____ any wonder that his friend doesn't like watching television much.

    A. no   B. such   C. nearly   D. hardly

2. [2004 广东]

Sometimes it was a bit boring to work there because there wasn't always _____ much to do.

    A. such   B. that   C. more   D. very

3. [2004 广东]

The great success of this programme has been _____ due to the support given by the local businessmen.

    A. rather   B. very   C. quickly   D. largely

4. [2005 春季 上海]

—What a nice fire you have in your fireplace!

—During the winter I like my house _____.

    A. warmly and comfortably   B. warm and comfortable

    C. warm and comfortably   D. warmly and comfortable

5. [2005 春季 上海]

We have only a sofa, a table and a bed in our new apartment. We need to buy _____ more furniture.

    A. any   B. many   C. little   D. some

6. [2005 全国 I／II]

My parents will move back into town in a year or _____.

    A. later   B. after   C. so   D. about

7. [2005 全国III]

—Is your headache getting _____?

—No, it's worse.

    A. better   B. bad   C. less   D. well

8. [2005 北京]

This _____ girl is Linda's cousin.

    A. pretty little Spanish   B. Spanish little pretty

    C. Spanish pretty little   D. little pretty Spanish

9. [2005 山东]

—Have you been to New Zealand?

—No, I'd like to, _____.

    A. too   B. though   C. yet   D. either

10. [2005 山东]

Mr. Smith owns _____ collection of coins than anyone else I have ever met.

A. larger   B. a larger   C. the larger   D. a large

11. [2005 江苏]

—How is everything going on with you in Europe?

—Quite well. Not so smoothly as I hoped, _____.

A. though   B. instead   C. either   D. too

12. [2005 江苏]

David has won the first prize in singing; he is still very excited now and feels _____ desire to go to bed.

A. the most   B. more   C. worse   D. the least

13. [2005 江西]

—Must I turn off the gas after cooking?

—Of course. You can never be _____ careful with that.

A. enough   B. too   C. so   D. very

14. [2005 福建]

—Why didn't you buy the camera you had longed for?

—I had planned to, but I was £ 50 _____.

A. fewer   B. less   C. cheap   D. short

15. [2005 湖南]

The more I think about him, the more reasons I find for loving him _____ I did.

A. as much as   B. as long as   C. as soon as   D. as far as

16. [2005 广东]

John is very lazy. He falls _____ behind in his studies.

A. very   B. far   C. more   D. still

17. [2006 春季 上海]

Some experts think that language learning is much _____ for children as their tongues are more flexible.

A. easy   B. easier   C. easily   D. more easily

18. [2006 全国 I]

Your story is perfect. I've never heard _____ before.

A. the better one   B. the best one   C. a better one   D. a good one

19. [2006 全国 I]

—Did you take enough money with you?

—No, I needed _____ I thought I would.

A. not so much as   B. as much as   C. much more than   D. much less than

20. [2006 北京]

This washing machine is environmentally friendly because it uses _____ water and electricity than _____ models.

A. less; older   B. less; elder   C. fewer; older   D. fewer; elder

班级_____姓名_____分数_____

1. [2006 上海]

A typhoon swept across the area with heavy rains and winds _____ strong as 113 miles per hour.

A. too   B. very   C. so   D. as

2. [2006 辽宁]

I hear _____ boys in your school like playing football in their spare time, though others prefer basketball.

A. quite a lot   B. quite a few   C. quite a bit   D. quite a little

3. [2006 江苏]

I wish you'd do _____ talking and some more work. Thus things will become better.

A. a bit less   B. any less   C. much more   D. a little more

4. [2006 浙江]

_____ by keeping down costs will PowerData hold its advantage over other companies.

A. Only   B. Just   C. Still   D. Yet

5. [2006 浙江]

We always keep _____ spare paper, in case we run out.

A. too much   B. a number of   C. plenty of   D. a good many

6. [2006 安徽]

Of the two sisters, Betty is _____ one, and she is also the one who loves to be quiet.

A. a younger   B. a youngest   C. the younger   D. the youngest

7. [2006 江西]

Attention, coffee lovers! We have for you, the best coffee machine _____ invented.

A. ever   B. already   C. even   D. nowadays

8. [2006 江西]

I don't think this film is by far the most boring. I have seen _____ .

A. better   B. worse   C. the best   D. the worst

9. [2006 福建]

_____ homework did we have to do that we had no time to take a rest.

A. So much   B. Too much   C. Too little   D. So little

10. [2006 湖南]

Although she did not know Boston well, she made her way _____ to the Home Circle Building.

A. easy enough   B. enough easy   C. easily enough   D. enough easily

11. [2006 四川]

—Did you enjoy yourself at the party?

—Yes, I've never been to _____ one before.

A. a more excited　　　　　　　　B. the most excited

C. a more exciting　　　　　　　　D. the most exciting

12. [2006 陕西]

I used to earn _____ than a pound a week when I first started work.

A. less　　　　B. fewer　　　　C. a few　　　　D. a little

13. [2007 春季 上海]

Nowadays the roles of husband and wife are not as _____ defined as before, especially when both partners work and earn money for the family.

A. clear　　　　B. clearer　　　　C. clearly　　　　D. more clearly

14. [2007 全国Ⅱ]

After two years' research, we have a _____ better understanding of the disease.

A. very　　　　B. far　　　　C. fairly　　　　D. quite

15. [2007 全国Ⅱ]

Speaking of all the songs he has written, I think this is probably his _____ one.

A. better-known　　　B. well-known　　　C. best-known　　　D. most-known

16. [2007 北京]

The new group of students is better-behaved than the other group who stayed here _____ .

A. early　　　　B. earlier　　　　C. earliest　　　　D. the earliest

17. [2007 上海]

Alan is a careful driver, but he drives _____ of my friends.

A. more carefully　　　　　　　　B. the most carefully

C. less carefully　　　　　　　　D. the least carefully

18. [2007 江苏]

With April 18's railway speedup, highway and air transport will have to compete with _____ service for passengers.

A. good　　　　B. better　　　　C. best　　　　D. the best

19. [2007 浙江]

Work gets done _____ when people do it together, and the rewards are higher too.

A. easily　　　　B. very easy　　　　C. more easily　　　　D. easier

20. [2007 江西]

The melon the Smiths served at dinner would have tasted _____ if it had been put in the fridge for a little while.

A. good　　　　B. better　　　　C. best　　　　D. well

21. [2007 福建]

—Do you need any help, Lucy?

—Yes. The job is _____ I could do myself.

A. less than　　　　B. more than　　　　C. no more than　　　　D. not more than

第六章 情态动词和虚拟语气

历届高考题选1（测试时间20分钟）

班级_____ 姓名_____ 分数_____

1. [1998 全国]
—When can I come for the photos? I need them tomorrow afternoon.
—They _____ be ready by 12:00.
A. can   B. should   C. might   D. need

2. [1998 全国]
—I stayed at a hotel while in New York.
—Oh, did you? You _____ with Barbara.
A. could have stayed   B. could stay
C. would stay   D. must have stayed

3. [1998 上海]
—Could I call you by your first name?
—Yes, you _____.
A. will   B. could   C. may   D. might

4. [1999 全国]
—Will you stay for lunch?
—Sorry, _____. My brother is coming to see me.
A. I mustn't   B. I can't   C. I needn't   D. I won't

5. [1999 上海]
There was a lot of fun at yesterday's party. You _____ come, but why didn't you?
A. must have   B. should   C. need have   D. ought to have

6. [2000 春季 北京/安徽]
Sorry I'm late. I _____ have turned off the alarm clock and gone back to sleep again.
A. might   B. should   C. can   D. will

7. [2000 春季 上海]
I should have been there, but I _____ not find the time.
A. would   B. could   C. might   D. should

8. [2000 全国]
—Are you coming to Jeff's party?
—I'm not sure. I _____ go to the concert instead.
A. must   B. would   C. should   D. might

9. [2000 上海]
My sister met him at the Grand Theatre yesterday afternoon, so he _____ your lecture.

A. couldn't have attended   B. needn't have attended

C. mustn't have attended   D. shouldn't have attended

10. [2000 上海]

If only he _____ quietly as the doctor instructed, he would not suffer so much now.

A. lies   B. lay   C. had lain   D. should lie

11. [2001 春季 上海]

Mr. Bush is on time for everything. How _____ it be that he was late for the opening ceremony?

A. can   B. should   C. may   D. must

12. [2001 春季 上海]

He hesitated for a moment before kicking the ball, otherwise he _____ a goal.

A. had scored   B. scored

C. would score   D. would have scored

13. [2001 全国]

I was really anxious about you. You _____ home without a word.

A. mustn't leave   B. shouldn't have left

C. couldn't have left   D. needn't leave

14. [2001 上海]

You can't imagine that a well-behaved gentleman _____ be so rude to a lady.

A. might   B. need   C. should   D. would

15. [2001 上海]

What would have happened _____, as far as the river bank?

A. Bob had walked farther   B. if Bob should walk farther

C. had Bob walked farther   D. if Bob walked farther

16. [2002 春季 北京/安徽/内蒙古]

—I hear you've got a set of valuable Australian coins. _____ I have a look?

—Yes, certainly.

A. Do   B. May   C. Shall   D. Should

17. [2002 春季 上海]

Oh, I'm not feeling well in the stomach. I _____ so much fried chicken just now.

A. shouldn't eat   B. mustn't have eaten

C. shouldn't have eaten   D. mustn't eat

18. [2002 春季 上海]

How I wish every family _____ a large house with a beautiful garden!

A. has   B. had   C. will have   D. had had

19. [2002 全国]

—Is John coming by train?

—He should, but he _____ not. He likes driving his car.

A. must   B. can   C. need   D. may

1. [2002 北京]

—I heard they went skiing in the mountains last winter.

—It _____ true because there was little snow there.

A. may not be   B. won't be   C. couldn't be   D. mustn't be

2. [2002 上海]

It has been announced that candidates _____ remain in their seats until all the papers have been collected.

A. can   B. will   C. may   D. shall

3. [2002 上海]

It is hard for me to imagine what I would be doing today if I _____ in love, at the age of seven, with the Melinda Cox Library in my hometown.

A. wouldn't have fallen   B. had not fallen

C. should fall   D. were to fall

4. [2003 春季 安徽]

Naturally, after I told her what to do, my daughter _____ go and do the opposite!

A. may   B. can   C. must   D. should

5. [2003 春季 北京]

—The room is so dirty. _____ we clean it?

—Of course.

A. Will   B. Shall   C. Would   D. Do

6. [2003 春季 上海]

My English-Chinese dictionary has disappeared. Who _____ have taken it?

A. should   B. must   C. could   D. would

7. [2003 春季 上海]

Look at the trouble I am in! If only I _____ your advice.

A. followed   B. would follow   C. had followed   D. should follow

8. [2003 全国]

A left-luggage office is a place where bags _____ be left for a short time, especially at a railway station.

A. should   B. can   C. must   D. will

9. [2003 上海]

How _____ you say that you really understand the whole story if you have covered only part of the article?

A. can   B. must   C. need   D. may

10. [2004 春季 上海]

You might just as well tell the manufacturer that male customers _____ not like the design of the furniture.

A. must   B. shall   C. may   D. need

11. [2004 全国 I]

—Isn't that Ann's husband over there?

—No, it _____ be him—I'm sure he doesn't wear glasses.

A. can't   B. must not   C. won't   D. may not

12. [2004 全国 II]

You _____ be tired—you've only been working for an hour.

A. must not   B. won't   C. can't   D. may not

13. [2004 全国 III]

I often see lights in that empty house. Do you think I _____ report it to the police?

A. should   B. may   C. will   D. can

14. [2004 全国 III]

Mr. White _____ at 8:30 for the meeting, but he didn't show up.

A. should have arrived   B. should arrive

C. should have had arrived   D. should be arriving

15. [2004 全国 IV]

—Tom graduated from college at a very young age.

—Oh, he _____ have been a very smart boy then.

A. could   B. should   C. might   D. must

16. [2004 上海]

Children under 12 years of age in that country _____ be under adult supervision when in a public library.

A. must   B. may   C. can   D. need

17. [2004 天津]

—Who is the girl standing over there?

—Well, if you _____ know, her name is Mabel.

A. may   B. can   C. must   D. shall

18. [2004 重庆]

"The interest _____ be divided into five parts, according to the agreement made by both sides," declared the judge.

A. may   B. should   C. must   D. shall

19. [2004 辽宁]

—Mum, I've been studying English since 8 o'clock. _____ I go out and play with Tom for a while?

—No, I'm afraid not. Besides, it's raining outside now.

A. Can't   B. Wouldn't   C. May not   D. Won't

1. [2004 江苏]

—I don't mind telling you what I know.

—You _____ . I'm not asking you for it.

A. mustn't   B. may not   C. can't   D. needn't

2. [2004 浙江]

I _____ pay Tracy a visit, but I'm not sure whether I will have time this Sunday.

A. should   B. might   C. would   D. could

3. [2004 福建]

—I'll tell Mary about her new job tomorrow.

—You _____ her last week.

A. ought to tell   B. would have told   C. must tell   D. should have told

4. [2004 湖北]

—Excuse me. Is this the right way to the Summer Palace?

—Sorry, I am not sure. But it _____ be.

A. might   B. will   C. must   D. can

5. [2004 湖南]

—Excuse me, but I want to use your computer to type a report.

—You _____ have my computer if you don't take care of it.

A. shan't   B. might not   C. needn't   D. shouldn't

6. [2005 春季 上海]

According to the local regulations, anyone who intends to get a driver's licence _____ take an eye test.

A. can   B. must   C. would   D. may

7. [2005 全国 I／II]

Tom, you _____ leave all your clothes on the floor like this!

A. wouldn't   B. mustn't   C. needn't   D. may not

8. [2005 全国III]

John, look at the time. _____ you play the piano at such a late hour?

A. Must   B. Can   C. May   D. Need

9. [2005 北京]

He _____ have completed his work; otherwise, he wouldn't be enjoying himself by the seaside.

A. should   B. must   C. wouldn't   D. can't

10. [2005 上海]

There _____ be any difficulty about passing the road test since you have practised a lot in the driving school.

A. mustn't   B. shan't   C. shouldn't   D. needn't

11. [2005 天津]

I _____ have been more than six years old when the accident happened.

A. shouldn't   B. couldn't   C. mustn't   D. needn't

12. [2005 重庆]

I was on the highway when this car went past followed by a police car. They _____ at least 150 kilometers an hour.

A. should have been doing   B. must have been doing

C. could have done   D. would have done

13. [2005 辽宁]

This cake is very sweet. You _____ a lot of sugar in it.

A. should put   B. could have put   C. might put   D. must have put

14. [2005 山东]

He paid for a seat, when he _____ have entered free.

A. could   B. would   C. must   D. need

15. [2005 江苏]

—The woman biologist stayed in Africa studying wild animals for 13 years before she returned.

—Oh, dear! She _____ a lot of difficulties!

A. may go through   B. might go through

C. ought to have gone through   D. must have gone through

16. [2005 江苏]

—Don't you think it necessary that he _____ to Miami but to New Youk?

—I agree, but the problem is _____ he has refused to.

A. will not be sent; that   B. not be sent; that

C. should not be sent; what   D. should not send; what

17. [2005 浙江]

The World Wide Web is sometimes jokingly called the World Wide Wait because it _____ be very slow.

A. should   B. must   C. will   D. can

18. [2005 安徽]

Helen _____ go on the trip with us, but she isn't quite sure yet.

A. shall   B. must   C. may   D. can

19. [2005 江西]

—Tom is never late for work. Why is he absent today?

—Something _____ to him.

A. must happen   B. should have happened

C. could have happened   D. must have happened

1. [2005 福建]

   —Catherine, I have cleaned the room for you.

   —Thanks. You _____ it. I could manage it myself.

   A. needn't do   B. needn't have done

   C. mustn't do   D. shouldn't have done

2. [2005 湖北]

   —Do you know where David is? I couldn't find him anywhere.

   —Well. He _____ have gone far—his coat's still here.

   A. shouldn't   B. mustn't   C. can't   D. wouldn't

3. [2005 湖北]

   If I _____ plan to do anything I wanted to, I'd like to go to Tibet and travel through as much of it as possible.

   A. would   B. could   C. had to   D. ought to

4. [2005 湖南]

   —Lucy doesn't mind lending you her dictionary.

   —She _____. I've already borrowed one.

   A. can't   B. mustn't   C. needn't   D. shouldn't

5. [2005 广东]

   —I've taken someone else's green sweater by mistake.

   —It _____ Harry's. He always wears green.

   A. has to be   B. will be   C. mustn't be   D. could be

6. [2006 春季 上海]

   You know he is not going to let us leave early if we _____ get the work done.

   A. can't   B. may not   C. shouldn't   D. mustn't

7. [2006 全国 I]

   We forgot to bring our tickets, but please let us enter, _____?

   A. do you   B. can we   C. will you   D. shall we

8. [2006 全国 I]

   We hope that as many people as possible _____ join us for the picnic tomorrow.

   A. need   B. must   C. should   D. can

9. [2006 全国 II]

   There's no light on—they _____ be at home.

   A. can't   B. mustn't   C. needn't   D. shouldn't

10. [2006 北京]

    —What's the name?

—Khulaifi,_____ I spell that for you?

A. Shall   B. Would   C. Can   D. Might

11. [2006 上海]

Black holes _____ not be seen directly, so determining the number of them is a tough task.

A. can   B. should   C. must   D. need

12. [2006 天津]

We _____ have proved great adventurers, but we have done the greatest march ever made in the past ten years.

A. needn't   B. may not   C. shouldn't   D. mustn't

13. [2006 山东]

—May I smoke here?

—If you _____, choose a seat in the smoking section.

A. should   B. could   C. may   D. must

14. [2006 江苏]

—I think I'll give Bob a ring.

—You _____. You haven't been in touch with him for ages.

A. will   B. may   C. have to   D. should

15. [2006 浙江]

—Could I have a word with you, mum?

—Oh dear, if you _____.

A. can   B. must   C. may   D. should

16. [2006 江西]

The weather turned out to be fine yesterday. I _____ the trouble to carry my umbrella with me.

A. should have taken   B. could have taken

C. needn't have taken   D. mustn't have taken

17. [2006 福建]

If it were not for the fact that she _____ sing, I would invite her to the party.

A. couldn't   B. shouldn't   C. can't   D. might not

18. [2006 湖南]

Some aspects of a pilot's job _____ be boring, and pilots often _____ work at inconvenient hours.

A. can; have to   B. may; can   C. have to; may   D. ought to; must

19. [2006 四川]

—Is Jack on duty today?

—It _____ be him. It's his turn tomorrow.

A. mustn't   B. won't   C. can't   D. needn't

20. [2006 陕西]

As you worked late yesterday, you _____ have come this morning.

A. needn't   B. mayn't   C. can't   D. mustn't

班级_____ 姓名_____ 分数_____

1. [2007 春季 上海]

The boss has given everyone a special holiday, so we _____ go to work tomorrow.

A. can't   B. mustn't   C. needn't   D. shouldn't

2. [2007 全国 I]

—How's your tour around the North Lake? Is it beautiful?

—It _____ be, but it is now heavily polluted.

A. will   B. would   C. should   D. must

3. [2007 北京]

In crowded places like airports and railway stations, you _____ take care of your luggage.

A. can   B. may   C. must   D. will

4. [2007 上海]

—Guess what! I have got A for my term paper.

—Great! You _____ read widely and put a lot of work into it.

A. must   B. should   C. must have   D. should have

5. [2007 重庆]

—What do you think we can do for our aged parents?

—You _____ do anything except to be with them and be yourself.

A. don't have to   B. oughtn't to   C. mustn't   D. can't

6. [2007 辽宁]

—Turn off the TV, Jack. _____ your homework now?

—Mum, just ten more minutes, please.

A. Should you be doing   B. Shouldn't you be doing

C. Couldn't you be doing   D. Will you be doing

7. [2007 江苏]

—She looks very happy. She _____ have passed the exam.

—I guess so. It's not difficult after all.

A. should   B. could   C. must   D. might

8. [2007 浙江]

—My cat's really fat.

—You _____ have given her so much food.

A. wouldn't   B. couldn't   C. shouldn't   D. mustn't

9. [2007 安徽]

The teacher _____ have thought Johnson was worth it or she wouldn't have wasted time on him, I suppose.

A. should   B. can   C. would   D. must

10. [2007 江西]

—Where is my dictionary? I remember I put it here yesterday.

—You _____ it in the wrong place.

A. must put   B. should have put   C. might put   D. might have put

11. [2007 福建]

My MP4 player isn't in my bag. Where _____ I have put it?

A. can   B. must   C. should   D. would

12. [2007 湖南]

The biggest problem for most plants, which _____ just get up and run away when threatened, is that animals like to eat them.

A. shan't   B. can't   C. needn't   D. mustn't

13. [2007 四川]

—What does the sign over there read?

—"No person _____ smoke or carry a lighted cigarette, cigar or pipe in this area."

A. will   B. may   C. shall   D. must

14. [2007 陕西]

I told your friend how to get to the hotel, but perhaps I _____ have driven her there.

A. could   B. must   C. might   D. should

第七章　动词的时态和语态

班级_____姓名_____分数_____

1. [1998 全国]

—Nancy is not coming tonight.

—But she _____!

A. promises　　　　B. promised　　　　C. will promise　　　　D. had promised

2. [1998 全国]

Shirley _____ a book about China last year but I don't know whether she has finished it.

A. has written　　　　B. wrote　　　　C. had written　　　　D. was writing

3. [1998 全国]

—Hi, Tracy, you look tired.

—I am tired. I _____ the living room all day.

A. painted

B. had painted

C. have been painting

D. have painted

4. [1999 全国]

The price _____, but I doubt whether it will remain so.

A. went down　　　　B. will go down　　　　C. has gone down　　　　D. was going down

5. [1999 全国]

—Hey, look where you are going!

—Oh, I'm terribly sorry. _____.

A. I'm not noticing

B. I wasn't noticing

C. I haven't noticed

D. I don't notice

6. [1999 上海]

He _____ to the lab than he set out to do the experiment.

A. has no sooner got

B. no sooner got

C. will no sooner get

D. had no sooner got

7. [2000 春季 北京/安徽]

Old McDonald gave up smoking for a while, but soon _____ to his old ways.

A. returned　　　　B. returns　　　　C. was returning　　　　D. had returned

8. [2000 春季 北京/安徽]

—You're drinking too much.

—Only at home. No one _____ me but you.

A. is seeing　　　　B. had seen　　　　C. sees　　　　D. saw

9. [2000 春季 北京/安徽]

All the preparations for the task _____, and we're ready to start.

A. completed
B. complete
C. had been completed
D. have been completed

10. [2000 春季 上海]

The manager entered the office and was happy to learn that four-fifths of the tickets _____.

A. was booked
B. had been booked
C. were booked
D. have been booked

11. [2000 春季 上海]

I told him what I was surprised _____ his attitude towards his study.

A. is
B. was
C. at is
D. at was

12. [2000 全国]

—You've left the light on.

—Oh, so I have. _____ and turn it off.

A. I'll go
B. I've gone
C. I go
D. I'm going

13. [2000 全国]

—How are you today?

—Oh, I _____ as ill as I do now for a very long time.

A. didn't feel
B. wasn't feeling
C. don't feel
D. haven't felt

14. [2000 全国]

The reporter said that the UFO _____ east to west when he saw it.

A. was travelling
B. travelled
C. had been travelling
D. was to travel

15. [2000 上海]

My uncle _____ until he was forty-five.

A. married
B. didn't marry
C. was not marrying
D. would marry

16. [2001 春季 北京/安徽/内蒙古]

Hundreds of jobs _____ if the factory closes.

A. lose
B. will be lost
C. are lost
D. will lose

17. [2001 春季 北京/安徽/内蒙古]

I've won a holiday for two to Florida. I _____ my mum.

A. am taking
B. have taken
C. take
D. will have taken

18. [2001 春季 北京/安徽/内蒙古]

A new cinema _____ here. They hope to finish it next month.

A. will be built
B. is built
C. has been built
D. is being built

19. [2001 春季 上海]

The new suspension bridge _____ by the end of last month.

A. has been designed
B. had been designed
C. was designed
D. would be designed

班级_____ 姓名_____ 分数_____

1. ［2001 全国］
Selecting a mobile phone for personal use is no easy task because technology _____ so rapidly.
A. is changing
B. has changed
C. will have changed
D. will change

2. ［2001 全国］
I _____ ping-pong quite well, but I haven't had time to play since the new year.
A. will play
B. have played
C. played
D. play

3. ［2001 全国］
Visitors _____ not to touch the exhibits.
A. will request
B. request
C. are requesting
D. are requested

4. ［2001 上海］
In such dry weather, the flowers will have to be watered if they _____.
A. have survived
B. are to survive
C. would survive
D. will survive

5. ［2002 春季 北京/安徽/内蒙古］
John and I _____ friends for eight years. We first got to know each other at a Christmas party. But we _____ each other a couple of times before that.
A. had been; have seen
B. have been; have seen
C. had been; had seen
D. have been; had seen

6. ［2002 春季 北京/安徽/内蒙古］
This is Ted's photo. We miss him a lot. He _____ trying to save a child in the earthquake.
A. killed
B. is killed
C. was killed
D. was killing

7. ［2002 春季 上海］
Rainforests _____ and burned at such a speed that they will disappear from the earth in the near future.
A. cut
B. are cut
C. are being cut
D. had been cut

8. ［2002 全国］
—You haven't said a word about my new coat, Brenda. Do you like it?
—I'm sorry I _____ anything about it sooner. I certainly think it's pretty on you.
A. wasn't saying
B. don't say
C. won't say
D. didn't say

9. ［2002 全国］
I wonder why Jenny _____ us recently. We should have heard from her by now.
A. hasn't written
B. doesn't write
C. won't write
D. hadn't written

10. ［2002 北京］
The little girl _____ her heart out because she _____ her toy bear and beileved she

wasn't ever going to find it.

A. had cried ; lost   B. cried ; had lost

C. cries ; has lost   D. has cried ; has lost

11. [2002 北京]

—Excuse me, sir. Would you do me a favor?

—Of course. What is it?

—I _____ if you could tell me how to fill out this form.

A. had wondered   B. was wondering   C. would wonder   D. did wonder

12. [2002 上海]

He will have learned English for eight years by the time he _____ from the university next year.

A. will graduate   B. will have graduated

C. graduates   D. is to graduate

13. [2002 上海]

I feel it is your husband who _____ for the spoiled child.

A. is to blame   B. is going to blame

C. is to be blamed   D. should blame

14. [2003 春季 安徽]

With the rapid growth of population, the city _____ in all directions in the past five years.

A. spreads   B. has spread   C. spread   D. had spread

15. [2003 春季 安徽]

The silence of the library _____ only by the sound of pages being turned over.

A. has been broken   B. breaks   C. broke   D. was broken

16. [2003 春季 北京]

—When will you come to see me, Dad?

—I will go to see you when you _____ the training course.

A. will have finished   B. will finish

C. are finishing   D. finish

17. [2003 春季 北京]

—How long _____ at this job?

—Since 1990.

A. were you employed   B. have you been employed

C. had you been employed   D. will you be employed

18. [2003 春季 北京]

—What happened to the priceless works of art?

—_____ .

A. They were destroyed in the earthquake

B. The earthquake was destroying them

C. They destroyed in the earthquake

D. The earthquake destroyed them

历届高考题选 3 (测试时间 20 分钟)

班级_____ 姓名_____ 分数_____

1. [2003 春季 上海]

By the end of last year, another new gymnasium _____ in Beijing.

A. would be completed   B. was being completed

C. has been completed   D. had been completed

2. [2003 全国]

All morning as she waited for the medical report from the doctor, her nervousness _____.

A. has grown   B. is growing   C. grew   D. had grown

3. [2003 全国]

Why don't you put the meat in the fridge? It will _____ fresh for several days.

A. be stayed   B. stay   C. be staying   D. have stayed

4. [2003 北京]

At this time tomorrow _____ over the Atlantic.

A. we're going to fly   B. we'll be flying

C. we'll fly   D. we're to fly

5. [2003 北京]

—_____ David and Vicky _____ married?

—For about three years.

A. How long were; being   B. How long have; got

C. How long have; been   D. How long did; get

6. [2003 北京]

The news came as no surprise to me. I _____ for some time that the factory was going to shut down.

A. had known   B. knew   C. have known   D. know

7. [2003 北京]

Come and see me whenever _____.

A. you are convenient   B. you will be convenient

C. it is convenient to you   D. it will be convenient to you

8. [2003 上海]

I thought Jim would say something about his school report, but he _____ it.

A. doesn't mention   B. hadn't mentioned

C. didn't mention   D. hasn't mentioned

9. [2004 春季 北京/安徽]

How can you possibly miss the news? It _____ on TV all day long.

A. has been   B. had been   C. was   D. will be

10. [**2004 春季 北京/安徽**]

—Sorry to have interrupted you. Please go on.

—Where was I?

—You _____ you didn't like your father's job.

A. had said　　　　B. said　　　　C. were saying　　　　D. had been saying

11. [**2004 春季 北京/安徽**]

I arrived late; I _____ the road to be so icy.

A. wouldn't expect　　　　　　　　B. haven't expected

C. hadn't expected　　　　　　　　D. wasn't expecting

12. [**2004 春季 北京/安徽**]

I _____ while reading the English textbook. Luckily, my roommate woke me up in time!

A. had fallen asleep　　　　　　　　B. have fallen asleep

C. fell asleep　　　　　　　　　　　D. fall asleep

13. [**2004 春季 上海**]

Although he has lived with us for years, he _____ us much impression.

A. hadn't left　　B. didn't leave　　C. doesn't leave　　D. hasn't left

14. [**2004 全国Ⅰ**]

Let's keep to the point or we _____ any decisions.

A. will never reach　　　　　　　　B. have never reached

C. never reach　　　　　　　　　　D. never reached

15. [**2004 全国Ⅰ**]

My mind wasn't on what he was saying, so I'm afraid I _____ half of it.

A. was missing　　B. had missed　　C. will miss　　D. missed

16. [**2004 全国Ⅱ**]

—Has Sam finished his homework today?

—I have no idea. He _____ it this morning.

A. did　　　　B. has done　　　　C. was doing　　　　D. had done

17. [**2004 全国Ⅱ**]

I _____ you not to move my dictionary—now I can't find it.

A. asked　　　　B. ask　　　　C. was asking　　　　D. had asked

18. [**2004 全国Ⅱ**]

According to the art dealer, the painting _____ to go for at least a million dollars.

A. is expected　　B. expects　　C. expected　　D. is expecting

19. [**2004 全国Ⅲ**]

—The window is dirty.

—I know. It _____ for weeks.

A. hasn't cleaned　　　　　　　　B. didn't clean

C. wasn't cleaned　　　　　　　　D. hasn't been cleaned

1. [2004 全国Ⅳ]

—Thank goodness, you're here! What _____ you?

—Traffic jam.

A. keeps   B. is keeping   C. had kept   D. kept

2. [2004 全国Ⅳ]

The house could fall down soon if no one _____ some quick repair work.

A. has done   B. is doing   C. does   D. had done

3. [2004 北京]

—What's that terrible noise?

—The neighbors _____ for a party.

A. have prepared   B. are preparing   C. prepare   D. will prepare

4. [2004 北京]

Now that she is out of a job, Lucy _____ going back to school, but she hasn't decided yet.

A. had considered

B. has been considering

C. considered

D. is going to consider

5. [2004 北京]

The mayor of Beijing says that all construction work for the Beijing Olympics _____ by 2006.

A. has been completed

B. has completed

C. will have been completed

D. will have completed

6. [2004 上海]

The first use of atomic weapons was in 1945, and their power _____ increased enormously ever since.

A. is   B. was   C. has been   D. had been

7. [2004 上海]

The number of deaths from heart disease will be reduced greatly if people _____ to eat more fruit and vegetables.

A. persuade   B. will persuade   C. be persuaded   D. are persuaded

8. [2004 天津]

—What were you doing when Tony phoned you?

—I had just finished my work and _____ to take a shower.

A. had started   B. started   C. have started   D. was starting

9. [2004 重庆]

The crazy fans _____ patiently for two hours, and they would wait till the movie star arrived.

A. were waiting

B. had been waiting

C. had waited

D. would wait

10. [2004 重庆]

She _____ her hairstyle in her hometown before she came to Chongqing for a better job.

A. would change   B. has changed   C. changed   D. was changing

11. [2004 辽宁]

It is said in the book that Thomas Edison(1847 ~ 1931) _____ the world leading inventor for sixty years.

A. would be   B. has been   C. had been   D. was

12. [2004 江苏]

More patients _____ in hospital this year than last year.

A. treated   B. have treated

C. had been treated   D. have been treated

13. [2004 江苏]

Sales of CDs have greatly increased since the early 1990s, when people _____ to enjoy the advantages of this new technology.

A. begin   B. began   C. have begun   D. had begun

14. [2004 浙江]

The discussion _____ alive when an interesting topic was brought in.

A. was coming   B. had come   C. has come   D. came

15. [2004 浙江]

Because the shop _____, all the T-shirts are sold at half price.

A. has closed down   B. closed down   C. is closing down   D. had closed down

16. [2004 福建]

—You were out when I dropped in at your house.

—Oh, I _____ for a friend from England at the airport.

A. was waiting   B. had waited   C. am waiting   D. have waited

17. [2004 福建]

She has set a new record, that is, the sales of her latest book _____ 50 million.

A. have reached   B. has reached   C. are reaching   D. had reached

18. [2004 湖北]

He kept looking at her, wondering whether he _____ her somewhere.

A. saw   B. has seen   C. sees   D. had seen

19. [2004 湖北]

—George and Lucy got married last week. Did you go to their wedding?

—No, I _____. Did they have a big wedding?

A. was not invited   B. have not been invited

C. hadn't been invited   D. didn't invite

1. [2004 湖南]

Turn on the television or open a magazine and you _____ advertisements showing happy families.

A. will often see   B. often see   C. are often seeing   D. have often seen

2. [2004 湖南]

—I hear Jane has gone to the Holy Island for her holiday.

—Oh, how nice! Do you know when she _____ ?

A. was leaving   B. had left   C. has left   D. left

3. [2005 春季 北京]

When Mark opened the door, he saw a woman standing there. He _____ her before.

A. never saw   B. had never seen   C. never sees   D. has never seen

4. [2005 春季 北京]

After a fire broke out in the lab, a lot of equipment _____ .

A. is damaged   B. had damaged   C. damaged   D. was damaged

5. [2005 春季 北京]

I have lost one of my gloves. I must _____ it somewhere.

A. drop

B. have dropped

C. be dropping

D. have been dropped

6. [2005 春季 北京]

I can't see any coffee in this cupboard. _____ ?

A. Has it all been finished

B. Was it all finished

C. Has it all finished

D. Did it all finish

7. [2005 春季 北京]

_____ my sister three times today but her line was always busy.

A. I'd phoned

B. I've been phoning

C. I've phoned

D. I was phoning

8. [2005 春季 上海]

The year 2002 _____ remarkable changes in Shanghai's landscape.

A. sees   B. has seen   C. saw   D. had seen

9. [2005 全国 I / II]

—What would you do if it _____ tomorrow?

—We have to carry it on, since we've got everything ready.

A. rain   B. rains   C. will rain   D. is raining

10. [2005 全国 I / II]

The hero's story _____ differently in the newspapers.

A. was reported   B. was reporting   C. reports   D. reported

11. [2005 全国Ⅰ/Ⅱ]

The coffee is wonderful! It doesn't taste like anything I _____ before.

A. was having   B. have   C. have ever had   D. had ever had

12. [2005 全国Ⅲ]

Listen to the two girls by the window. What language _____?

A. did they speak   B. were they speaking

C. are they speaking   D. have they been speaking

13. [2005 全国Ⅲ]

—Did you tell Julia about the result?

—Oh, no, I forgot. I _____ her now.

A. will be calling   B. will call   C. call   D. am to call

14. [2005 北京]

He _____ more than 5 000 English words when he entered the university at the age of 15.

A. has learned   B. would have learned

C. learned   D. had learned

15. [2005 北京]

Scientists think that the continents _____ always where they _____ today.

A. aren't; are   B. aren't; were   C. weren't; are   D. weren't; were

16. [2005 北京]

—Why did you leave that position?

—I _____ a better position at IBM.

A. offer   B. offered   C. am offered   D. was offered

17. [2005 上海]

More than a dozen students in that school _____ abroad to study medicine last year.

A. sent   B. were sent   C. had sent   D. had been sent

18. [2005 天津]

By the time Jane gets home, her aunt _____ for London to attend a meeting.

A. will leave   B. leaves   C. will have left   D. left

19. [2005 重庆]

—What's wrong with your coat?

—Just now when I wanted to get off the bus, the man next to me _____ on it.

A. sat   B. had sat   C. had been sitting   D. was sitting

20. [2005 重庆]

—What are you going to do this afternoon?

—I am going to the cinema with some friends. The film _____ quite early, so we _____
to the bookstore after that.

A. finished; are going   B. finished; go

C. finishes; are going   D. finishes; go

班级_____姓名_____分数_____

1. [2005 重庆]

Millions of pounds' worth of damage _____ by a storm which swept across the north of England last night.

A. has been caused

B. had been caused

C. will be caused

D. will have been caused

2. [2005 辽宁]

Susan decided not to work on the program at home because she didn't want her parents to know what she _____.

A. has done   B. had done   C. was doing   D. is doing

3. [2005 辽宁]

Months ago we sailed ten thousand miles across this open sea, which _____ the Pacific, and we met no storms.

A. was called   B. is called   C. had been called   D. has been called

4. [2005 江苏]

They _____ on the program for almost one week before I joined them, and now we _____ on it as no good results have come out so far.

A. had been working; are still working   B. had worked; were still working

C. have been working; have worked   D. have worked; are still working

5. [2005 浙江]

My brother is an actor. He _____ in several films so far.

A. appears   B. appeared   C. has appeared   D. is appearing

6. [2005 浙江]

—Are you still busy?

—Yes, I _____ my work, and it won't take long.

A. just finish   B. am just finishing

C. have just finished   D. am just going to finish

7. [2005 安徽]

The manager had fallen asleep where he _____, without undressing.

A. was laying   B. was lying   C. had laid   D. had lied

8. [2005 江西]

—Hurry up! Alice and Sue are waiting for you at the school gate.

—Oh! I thought they _____ without me.

A. went   B. are going   C. have gone   D. had gone

9. [2005 福建]

Father _____ for London on business upon my arrival, so I didn't see him.

A. has left   B. left   C. was leaving   D. had left

10. [2005 湖北]

When the old man _____ to walk back to his house, the sun _____ itself behind the mountain.

A. started; had already hidden   B. had started; had already hidden

C. had started; was hiding   D. was starting; hid

11. [2005 湖北]

He was hoping to go abroad but his parents _____ that they won't support him unless he can borrow money from the bank.

A. were deciding   B. have decided   C. decided   D. will decide

12. [2005 湖南]

—If the traffic hadn't been so heavy, I could have been back by 6 o'clock.

—What a pity! Tina _____ here to see you.

A. is   B. was   C. would be   D. has been

13. [2005 湖南]

Since I won the big prize, my telephone hasn't stopped ringing. People _____ to ask how I am going to spend the money.

A. phone   B. will phone   C. were phoning   D. are phoning

14. [2005 广东]

Years ago we didn't know this, but recent science _____ that people who don't sleep well soon get ill.

A. showed   B. has shown   C. will show   D. is showing

15. [2005 广东]

The policeman's attention was suddenly caught by a small box which _____ placed under the Minister's car.

A. has been   B. was being   C. had been   D. would be

16. [2006 春季 上海]

We _____ our new neighbours yet, so we don't know their names.

A. don't meet   B. won't meet   C. haven't met   D. hadn't met

17. [2006 全国 I]

John, a friend of mine, who got married only last week, spent $3000 more than he _____ for the wedding.

A. will plan   B. has planned   C. would plan   D. had planned

18. [2006 全国 II]

The house belongs to my aunt but she _____ here any more.

A. hasn't lived   B. didn't live   C. hadn't lived   D. doesn't live

19. [2006 全国 II]

The water _____ cool when I jumped into the pool for morning exercise.

A. was felt   B. is felt   C. felt   D. feels

班级_____姓名_____分数_____

1. [2006 全国 II]

Eliza remembers everything exactly as if it _____ yesterday.

A. was happening   B. happens   C. has happened   D. happened

2. [2006 北京]

—Your job _____ open for your return.

—Thanks.

A. will be kept   B. will keep   C. had kept   D. had been kept

3. [2006 北京]

—_____ leave at the end of this month.

—I don't think you should do that until _____ another job.

A. I'm going to;you'd found   B. I'm going to;you've found

C. I'll;you'll find   D. I'll;you'd find

4. [2006 北京]

—Where did you put the car keys?

—Oh,I _____ I put them on the chair because the phone rang as I _____ in.

A. remembered;come   B. remembered;was coming

C. remember;come   D. remember;was coming

5. [2006 上海]

Send my regards to your lovely wife when you _____ home.

A. wrote   B. will write   C. have written   D. write

6. [2006 上海]

When he turned professional at the age of 11,Mike _____ to become a world champion by his coach and parents.

A. expected   B. was expecting

C. was expected   D. would be expected

7. [2006 天津]

What we used to think _____ impossible now does seem possible.

A. is   B. was   C. has been   D. will be

8. [2006 重庆]

I have to go to work by taxi because my car _____ at the garage.

A. will be repaired   B. is repaired

C. is being repaired   D. has been repaired

9. [2006 重庆]

Customers are asked to make sure that they _____ the right change before leaving the shop.

A. will give   B. have been given   C. have given   D. will be given

10. [2006 重庆]

I _____ in London for many years, but I've never regretted my final decision to move back to China.

A. lived   B. was living   C. have lived   D. had lived

11. [2006 辽宁]

I think it is necessary for my 19-year-old son to have his own mobile phone, for I sometimes want to make sure if he _____ home for dinner.

A. come   B. comes   C. has come   D. will come

12. [2006 辽宁]

It is said that the early European playing-cards _____ for entertainment and education.

A. were being designed   B. have designed

C. have been designed   D. were designed

13. [2006 山东]

Although the causes of cancer _____, we do not yet have any practical way to prevent it.

A. are being uncovered   B. have been uncovering

C. are uncovering   D. have uncovered

14. [2006 江苏]

—I don't suppose the police know who did it.

—Well, surprisingly they do. A man has been arrested and _____ now.

A. has been questioned   B. is being questioned

C. is questioning   D. has questioned

15. [2006 江苏]

Although medical science _____ control over several dangerous diseases, what worries us is that some of them are returning.

A. achieved   B. has achieved   C. will achieve   D. had achieved

16. [2006 浙江]

This machine _____. It hasn't worked for years.

A. didn't work   B. wasn't working   C. doesn't work   D. isn't working

17. [2006 浙江]

My friend, who _____ on the International Olympic all his life, is retiring next month.

A. served   B. is serving   C. had served   D. has served

18. [2006 安徽]

I _____ along the street looking for a place to park when the accident _____.

A. went; was occurring   B. went; occurred

C. was going; occurred   D. was going; had occurred

19. [2006 江西]

My cousin went to Canada two years ago. He _____ there for a few months and then went to America.

A. worked   B. would work

C. would be working   D. has been working

班级_____姓名_____分数_____

1. [2006 福建]

Ladies and gentlemen, please fasten your seat belts. The plane _____.

A. takes off   B. is taking off   C. has taken off   D. took off

2. [2006 福建]

The moment the 28th Olympic Games _____ open, the whole world cheered.

A. declared   B. have been declared

C. have declared   D. were declared

3. [2006 福建]

The workers will go on strike if the demands they _____ put forward are turned down.

A. could   B. would   C. /   D. had

4. [2006 湖北]

I won't tell the student the answer to the math problem until he _____ on it for more than an hour.

A. has been working   B. will have worked

C. will have been working   D. had worked

5. [2006 湖南]

I was giving a talk to a large group of people, the same talk I _____ to half a dozen other groups.

A. was giving   B. am giving   C. had given   D. have given

6. [2006 湖南]

In a room above the store, where a party _____, some workers were busily setting the table.

A. was to be held   B. has been held   C. will be held   D. is being held

7. [2006 四川]

Look at the timetable. Hurry up! Flight 4026 _____ off at 18:20.

A. takes   B. took   C. will be taken   D. has taken

8. [2006 陕西]

—You look very tired. _____ at all last night?

—No, not really. I'm tired out now.

A. Do you sleep   B. Did you sleep

C. Were you sleeping   D. Had you slept

9. [2007 春季 上海]

The unemployment rate in this district _____ from 6% to 5% in the past two years.

A. has fallen   B. had fallen   C. is falling   D. was falling

10. [2007 春季 上海]

John had to have his car repaired in a garage because it _____ seriously.

A. damaged   B. was being damaged

C. had damaged   D. had been damaged

11. [2007 全国 I]

I know a little bit about Italy as my wife and I _____ there several years ago.

A. are going   B. had been   C. went   D. have been

12. [2007 全国 I]

The flowers were so lovely that they _____ in no time.

A. sold   B. had been sold   C. were sold   D. would sell

13. [2007 全国 II]

—Is there anything wrong, Bob? You look sad.

—Oh, nothing much. In fact, I _____ of my friends back home.

A. have just thought   B. was just thinking

C. would just think   D. will just be thinking

14. [2007 全国 II]

—Tom, you didn't come to the party last night?

—I _____, but I suddenly remembered I had homework to do.

A. had to   B. didn't   C. was going to   D. wouldn't

15. [2007 北京]

—How can I apply for an online course?

—Just fill out this form and we _____ what we can do for you.

A. see   B. are seeing   C. have seen   D. will see

16. [2007 北京]

—It was really very kind of you to give me a lift home.

—Oh, don't mention it. I _____ past your house anyway.

A. was coming   B. will come   C. had come   D. have come

17. [2007 北京]

I got caught in the rain and my suit _____.

A. has ruined   B. had ruined   C. has been ruined   D. had been ruined

18. [2007 上海]

—Did you tidy your room?

—No, I was going to tidy my room but I _____ visitors.

A. had   B. have   C. have had   D. will have

19. [2007 上海]

With the help of high technology, more and more new substances _____ in the past years.

A. discovered   B. have discovered

C. had been discovered   D. have been discovered

20. [2007 天津]

If Newton lived today, he would be surprised by what _____ in science and technology.

A. had discovered   B. had been discovered

C. has discovered   D. has been discovered

1. [2007 重庆]

—Did Alan enjoy seeing his old friends yesterday?

—Yes, he did. He _____ his old friends for a long time.

A. didn't see   B. wouldn't see

C. hasn't seen   D. hadn't seen

2. [2007 重庆]

Leonardo da Vinci(1452 ~ 1519) _____ birds kept in cages in order to have the pleasure of setting them free.

A. is said to be buying   B. is said to have bought

C. had said to buy   D. has said to have bought

3. [2007 重庆]

When I called you this morning, nobody answered the phone. Where _____?

A. did you go   B. have you gone   C. were you   D. had you been

4. [2007 辽宁]

—Have you handed in your schoolwork yet?

—Yes, I have. I guess it _____ now.

A. has graded   B. is graded   C. is being graded   D. is grading

5. [2007 辽宁]

—Has your father returned from Africa yet?

—Yes, but he _____ here for only three days before his company sent him to Australia.

A. was   B. has been   C. will be   D. would be

6. [2007 山东]

They _____ two free tickets to Canada, otherwise they'd never have been able to afford to go.

A. had got   B. got   C. have got   D. get

7. [2007 江苏]

At the end of the meeting, it was anounced that an agreement _____.

A. has been reached   B. had been reached

C. has reached   D. had reached

8. [2007 江苏]

—_____ you _____ him around the museum yet?

—Yes. We had a great time there.

A. Have; shown   B. Do; show   C. Had; shown   D. Did; show

9. [2007 浙江]

—Jack bought a new mobile phone the other day.

—_____? That's his third one in just one month.

A. Had he   B. Did he   C. Does he   D. Has he

10. [2007 浙江]

The play had already been on for quite some time when we _____ at the New Theatre.

A. have arrived   B. arrived   C. had arrived   D. arrive

11. [2007 安徽]

They became friends again that day. Until then, they _____ to each other for nearly two years.

A. didn't speak   B. hadn't spoken

C. haven't spoken   D. haven't been speaking

12. [2007 江西]

—I have got a headache.

—No wonder. You _____ in front of that computer too long.

A. work   B. are working

C. have been working   D. worked

13. [2007 江西]

—Ouch! You hurt me!

—I am sorry. But I _____ any harm. I _____ to drive a rat out.

A. didn't mean; tried   B. don't mean; am trying

C. haven't meant; tried   D. didn't mean; was trying

14. [2007 福建]

—I saw Jane and her boyfriend in the park at eight yesterday evening.

—Impossible. She _____ TV with me in my home then.

A. watched   B. had watched   C. would watch   D. was watching

15. [2007 福建]

Danny _____ hard for long to realize his dream and now he is popular.

A. works   B. is working   C. has worked   D. worked

16. [2007 湖南]

As the years passed, many occasions—birthdays, awards, graduations—_____ with Dad's flowers.

A. are marked   B. were marked   C. have marked   D. had marked

17. [2007 湖南]

Cathy is taking notes of the grammatical rules in class at Sunshine School, where she _____ English for a year.

A. studies   B. studied   C. is studying   D. has been studying

18. [2007 四川]

When you get the paper back, pay special attention to what _____.

A. have marked   B. have been marked

C. had marked   D. had been marked

第八章 非谓语动词

班级_____姓名_____分数_____

1. [1998 全国]

Cleaning women in big cities usually get _____ by the hour.

A. pay   B. paying   C. paid   D. to pay

2. [1998 全国]

European football is played in 80 countries, _____ it the most popular sport in the world.

A. making   B. makes   C. made   D. to make

3. [1998 上海]

What worried the child most was _____ to visit his mother in the hospital.

A. his not allowing   B. his not being allowed

C. his being not allowed   D. having not been allowed

4. [1998 上海]

To fetch water before breakfast seemed to me a rule _____.

A. to never break   B. never to be broken

C. never to have broken   D. never to be breaking

5. [1998 上海]

He claimed _____ in the supermarket when he was doing shopping yesterday.

A. being badly treated   B. treating badly

C. to be treated badly   D. to have been badly treated

6. [1998 上海]

She asked me to help her, _____ that she couldn't move the heavy suitcase alone.

A. only to realize   B. realizing

C. having been realized   D. realized

7. [1998 上海]

Mrs Brown was much disappointed to see the washing machine she had _____ went wrong again.

A. it   B. it repaired   C. repaired   D. to be repaired

8. [1999 全国]

Robert is said to _____ abroad, but I don't know what country he studied in.

A. have studied   B. study

C. be studying   D. have been studying

9. [1999 全国]

The purpose of new technologies is to make life easier, _____ it more difficult.

A. not make   B. not to make   C. not making   D. do not make

10. ［1999 全国］

When I got back home I saw a message pinned to the door _____ "Sorry to miss you; will call later. "

A. read   B. reads   C. to read   D. reading

11. ［1999 上海］

A computer does only what thinking people _____.

A. have it do   B. have it done   C. have done it   D. having it done

12. ［1999 上海］

—Mum, why do you always make me eat an egg every day?

—_____ enough protein and nutrition as you are growing up.

A. Get   B. Getting   C. To get   D. To be getting

13. ［1999 上海］

There are five pairs _____, but I'm at a loss which to buy.

A. to be chosen   B. to choose from   C. to choose   D. for choosing

14. ［1999 上海］

The lady said she would buy a gift for her daughter with the _____.

A. 20 dollars remained   B. 20 dollars to remain

C. remained 20 dollars   D. remaining 20 dollars

15. ［1999 上海］

—Let me tell you something about the journalists.

—Don't you remember _____ me the story yesterday?

A. told   B. telling   C. to tell   D. to have told

16. ［2000 春季 北京/安徽］

The picture _____ on the wall is painted by my nephew.

A. having hung   B. hanging   C. hangs   D. being hung

17. ［2000 春季 北京/安徽］

_____ the general state of his health, it may take him a while to recover from the operation.

A. Given   B. To give   C. Giving   D. Having given

18. ［2000 春季 上海］

He let me repeat his instruction _____ sure that I understood what was _____ after he went away.

A. to make; to be done   B. making; doing

C. to make; to do   D. making; to do

19. ［2000 春季 上海］

Will those _____ the foreign children come to the headmaster's office?

A. teaching   B. teach   C. who teaches   D. who teaching

1. [2000 春季 上海]

While building a tunnel through the mountain,_____.

A. an underground lake was discovered

B. there was an underground lake discovered

C. a lake was discovered underground

D. the workers discovered an underground lake

2. [2000 全国]

I've worked with children before, so I know what _____ in my new job.

A. expected   B. to expect   C. to be expecting   D. expects

3. [2000 全国]

The managers discussed the plan that they would like to see _____ the next year.

A. carry out   B. carrying out   C. carried out   D. to carry out

4. [2000 上海]

They're not very good, but we like _____.

A. anyway to play basketball with them   B. to play basketball with them anyway

C. to play with them basketball anyway   D. with them to play basketball anyway

5. [2000 上海]

He sent me an e-mail, _____ to get further information.

A. hoped   B. hoping   C. to hope   D. hope

6. [2000 上海]

_____ in 1636, Harvard is one of the most famous universities in the United States.

A. Being founded   B. It was founded   C. Founded   D. Founding

7. [2000 上海]

The _____ boy was last seen _____ near the East Lake.

A. missing; playing   B. missing; play   C. missed; played   D. missed; to play

8. [2000 上海]

Tony was very unhappy for _____ to the party.

A. having not been invited   B. not having invited

C. having not invited   D. not having been invited

9. [2001 春季 北京/安徽/内蒙古]

_____ late in the morning, Bob turned off the alarm.

A. To sleep   B. Sleeping   C. Sleep   D. Having slept

10. [2001 春季 北京/安徽/内蒙古]

One learns a language by making mistakes and _____ them.

A. correct   B. correcting   C. corrects   D. to correct

11. [2001 春季 上海]

Sandy could do nothing but _____ to his teacher that he was wrong.

A. admit   B. admitted   C. admitting   D. to admit

12. [2001 春季 上海]

In order to improve English, _____.

A. Jenny's father bought her a lot of tapes

B. Jenny bought a lot of tapes for herself

C. a lot of tapes were bought by Jenny

D. a lot of tapes were bought by Jenny's father

13. [2001 春季 上海]

Mr. Reed made up his mind to devote all he had to _____ some schools for poor children.

A. set up   B. setting up   C. have set up   D. having set up

14. [2001 春季 上海]

_____ from heart trouble for years, Professor White has to take some medicine with him wherever he goes.

A. Suffered   B. Suffering

C. Having suffered   D. Being suffered

15. [2001 全国]

_____ such heavy pollution already, it may now be too late to clean up the river.

A. Having suffered   B. Suffering   C. That   D. Suffered

16. [2001 上海]

Finding her car stolen, _____.

A. a policeman was asked to help   B. the area was searched thoroughly

C. it was looked for everywhere   D. she hurried to a policeman for help

17. [2001 上海]

Do let your mother know all the truth. She appears to _____ everything.

A. tell   B. be told   C. be telling   D. have been told

18. [2001 上海]

I really appreciate _____ to relax with you on this nice island.

A. to have had time   B. having time   C. to have time   D. to having time

19. [2001 上海]

The bell _____ the end of the period rang, _____ our heated discussion.

A. indicating; interrupting   B. indicated; interrupting

C. indicating; interrupted   D. indicated; interrupted

20. [2001 上海]

Fishing is his favorite hobby, and _____.

A. he'd like to collect coins as well

B. he feels like collecting coins, too

C. to collect coins is also his hobby

D. collecting coins also gives him great pleasure

1. ［2002 春季 北京/安徽/内蒙古］

   Prices of daily goods _____ through a computer can be lower than store prices.

   A. are bought   B. bought   C. been bought   D. buying

2. ［2002 春季 上海］

   In some parts of London, missing a bus means _____ for another hour.

   A. waiting   B. to wait   C. wait   D. to be waiting

3. ［2002 春季 上海］

   When _____, the museum will be open to the public next year.

   A. completed   B. completing   C. being completed   D. to be completed

4. ［2002 春季 上海］

   In order to make our city green, _____.

   A. it is necessary to have planted more trees

   B. many more trees need to plant

   C. our city needs more trees

   D. we must plant more trees

5. ［2002 春季 上海］

   With a lot of difficult problems _____, the newly-elected president is having a hard time.

   A. settled   B. settling   C. to settle   D. being settled

6. ［2002 全国］

   Having a trip abroad is certainly good for the old couple, but it remains _____ whether they will enjoy it.

   A. to see   B. to be seen   C. seeing   D. seen

7. ［2002 全国］

   It is said in Australia there is more land than the government knows _____.

   A. it what to do with   B. what to do it with

   C. what to do with it   D. to do what with it

8. ［2002 全国］

   The research is so designed that once _____ nothing can be done to change it.

   A. begins   B. having begun   C. beginning   D. begun

9. ［2002 北京］

   —How do you deal with the disagreement between the company and the customers?

   —The key _____ the problem is to meet the demand _____ by the customers.

   A. to solving; making   B. to solving; made

   C. to solve; making   D. to solve; made

10. [2002 上海]

In order to gain a bigger share in the international market, many state-run companies are striving _____ their products more competitive.

A. to make   B. making   C. to have made   D. having made

11. [2002 上海]

Though _____ money, his parents managed to send him to university.

A. lacked   B. lacking of   C. lacking   D. lacked in

12. [2002 上海]

Don't use words, expressions, or phrases _____ only to people with specific knowledge.

A. being known   B. having been known

C. to be known   D. known

13. [2002 上海]

_____ to sunlight for too much time will do harm to one's skin.

A. Exposed   B. Having exposed

C. Being exposed   D. After being exposed

14. [2003 春季 安徽]

—Why did you go back to the shop?

—I left my friend _____ there.

A. waiting   B. to wait   C. wait   D. waits

15. [2003 春季 安徽]

The manager, _____ his factory's products were poor in quality, decided to give his workers further training.

A. knowing   B. known   C. to know   D. being known

16. [2003 春季 安徽]

The man we followed suddenly stopped and looked as if _____ whether he was going in the right direction.

A. seeing   B. having seen   C. to have seen   D. to see

17. [2003 春季 北京]

Mr. Smith, _____ of the _____ speech, started to read a novel.

A. tired; boring   B. tiring; bored   C. tired; bored   D. tiring; boring

18. [2003 春季 上海]

Friendship is like money: easier made than _____.

A. kept   B. to be kept   C. keeping   D. being kept

19. [2003 春季 上海]

_____ the meeting himself gave them a great deal of encouragement.

A. The president will attend   B. The president to attend

C. The president attended   D. The president's attending

20. [2003 春季 上海]

Unless _____ to speak, you should remain silent at the conference.

A. invited   B. inviting   C. being invited   D. having invited

班级_____ 姓名_____ 分数_____

1. [2003 春季 上海]

She will tell us why she feels so strongly that each of us has a role to _____ in making the earth a better place to live.

   A. have played   B. play   C. be played   D. be playing

2. [2003 全国]

A cook will be immediately fired if he is found _____ in the kitchen.

   A. smoke   B. smoking   C. to smoke   D. smoked

3. [2003 北京]

The teacher asked us _____ so much noise.

   A. don't make   B. not make   C. not making   D. not to make

4. [2003 北京]

_____ time, he'll make a first-class tennis player.

   A. Having given   B. To give   C. Giving   D. Given

5. [2003 上海]

The discovery of new evidence led to _____.

   A. the thief having caught   B. catch the thief

   C. the thief being caught   D. the thief to be caught

6. [2003 上海]

Generally speaking, when _____ according to the directions, the drug has no side effect.

   A. taking   B. taken   C. to take   D. to be taken

7. [2003 上海]

An army spokesman stressed that all the soldiers had been ordered _____ clear warnings before firing any shots.

   A. to issue   B. being issued   C. to have issued   D. to be issued

8. [2003 上海]

There is a new problem involved in the popularity of private cars _____ road conditions need _____.

   A. that; to be improved   B. which; to be improved

   C. where; improving   D. when; improving

9. [2004 春季 北京/安徽]

He looked around and caught a man _____ his hand into the pocket of a passenger.

   A. put   B. to be putting   C. to put   D. putting

10. [2004 春季 上海]

I'm going to the supermarket this afternoon. Do you have anything _____?

   A. to be buying   B. to buy   C. for buying   D. bought

11. [2004 春季 上海]

The pilot asked all the passengers on board to remain _____ as the plane was making a landing.

A. seat   B. seating   C. seated   D. to be seating

12. [2004 春季 上海]

Victor apologized for _____ to inform me of the change in the plan.

A. his being not able   B. him not to be able

C. his not being able   D. him to be not able

13. [2004 春季 上海]

After his journey from abroad, Richard Jones returned home, _____.

A. exhausting   B. exhausted   C. being exhausted   D. having exhausted

14. [2004 春季 上海]

Suddenly, a tall man driving a golden carriage _____ the girl and took her away, _____ into the woods.

A. seizing; disappeared   B. seized; disappeared

C. seizing; disappearing   D. seized; disappearing

15. [2004 全国 I]

Sarah, hurry up. I'm afraid you won't have time to _____ before the party.

A. get changed   B. get change   C. get changing   D. get to change

16. [2004 全国 II]

When first _____ to the market, these products enjoyed great success.

A. introducing   B. introduced   C. introduce   D. being introduced

17. [2004 全国 II]

"We can't go out in this weather," said Bob, _____ out of the window.

A. looking   B. to look   C. looked   D. having looked

18. [2004 全国 III]

Helen had to shout _____ above the sound of the music.

A. making herself hear   B. to make herself hear

C. making herself heard   D. to make herself heard

19. [2004 全国 III]

Reading is an experience quite different from watching TV; there are pictures _____ in your mind instead of before your eyes.

A. to form   B. form   C. forming   D. having formed

20. [2004 全国 IV]

It shames me to say it, but I told a lie when _____ at the meeting by my boss.

A. questioning   B. having questioned

C. questioned   D. to be questioned

21. [2004 全国 IV]

Alice returned from the manager's office, _____ me that the boss wanted to see me at once.

A. having told   B. tells   C. to tell   D. telling

1. ［2004 北京］

My advisor encouraged _____ a summer course to improve my writing skills.

A. for me taking   B. me taking   C. for me to take   D. me to take

2. ［2004 北京］

_____ in the queue for half an hour, Tom suddenly realized that he had left his wallet at home.

A. To wait   B. Have waited   C. Having waited   D. To have waited

3. ［2004 上海］

According to a recent U. S. survey, children spend up to 25 hours a week _____ TV.

A. to watch   B. to watching   C. watching   D. watch

4. ［2004 上海］

The flu is believed _____ by viruses that like to reproduce in the cells inside the human nose and throat.

A. causing   B. being caused   C. to be caused   D. to have caused

5. ［2004 上海］

The flowers _____ sweet in the botanic garden attract the visitors to the beauty of nature.

A. to smell   B. smelling   C. smelt   D. to be smelt

6. ［2004 上海］

The disc, digitally _____ in the studio, sounded fantastic at the party that night.

A. recorded   B. recording   C. to be recorded   D. having recorded

7. ［2004 上海］

Having been attacked by terrorists, _____.

A. doctors came to their rescue   B. the tall building collapsed

C. an emergency measure was taken   D. warnings were given to tourists

8. ［2004 天津］

Don't leave the water _____ while you brush your teeth.

A. run   B. running   C. being run   D. to run

9. ［2004 重庆］

Laws that punish parents for their little children's actions against the laws get parents _____.

A. worried   B. to worry   C. worrying   D. worry

10. ［2004 辽宁］

I don't know whether you happen to _____, but I'm going to study in the U. S. A. this September.

A. be heard   B. be hearing   C. hear   D. have heard

11. [2004 辽宁]

_____ by the beauty of nature, the girl from London decided to spend another two days on the farm.

A. Attracting   B. Attracted   C. To be attracted   D. Having attracted

12. [2004 江苏]

The man insisted _____ a taxi for me even though I told him I lived nearby.

A. find   B. to find   C. on finding   D. in finding

13. [2004 江苏]

The old man, _____ abroad for twenty years, is on the way back to his motherland.

A. to work   B. working   C. to have worked   D. having worked

14. [2004 浙江]

Linda worked for the Minnesota Manufacturing and Mining Company, _____ as 3M.

A. knowing   B. known   C. being known   D. to be known

15. [2004 浙江]

I've never seen anyone run so fast—just _____ David go.

A. watch   B. to watch   C. watching   D. having watched

16. [2004 福建]

The news reporters hurried to the airport, only _____ the film stars had left.

A. to tell   B. to be told   C. telling   D. told

17. [2004 福建]

Having been ill in bed for nearly a month, he had a hard time _____ the exam.

A. pass   B. to pass   C. passed   D. passing

18. [2004 湖北]

_____ with the size of the whole earth, the biggest ocean does not seem big at all.

A. Compare   B. When comparing

C. Comparing   D. When compared

19. [2004 湖南]

You were silly not _____ your car.

A. to lock   B. to have locked   C. locking   D. having locked

20. [2004 广东]

_____ the programme, they have to stay there for another two weeks.

A. Not completing   B. Not completed

C. Not having completed   D. Having not completed

21. [2005 春季 北京]

_____ with a difficult situation, Arnold decided to ask his boss for advice.

A. To face   B. Having faced   C. Faced   D. Facing

22. [2005 春季 上海]

Accustomed to _____ the steep mountains, he had no difficulty reaching the top.

A. climbing   B. climb   C. having climbed   D. have climbed

班级_____ 姓名_____ 分数_____

1. [**2005 春季 上海**]

When the first English settlers arrived in the New World, the Indians _____ jewellery made of animal bones greeted them warmly.

A. wearing   B. to wear   C. worn   D. having worn

2. [**2005 春季 上海**]

This company was the first _____ portable radios as well as cassette tape reccorders in the world.

A. producing   B. to produce   C. having produced   D. produced

3. [**2005 春季 上海**]

The purpose of new technology is to make life easier, _____ it more difficult.

A. not making   B. not make   C. not to make   D. nor to make

4. [**2005 全国 I／II**]

The storm left, _____ a lot of damage to this area.

A. caused   B. to have caused   C. to cause   D. having caused

5. [**2005 全国 III**]

While watching television, _____.

A. the doorbell rang   B. the doorbell rings

C. we heard the doorbell ring   D. we heard the doorbell rings

6. [**2005 北京**]

It's necessary to be prepared for a job interview. _____ the answers ready will be of great help.

A. To have had   B. Having had   C. Have   D. Having

7. [**2005 北京**]

When asked by the police, he said that he remembered _____ at the party, but not _____.

A. to arrive; leaving   B. to arrive; to leave

C. arriving; leaving   D. arriving; to leave

8. [**2005 北京**]

The prize of the game show is ＄30 000 and an all expenses _____ vacation to China.

A. paying   B. paid   C. to be paid   D. being paid

9. [**2005 北京**]

I couldn't do my homework with all that noise _____.

A. going on   B. goes on   C. went on   D. to go on

10. [**2005 上海**]

He got well-prepared for the job interview, for he couldn't risk _____ the good opportunity.

A. to lose   B. losing   C. to be lost   D. being lost

11. [2005 上海]

_____ into use in April 2000, the hotline was meant for residents reporting water and heating supply breakdowns.

A. Put   B. Putting   C. Having put   D. Being put

12. [2005 上海]

It was unbelievable that the fans waited outside the gym for three hours just _____ a look at the sports stars.

A. had   B. having   C. to have   D. have

13. [2005 上海]

More and more people are signing up for Yoga classes nowadays, _____ advantage of the health and relaxation benefits.

A. taking   B. taken   C. having taken   D. having been taken

14. [2005 天津]

You should understand the traffic rule by now. You've had it _____ often enough.

A. explaining   B. to explain   C. explain   D. explained

15. [2005 天津]

I don't want _____ like I'm speaking ill of anybody, but the manager's plan is unfair.

A. to sound   B. to be sounded   C. sounding   D. to have sounded

16. [2005 重庆]

Daddy didn't mind what we were doing, as long as we were together, _____ fun.

A. had   B. have   C. to have   D. having

17. [2005 辽宁]

All these gifts must be mailed immediately _____ in time for Christmas.

A. in order to have received   B. in order to receive

C. so as to be received   D. so as to be receiving

18. [2005 山东]

Oil prices have risen by 32 percent since the start of the year, _____ a record US $57.65 a barrel on April 4.

A. have reached   B. reaching   C. to reach   D. to be reaching

19. [2005 江苏]

—Is Bob still performing?

—I'm afraid not. He is said to _____ the stage already as he has become an official.

A. have left   B. leave   C. have been left   D. be left

20. [2005 江苏]

_____ in the mountains for a week, the two students were finally saved by the local police.

A. Having lost   B. Lost   C. Being lost   D. Losing

21. [2005 浙江]

_____ more about university courses, call (920) 7463789.

A. To find out   B. Finding out   C. Find out   D. Having found out

班级_____ 姓名_____ 分数_____

1. ［2005 安徽］

I really can't understand _____ her like that.

A. you treat   B. you to treat   C. why treat   D. you treating

2. ［2005 江西］

I think you'll grow _____ him when you know him better.

A. liking   2B. to be like   C. to like   D. to be liking

3. ［2005 江西］

The manager, _____ it clear to us that he didn't agree with us, left the meeting room.

A. who has made   B. having made   C. made   D. making

4. ［2005 福建］

—Can the project be finished as planned?

—Sure, _____ it completed in time, we'll work two more hours a day.

A. having got   B. to get   C. getting   D. get

5. ［2005 福建］

When _____ help, one often says "Thank you." or "It's kind of you."

A. offering   B. to offer   C. to be offered   D. offered

6. ［2005 湖北］

The repairs cost a lot, but it's money well _____.

A. to spend   B. spent   C. being spent   D. spending

7. ［2005 湖北］

_____ from other continents for millions of years, Australia has many plants and animals not found in any other country in the world.

A. Being separated   B. Having separated

C. Having been separated   D. To be separated

8. ［2005 湖南］

_____ in a white uniform, he looks more like a cook than a doctor.

A. Dressed   B. To dress   C. Dressing   D. Having dressed

9. ［2005 湖南］

I send you 100 dollars today, the rest _____ in a year.

A. follows   B. followed   C. to follow   D. being followed

10. ［2005 广东］

He glanced over at her, _____ that though she was tiny, she seemed very well put together.

A. noting   B. noted   C. to note   D. having noted

11. ［2005 广东］

He hurried to the station only _____ that the train had left.

A. to find   B. finding   C. found   D. to have found

12. [2006 春季 上海]

The parents suggested _____ in the hotel room but their kids were anxious to camp out during the trip.

A. sleep   B. to sleep   C. sleeping   D. having slept

13. [2006 春季 上海]

There are hundreds of visitors _____ in front of the Art Gallery to have a look at Van Gogh's paintings.

A. waited   B. to wait   C. waiting   D. wait

14. [2006 春季 上海]

_____ the employees' working efficiency, the supervisor will allow them to have a coffee break.

A. lmproving   B. To improve   C. Having improved   D. Improved

15. [2006 春季 上海]

In the dream Peter saw himself _____ by a fierce wolf, and he woke suddenly with a start.

A. chased   B. to be chased   C. be chased   D. having been chased

16. [2006 春季 上海]

China has promised to revise its existing regulations and _____ new policies according to WTO requirements.

A. forming   B. to form   C. to be forming   D. have formed

17. [2006 全国 I]

We often provide our children with toys, footballs or basketballs, _____ that all children like these things.

A. thinking   B. think   C. to think   D. thought

18. [2006 全国 II]

_____ and happy, Tony stood up and accepted the prize.

A. Surprising   B. Surprised   C. Being surprised   D. To be surprising

19. [2006 北京]

There have been several new events _____ to the program for the 2008 Beijing Olympic Games.

A. add   B. to add   C. adding   D. added

20. [2006 北京]

I can't stand _____ with Jane in the same office. She just refuses _____ talking while she works.

A. working; stopping   B. to work; stopping

C. working; to stop   D. to work; to stop

21. [2006 上海]

Eugene's never willing to alter any of his opinions. It's no use _____ with him.

A. to argue   B. arguing   C. argued   D. having argued

1. [2006 上海]
Energy drinks are not allowed _____ in Australia but are brought in from New Zealand.
A. to make
B. to be made
C. to have been made
D. to be making

2. [2006 上海]
Russ and Earl were auto mechanics _____ the same pay, but Earl had more ambition.
A. to earn
B. to have earned
C. earning
D. earned

3. [2006 上海]
The mother felt herself _____ cold and her hands trembled as she read the letter from the battlefield.
A. grow
B. grown
C. to grow
D. to have grown

4. [2006 上海]
_____ automatically the e-mail will be received by all the club members.
A. Mailed out
B. Mailing out
C. To be mailed out
D. having mailed out

5. [2006 天津]
A good story does not necessarily have to have a happy ending, but the reader must not be left _____.
A. unsatisfied
B. unsatisfying
C. to be unsatisfying
D. being unsatisfied

6. [2006 重庆]
Isn't it time you got down to _____ the papers?
A. mark
B. be marked
C. being marked
D. marking

7. [2006 山东]
Five people won the "China's Green Figure" award, a title _____ to ordinary people for their contributions to environmental protection.
A. being given
B. is given
C. given
D. was given

8. [2006 山东]
Police are now searching for a woman who is reported to _____ since the flood hit the area last Friday.
A. have been missing
B. have got lost
C. be missing
D. get lost

9. [2006 江苏]
—There is a story here in the paper about a 110-year-old man.
—My goodness! I can't imagine _____ that old.

A. to be   B. to have been   C. being   D. having been

10. [2006 浙江]

When _____ different cultures, we often pay attention only to the differences without noticing the many similarities.

A. compared   B. being compared   C. comparing   D. having compared

11. [2006 浙江]

It remains _____ whether Jim'll be fit enough to play in the finals.

A. seen   B. to be seen   C. seeing   D. to see

12. [2006 安徽]

My cousin came to see me from the country, _____ me a full basket of fresh fruits.

A. brought   B. bringing   C. to bring   D. had brought

13. [2006 安徽]

Tom sounds very much _____ in the job, but I'm not sure whether he can manage it.

A. interested   B. interesting   C. interestingly D. interestedly

14. [2006 安徽]

Mr. Green stood up in defence of the 16-year-old boy, saying that he was not the one _____ .

A. blamed   B. blaming   C. to blame   D. to be blamed

15. [2006 江西]

After he became conscious, he remembered _____ and _____ on the head with a rod.

A. to attack; hit   B. to be attacked; to be hit

C. attacking; be hit   D. having been attacked; hit

16. [2006 江西]

It took a long time for the connection between body temperature and illness _____ .

A. to make   B. to be made   C. making   D. being made

17. [2006 福建]

_____ for the breakdown of the school computer network, Alice was in low spirits.

A. Blaming   B. Blamed   C. To blame   D. To be blamed

18. [2006 湖北]

AIDS is said _____ the biggest health challenge to both men and women in that area over the past few years.

A. that it is   B. to be   C. that it has been   D. to have been

19. [2006 湖北]

Don't sit there _____ nothing. Come and help me with this table.

A. do   B. to do   C. doing   D. and doing

20. [2006 湖南]

The wild flowers looked like a soft orange blanket _____ the desert.

A. covering   B. covered   C. cover   D. to cover

班级_____ 姓名_____ 分数_____

1. [2006 湖南]

If you think that treating a woman well means always _____ her permission for things, think again.

A. gets   B. got   C. to get   D. getting

2. [2006 湖南]

As the twentieth century came to a close, the raw materials for a great national literature were at hand, waiting _____.

A. to use   B. to be used   C. to have used   D. to be using

3. [2006 四川]

The Chinese are proud of the 29th Olympic Games _____ in Beijing in 2008.

A. hold   B. holding   C. held   D. to be held

4. [2006 四川]

_____ with so much trouble, we failed to complete the task on time.

A. Faced   B. Face   C. Facing   D. To face

5. [2006 陕西]

It is difficult to imagine his _____ the decision without any consideration.

A. to accept   B. accept   C. accepting   D. accepted

6. [2006 陕西]

He hurried to the booking office only _____ that all the tickets had been sold out.

A. to be told   B. to tell   C. told   D. telling

7. [2006 陕西]

Faced with a bill for $10 000, _____.

A. an extra job has been given to John   B. the boss has given John an extra job

C. an extra job has been taken   D. John has taken an extra job

8. [2007 春季 上海]

All the staff in our company are considering _____ to the city centre for the fashion show.

A. to go   B. going   C. to have gone   D. having gone

9. [2007 春季 上海]

_____ the safety of gas, the government has checked the city's gas supply system thoroughly.

A. To ensure   B. Ensuring

C. Having ensured   D. To have ensured

10. [2007 春季 上海]

She wants her paintings _____ in the gallery, but we don't think they would be very popular.

A. display   B. to display   C. displaying   D. displayed

11 [2007 全国 I]

—It's a long time since I saw my sister.

—_____ her this weekend?

A. Why not visit　　　　　　B. Why not to visit

C. Why not visiting　　　　　D. Why don't visit

12. [2007 全国 I]

—The last one _____ pays the meal.

—Agreed！

A. arrived　　　　B. arrives　　　　C. to arrive　　　　D. arriving

13. [2007 全国 I]

I smell something _____ in the kitchen. Can I call you back in a minute?

A. burning　　　　B. burnt　　　　C. being burnt　　　　D. to be burnt

14. [2007 全国 II]

At the beginning of class, the noise of desks _____ could be heard outside the classroom.

A. opened and closed　　　　　　B. to be opened and closed

C. being opened and closed　　　　D. to open and close

15. [2007 北京]

—Excuse me, sir, where is Room 301?

—Just a minute. I'll have Bob _____ you to your room.

A. show　　　　B. shows　　　　C. to show　　　　D. showing

16. [2007 北京]

He is a student at Oxford University, _____ for a degree in computer science.

A. studied　　　　　　B. studying

C. to have studied　　　D. to be studying

17. [2007 上海]

After a knock at the door, the child heard his mother's voice _____ him.

A. calling　　　　B. called　　　　C. being called　　　　D. to call

18. [2007 上海]

There is nothing more I can try _____ you to stay, so I wish you good luck.

A. being persuaded　　　　B. persuading

C. to be persuaded　　　　D. to persuade

19. [2007 上海]

The Town Hall _____ in the 1800's was the most distinguished building at that time.

A. to be completed　　　　B. having been completed

C. completed　　　　　　　D. being completed

20. [2007 天津]

The glass doors have taken the place of the wooden ones at the entrance, _____ in the natural light during the day.

A. to let　　　　B. letting　　　　C. let　　　　D. having let

班级_____ 姓名_____ 分数_____

1. [2007 重庆]

The children went home from the grammar school, their lessons _____ for the day.

A. finishing   B. finished   C. had finished   D. were finished

2. [2007 辽宁]

The crowd cheered wildly at the sight of Liu Xiang, who was reported _____ the world record in the 110-meter hurdle race.

A. breaking   B. having broken   C. to have broken   D. to break

3. [2007 辽宁]

You can't imagine what difficulty we had _____ home in the snowstorm.

A. walked   B. walk   C. to walk   D. walking

4. [2007 山东]

Please remain _____ until the plane has come to a complete stop.

A. to seat   B. to be seated   C. seating   D. seated

5. [2007 山东]

The country has already sent up three unmanned spacecraft, the most recent _____ at the end of last March.

A. has been launched   B. having been launched

C. being launched   D. to be launched

6. [2007 江苏]

—Can I smoke here?

—Sorry. We don't allow _____ here.

A. people smoking   B. people smoke   C. to smoke   D. smoking

7. [2007 江苏]

He is very popular among his students as he always tries to make them _____ in his lectures.

A. interested   B. interesting   C. interest   D. to interest

8. [2007 江苏]

My parents have always made me _____ about myself, even when I was twelve.

A. feeling well   B. feeling good   C. feel well   D. feel good

9. [2007 浙江]

The children talked so loudly at dinner table I had to struggle _____ .

A. to be heard   B. to have heard   C. hearing   D. being heard

10. [2007 浙江]

_____ by a greater demand for vegetables, farmers have built more green houses.

A. Driven   B. Being driven   C. To drive   D. Having driven

11. [2007 安徽]

—Robert is indeed a wise man.

—Oh, yes. How often I have regretted _____ his advice!

A. to take   B. taking   C. not to take   D. not taking

12. [2007 安徽]

John received an invitation to dinner, and with his work _____, he gladly accepted it.

A. finished   B. finishing   C. having finished   D. was finished

13. [2007 安徽]

—Did Peter fix the computer himself?

—He _____, because he doesn't know much about computers.

A. has it fixed   B. had fixed it   C. had it fixed   D. fixed it

14. [2007 江西]

When asked why he went there, he said he was sent there _____ for a space flight.

A. training

C. to have trained

B. being trained

D. to be trained

15. [2007 福建]

Jenny hopes that Mr. Smith will suggest a good way to have her written English _____ in a short period.

A. improved   B. improving   C. to improve   D. improve

16. [2007 福建]

—Come on, please give me some ideas about the project.

—Sorry. With so much work _____ my mind, I almost break down.

A. filled   B. filling   C. to fill   D. being filled

17. [2007 湖南]

As the light turned green, I stood for a moment, not _____, and asked myself what I was going to do.

A. moved   B. moving   C. to move   D. being moved

18. [2007 湖南]

"Things _____ never come again!" I couldn't help talking to myself.

A. lost   B. losing   C. to lose   D. have lost

19. [2007 四川]

Peter received a letter just now _____ his grandma would come to see him soon.

A. said   B. says   C. saying   D. to say

20. [2007 陕西]

_____ that she didn't do a good job, I don't think I am abler than her.

A. To have said   B. Having said   C. To say   D. Saying

第九章 主谓一致

班级_____ 姓名_____ 分数_____

1. [1999 上海]

E-mail, as well as telephones, _____ an important part in daily communication.

A. is playing   B. have played   C. are playing   D. play

2. [1999 上海]

Books of this kind _____ well.

A. sell   B. sells   C. are sold   D. is sold

3. [2000 春季 上海]

Every possible means _____ to prevent the air pollution, but the sky is still not clear.

A. is used   B. are used   C. has been used   D. have been used

4. [2000 上海]

_____ of the land in that district _____ covered with trees and grass.

A. Two fifth; is   B. Two fifth; are   C. Two fifths; is   D. Two fifths; are

5. [2001 上海]

As a result of destroying the forests, a large _____ of desert _____ covered the land.

A. number; has   B. quantity; has   C. number; have   D. quantity; have

6. [2002 春季 上海]

He is the only one of the students who _____ a winner of scholarship for three years.

A. is   B. are   C. have been   D. has been

7. [2003 春季 上海]

When and where to go for the on-salary holiday _____ yet.

A. are not decided   B. have not been decided

C. is not being decided   D. has not been decided

8. [2004 春季 上海]

No one in the department but Tom and I _____ that the director is going to resign.

A. knows   B. know   C. have known   D. am to know

9. [2004 北京]

The teacher, with 6 girls and 8 boys of her class, _____ visiting a museum when the earthquake struck.

A. was   B. were   C. had been   D. would be

10. [2004 广东]

All the employees except the manager _____ to work online at home.

A. encourages   B. encourage   C. is encouraged   D. are encouraged

11. [2005 春季 上海]

On top of the books _____ the photo album you're looking for.

A. is   B. are   C. has   D. have

12. [2005 春季 上海]

Telephone messages for the manager _____ on her desk but she didn't notice them.

A. were left   B. was left   C. was leaving   D. were leaving

13. [2005 上海]

Professor Smith, along with his assistants, _____ on the project day and night to meet the deadline.

A. work   B. working   C. is working   D. are working

14. [2005 辽宁]

Nowadays, a large number of women, especially those from the countryside, _____ in the clothing industry.

A. is working   B. works   C. work   D. worked

15. [2005 山东]

With more forests being destroyed, huge quantities of good earth _____ each year.

A. is washing away   B. is being washed away

C. are washing away   D. are being washed away

16. [2005 山东]

The country life he was used to _____ greatly since 1992.

A. change   B. has changed   C. changing   D. have changed

17. [2006 全国Ⅰ]

As you can see, the number of cars on roads _____ rising these days.

A. was keeping   B. keep   C. keeps   D. were keeping

18. [2006 辽宁]

The father as well as his three children _____ skating on the frozen river every Sunday afternoon in winter.

A. is going   B. go   C. goes   D. are going

19. [2006 江苏]

A poet and artist _____ coming to speak to us about Chinese literature and painting tomorrow afternoon.

A. is   B. are   C. was   D. were

20. [2006 浙江]

The company had about 20 notebook computers but only one-third _____ used regularly. Now we have 60 working all day long.

A. is   B. are   C. was   D. were

21. [2006 安徽]

Most of what has been said about the Smiths _____ also true of the Johnsons.

A. are   B. is   C. being   D. to be

历届高考题选（测试时间20分钟）

班级_____姓名_____分数_____

1. [**2000 上海**]

The news that they failed their driving test discouraged him,_____?

A. did they　　　　B. didn't they　　　　C. did it　　　　D. didn't it

2. [**2001 春季 北京/安徽/内蒙古**]

_____ at the door before entering please.

A. Knocked　　　　B. To knock　　　　C. Knocking　　　　D. Knock

3. [**2001 春季 上海**]

_____ blood if you can and many lives will be saved.

A. Giving　　　　B. Give　　　　C. Given　　　　D. To give

4. [**2001 上海**]

I don't suppose anyone will volunteer,_____?

A. do I　　　　B. don't I　　　　C. will they　　　　D. won't they

5. [**2002 春季 上海**]

_____ role she played in the film! No wonder she has won an Oscar.

A. How interesting　　　　　　B. How an interesting

C. What interesting　　　　　　D. What an interesting

6. [**2002 春季 上海**]

Brian told you that there wasn't anyone in the room at that time,_____?

A. was there　　　　B. wasn't there　　　　C. didn't he　　　　D. did he

7. [**2002 上海**]

Mrs. Black doesn't believe her son is able to design a digital camera,_____?

A. is he　　　　B. isn't he　　　　C. doesn't she　　　　D. does she

8. [**2003 春季 上海**]

If you want help—money or anything, let me know,_____ you?

A. don't　　　　B. will　　　　C. shall　　　　D. do

9. [**2003 春季 上海**]

Don't be discouraged. _____ things as they are and you will enjoy every day of your life.

A. Taking　　　　B. To take　　　　C. Take　　　　D. Taken

10. [**2003 全国**]

—Sorry, Joe. I didn't mean to. . .

—Don't call me "Joe". I'm Mr Parker to you, and _____ you forget it!

A. do　　　　B. didn't　　　　C. did　　　　D. don't

11. [2004 春季 上海]

There is no light in the dormitory. They must have gone to the lecture,_____?

A. didn't they   B. don't they   C. mustn't they   D. haven't they

12. [2004 上海]

Bill's aim is to inform the viewers that cigarette advertising on TV is illegal,_____?

A. isn't it   B. is it   C. isn't he   D. is he

13. [2004 重庆]

There are eight tips in Dr. Roger's lecture on sleep, and one of them is:_____ to bed early unless you think it is necessary.

A. doesn't go   B. not to go   C. not going   D. don't go

14. [2005 春季 北京]

He never said that he was good at mathematics,_____?

A. was he   B. wasn't he   C. did he   D. didn't he

15. [2005 上海]

There was a loud scream from the backstage immediately after the concert ended,_____?

A. wasn't there   B. was there   C. didn't it   D. did it

16. [2004 重庆]

—What should I do with this passage?

—_____ the main idea of each paragraph.

A. Finding out   B. Found out   C. Find out   D. To find out

17. [2006 全国Ⅱ]

Mary,_____ here—everybody else, stay where youe are.

A. come   B. comes   C. to come   D. coming

18. [2006 重庆]

—Mr. Gordon asked me to remind you of the meeting this afternoon. Don't you forget it!

—OK, I _____.

A. won't   B. don't   C. will   D. do

19. [2006 福建]

I'm sure you'd rather she went to school by bus,_____?

A. hadn't you   B. wouldn't you   C. aren't I   D. didn't she

20. [2007 春季 上海]

If you talk nice and polite, people listen to you. If you shout, this is no good,_____?

A. do you   B. don't you   C. is it   D. isn't it

21. [2007 北京]

When you've finished with that book, don't forget to put it back on the shelf,_____?

A. do you   B. don't you   C. will you   D. won't you

22. [2007 上海]

The little boy came riding full speed down the motorway on his bicycle._____ it was!

A. What a dangerous scene   B. What dangerous a scene

C. How a dangerous scene   D. How dangerous the scene

第十一章 it 用法和强调句 there be 句型

历届高考题选 1(测试时间 20 分钟)

班级_____姓名_____分数_____

1. [**1998 全国**]

I hate _____ when people talk with their mouths full.

A. it   B. that   C. these   D. them

2. [**1998 全国**]

It was only when I reread his poems recently _____ I began to appreciate their beauty.

A. until   B. that   C. then   D. so

3. [**1998 上海**]

_____ was in 1979 _____ I graduated from the university.

A. That;that   B. It;that   C. That;when   D. It;when

4. [**1999 上海**]

What a pity my new computer doesn't work. _____ must be something wrong with it.

A. It   B. There   C. This   D. That

5. [**1999 上海**]

It was _____ he said _____ disappointed me.

A. what;that   B. that;that   C. what;what   D. that;what

6. [**2000 春季 上海**]

It was how the young man had learned five foreign languages _____ attracted the audience's interest.

A. which   B. that   C. what   D. in which

7. [**2000 全国**]

It is the ability to do the job _____ matters not where you come from or what you are.

A. one   B. that   C. what   D. it

8. [**2000 上海**]

An awful accident _____,however,occur the other day.

A. does   B. did   C. has to   D. had to

9. [**2001 春季 上海**]

_____ is no possibility _____ Bob can win the first prize in the match.

A. There;that   B. It;that   C. There;whether   D. It;whether

10. [**2001 全国**]

The Parkers bought a new house but _____ will need a lot of work before they can move in.

A. they   B. it   C. one   D. which

11. [2001 上海]

In fact _____ is a hard job for the police to keep order in an important football match.

A. this   B. that   C. there   D. it

12. [2002 春季 上海]

Since you have repaired my TV set, _____ is no need for me to buy a new one.

A. it   B. there   C. this   D. that

13. [2003 春季 上海]

It was because of bad weather _____ the football match had to be put off.

A. so   B. so that   C. why   D. that

14. [2003 上海]

It is these poisonous products _____ can cause the symptoms of the flu, such as headache and aching muscles.

A. who   B. that   C. how   D. what

15. [2003 上海]

It is pretty well understood _____ controls the flow of carbon dioxide in and out the atmosphere today.

A. that   B. when   C. what   D. how

16. [2004 春季 上海]

It was only with the help of the local guide _____.

A. was the mountain climber rescued

B. that the mountain climber was rescued

C. when the mountain climber was rescued

D. then the mountain climber was rescued

17. [2004 全国 I]

I like _____ in the autumn when the weather is clear and bright.

A. this   B. that   C. it   D. one

18. [2004 全国 II]

—Do you like _____ here?

—Oh, yes. The air, the weather, the way of life. Everything is so nice.

A. this   B. these   C. that   D. it

19. [2004 北京]

The Foreign Minister said, "_____ our hope that the two sides will work towards peace."

A. This is   B. There is   C. That is   D. It is

20. [2004 福建]

It was with great joy _____ he received the news that his lost daughter had been found.

A. because   B. which   C. since   D. that

21. [2004 湖北]

It was _____ back home after the experiment.

A. not until midnight did he go   B. until midnight that he didn't go

C. not until midnight that he went   D. until midnight when he didn't go

班级＿＿＿＿＿姓名＿＿＿＿＿分数＿＿＿＿＿

1. ［2005 春季 上海］

Our club is open to adults only. ＿＿＿＿＿＿ your children have entered without permission.

A. There seems that　　　　　　B. It seems to be

C. There seems to be　　　　　　D. It seems that

2. ［2005 春季 上海］

It was after the invention of printing ＿＿＿＿＿＿ to publish large numbers of books and pictures.

A. were people able　　　　　　B. that people were able

C. when were people able　　　　D. people were able

3. ［2005 全国 I／II］

It wasn't until nearly a month later ＿＿＿＿＿＿ I received the manager's reply.

A. since　　　　B. when　　　　C. as　　　　D. that

4. ［2005 全国 I／II］

The chairman thought ＿＿＿＿＿＿ necessary to invite Professor Smith to speak at the meeting.

A. that　　　　B. it　　　　C. this　　　　D. him

5. ［2005 全国III］

The doctor advised Vera strongly that she should take a holiday, but ＿＿＿＿＿＿ didn't help.

A. it　　　　B. she　　　　C. which　　　　D. he

6. ［2005 天津］

It is what you do rather than what you say ＿＿＿＿＿＿ matters.

A. that　　　　B. what　　　　C. which　　　　D. this

7. ［2005 山东］

—＿＿＿＿＿＿ that he managed to get the information?

—Oh, a friend of his helped him.

A. Where was it　　B. What was it　　C. How was it　　D. Why was it

8. ［2006 春季 上海］

David said that it was because of his strong interest in literature ＿＿＿＿＿＿ he chose the course.

A. that　　　　B. what　　　　C. why　　　　D. how

9. ［2006 全国 I］

It was not until she got home ＿＿＿＿＿＿ Jennifer realized she had lost her keys.

A. when　　　　B. that　　　　C. where　　　　D. before

10. ［2006 全国 II］

If I can help ＿＿＿＿＿＿, I don't like working late into the night.

A. so　　　　B. that　　　　C. it　　　　D. them

11. ［2006 天津］

It was after he got what he had desired ＿＿＿＿＿＿ he realized it was not so important.

A. that   B. when   C. since   D. as

12. [2006 山东]

I'd appreciate _____ if you would like to teach me how to use the computer.

A. that   B. it   C. this   D. you

13. [2006 浙江]

_____ is our belief that improvements in health care will lead to a stronger, more prosperous economy.

A. As   B. That   C. This   D. It

14. [2006 湖南]

As the busiest woman in Norton, she made _____ her duty to look after all the other people's affairs in that town.

A. this   B. that   C. one   D. it

15. [2007 春季 上海]

It is imagination _____ makes the world colourful, full of vigour and vitality.

A. where   B. what   C. that   D. when

16. [2007 全国 I]

—Have you heard the latest news?

—No, what _____?

A. is it   B. is there   C. are they   D. are those

17. [2007 全国 II]

_____ felt funny watching myself on TV.

A. One   B. This   C. It   D. That

18. [2007 天津]

He didn't make _____ clear when and where the meeting would be held.

A. this   B. that   C. it   D. these

19. [2007 重庆]

It is not who is right but what is right _____ is of importance.

A. which   B. it   C. that   D. this

20. [2007 山东]

_____ worries me the way he keeps changing his mind.

A. This   B. That   C. What   D. It

21. [2007 山东]

—Where did you get to know her?

—It was on the farm _____ we worked.

A. that   B. there   C. which   D. where

22. [2007 浙江]

It _____ we had stayed together for a couple of weeks _____ I found we had a lot in common.

A. was until; when   B. was until; that

C. wasn't until; when   D. wasn't until; that

第十二章 省略与倒装

班级_____ 姓名_____ 分数_____

1. [1998 上海]

—Does your brother intend to study German?

—Yes, he intends _____.

A. /   B. to   C. so   D. that

2. [1998 上海]

If _____ the same treatment again, he is sure to get well.

A. giving   B. give   C. given   D. being given

3. [1999 全国]

We'll have to finish the job, _____.

A. long it takes however   B. it takes however long

C. long however it takes   D. however long it takes

4. [2000 春季 北京/安徽]

I finally got the job I dreamed about. Never in all my life _____ so happy!

A. did I feel   B. I felt   C. I had felt   D. had I felt

5. [2000 春季 上海]

—You should have thanked her before you left.

—I meant _____, but when I was leaving I couldn't find her anywhere.

A. to do   B. to   C. doing   D. doing so

6. [2000 上海]

Not a single song _____ at yesterday's party.

A. she sang   B. sang she   C. did she sing   D. she did sing

7. [2001 春季 北京/安徽/内蒙古]

_____ can you expect to get a pay rise.

A. With hard work   B. Although work hard

C. Only with hard work   D. Now that he works hard

8. [2001 春季 上海]

Only when the war was over _____ to his hometown.

A. did the young soldier return   B. the young soldier returned

C. returned the young soldier   D. the young soldier did return

9. [2001 上海]

_____, I have never seen anyone who's as capable as John.

A. As long as I have traveled   B. Now that I have traveled so much

C. Much as I have traveled   D. As I have traveled so much

10. [2001 上海]

So difficult _____ it to live in an English-speaking country that I am determined to learn English well.

A. I have felt   B. have I felt   C. I did feel   D. did I feel

11. [2002 春季 上海]

Not only _____ interested in football but _____ beginning to show an interest in it.

A. the teacher himself is;all his students are

B. the teacher himself is;are all his students

C. is the teacher himself;are all his students

D. is the teacher himself;all his students are

12. [2002 上海]

—You forgot your purse when you went out.

—Good heavens! _____.

A. So did I   B. So I did   C. I did so   D. I so did

13. [2003 春季 北京]

—The boys are not doing a good job at all,are they?

—_____.

A. I guess not so   B. I don't guess   C. I don't guess so   D. I guess not

14. [2003 春季 上海]

Only in this way _____ to make improvement in the operating system.

A. you can hope   B. you did hope   C. can you hope   D. did you hope

15. [2003 全国]

The old couple have been married for 40 years and never once _____ with each other.

A. they had quarreled   B. they have quarreled

C. have they quarreled   D. had they quarreled

16. [2003 上海]

Only when your identity has been checked,_____.

A. you are allowed in   B. you will be allowed in

C. will you allow in   D. will you be allowed in

17. [2004 全国Ⅲ]

—I would never come to this restaurant again. The food is terrible!

—_____.

A. Nor am I   B. Neither would I   C. Same with me   D. So do I

18. [2004 上海]

_____ snacks and drinks,bu they also brought cards for entertainment when they had a picnic in the forest.

A. Not only they brought   B. Not only did they bring

C. Not only brought they   D. Not only they did bring

1. [2004 重庆]

I failed in the final examination last term and only then _____ the importance of studies.

A. I realized   B. I had realized   C. had I realized   D. did I realize

2. [2004 辽宁]

Maybe you have been to many countries, but nowhere else _____ such a beautiful palace.

A. can you find   B. you could find   C. you can find   D. could you find

3. [2004 江苏]

—You haven't lost the ticket, have you?

—_____. I know it's not easy to get another one at the moment.

A. I hope not

C. I hope so

B. Yes, I have

D. Yes, I'm afraid so

4. [2004 广东]

Of the making of good books there is no end; neither _____ any end to their influence on man's lives.

A. there is   B. there are   C. is there   D. are there

5. [2005 春季 上海]

So little _____ with each other that the neighbouring countries could not settle their difference.

A. they agreed   B. agreed they   C. did they agree   D. they did agree

6. [2005 春季 上海]

Sugar, when _____ with water, dissolves quickly.

A. mixed   B. mixing   C. mix   D. is mixed

7. [2005 全国Ⅲ]

Mary never does any reading in the evening, _____.

A. so does John

C. John doesn't too

B. John does too

D. nor does John

8. [2005 上海]

Never before _____ in greater need of modern public transport than it is today.

A. has this city been

C. was this city

B. this city has been

D. this city was

9. [2005 天津]

They have a good knowledge of English but little _____ they know about German.

A. have   B. did   C. had   D. do

10. [2005 重庆]

_____, he talks a lot about his favorite singers after class.

A. A quiet student as he may be   B. Quiet student as he may be

C. Be a quiet student as he may   D. Quiet as he may be a student

11. [2005 辽宁]

—Well, I do think the rabbit is a beautiful, gentle animal which can run very fast.

—_____.

A. So it is   B. So is it   C. So does it   D. So it does

12. [2005 辽宁]

In the dark forests _____, some large enough to hold several English towns.

A. stand many lakes   B. lie many lakes

C. many lakes lie   D. many lakes stand

13. [2005 江苏]

_____ about wild plants that they decided to make a trip to Madagascar for further research.

A. So curious the couple was   B. So curious were the couple

C. How curious the couple were   D. The couple was such curious

14. [2005 湖北]

—Father, you promised!

—Well, _____. But it was you who didn't keep your word first.

A. so was I   B. so did I   C. so I was   D. so I did

15. [2005 安徽]

—Maggie had a wonderful time at the party.

—_____, and so did I.

A. So she had   B. So had she   C. So she did   D. So did she

16. [2005 福建]

Only after my friend came _____.

A. did the computer repair   B. he repaired the computer

C. was the computer repaired   D. the computer was repaired

17. [2005 广东]

_____, Carolina couldn't get the door open.

A. Try as she might   B. As she might try

C. She might as try   D. Might she as try

18. [2006 春季 上海]

Just in front of our house _____ with a history of 1 000 years.

A. does a tall tree stand   B. stands a tall tree

C. a tall tree is standing   D. a tall tree stands

19. [2006 全国 I]

—Will you be able to finish your report today?

—_____.

A. I like it   B. I hope so   C. I'll do so   D. I'd love it

班级_____姓名_____分数_____

1. [2006 天津]

—Did Linda see the traffic accident?

—No, no sooner _____ than it happened.

A. had she gone   B. she had gone   C. has she gone   D. she has gone

2. [2006 重庆]

I've tried very hard to improve my English. But by no means _____ with my progress.

A. the teacher is not satisfied   B. is the teacher not satisfied

C. the teacher is satisfied   D. is the teacher satisfied

3. [2006 重庆]

_____ and I'll get the work finished.

A. Have one more hour   B. One more hour

C. Given one more hour   D. If I have one more hour

4. [2006 安徽]

Never in my wildest dreams _____ these people are living in such poor conditions.

A. I could imagine   B. could I imagine

C. I couldn't imagine   D. couldn't I imagine

5. [2006 江西]

—I reminded you not to forget the appointment.

—_____.

A. So you did   B. So I do not   C. So did you   D. So do I.

6. [2006 福建]

—It's burning hot today, isn't it?

—Yes. _____ yesterday.

A. So was it   B. So it was   C. So it is   D. So is it

7. [2006 湖北]

_____ fired, your health care and other benefits will not be immediately cut off.

A. Would you be   B. Should you be   C. Could you be   D. Might you be

8. [2006 四川]

At the foot of the mountain _____.

A. a village lie   B. lies a village

C. does a village lie   D. lying a village

9. [2006 陕西]

Only then _____ how much damage had been caused.

A. had she realized   B. she realized

C. did she realize   D. she had realized

10. [2007 春季 上海]

—Did you see who the driver was?

—No, so quickly _____ that I couldn't get a good look at his face.

A. did the car speed by   B. the car sped by

C. does the car speed by   D. the car speeds by

11. [2007 春季 上海]

_____ tomorrow, our ship will set sail for Macao.

A. However the weather is like   B. However is the weather like

C. Whatever is the weather like   D. Whatever the weather is like

12. [2007 全国 I]

We all know that, _____, the situation will get worse.

A. not if dealt carefully with   B. if not carefully dealt with

C. if dealt not carefully with   D. not if carefully dealt with

13. [2007 全国 II]

If Joe's wife won't go to the party, _____.

A. he will either   B. neither will he

C. he neither will   D. either he will

14. [2007 上海]

—How was the televised debate last night?

—Super! Rarely _____ so much media attention.

A. a debate attracted   B. did a debate attract

C. a debate did attract   D. attracted a debate

15. [2007 重庆]

—Do you have any idea what Paul does all day?

—As I know, he spends at least as much time playing as he _____.

A. writes   B. does writing   C. is writing   D. does write

16. [2007 重庆]

_____, his idea was accepted by all the people at the meeting.

A. Strange as might it sound   B. As it might sound strange

C. As strange it might sound   D. Strange as it might sound

17. [2007 辽宁]

I have been living in the United States for twenty years, but seldom _____ so lonely as now.

A. have I felt   B. I had felt   C. I have felt   D. had I felt

18. [2007 江苏]

—My room gets very cold at night.

—_____.

A. So is mine   B. So mine is

C. So does mine   D. So mine does

第十三章 并列句

班级_____ 姓名_____ 分数_____

1. [1998 上海]

Tommy caught the school bus,_____.

A. and Jane did neither   B. but so did Jane

C. and Jane didn't either   D. but Jane didn't

2. [1999 全国]

Your performance in the driving test didn't reach the required standard—_____, you failed.

A. in the end   B. after all   C. in other words   D. at the same time

3. [1999 上海]

One more week,_____ we will accomplish the task.

A. or   B. so that   C. and   D. if

4. [2000 春季 北京/安徽]

The changes in the city will cost quite a lot,_____ they will save us money in the long run.

A. or   B. since   C. for   D. but

5. [2000 春季 上海]

There was no news,_____, she did not give up hope.

A. moreover   B. therefore   C. but   D. nevertheless

6. [2000 上海]

He holds an important position in the company;_____, I don't quite trust him.

A. thus   B. furthermore   C. otherwise   D. nevertheless

7. [2002 全国]

Excuse me for breaking in,_____ I have some news for you.

A. so   B. and   C. but   D. yet

8. [2002 北京]

It is so nice to hear from her._____, we last met more than thirty years ago.

A. What's more   B. That is to say

C. In other words   D. Believe it or not

9. [2002 北京]

—Would you like to come to the dinner party here on Saturday?

—Thank you. I'd love to,_____ I'll be out of town at the weekend.

A. because   B. and   C. so   D. but

10. [2003 全国]

We're going to the bookstore in John's car. You can come with us _____ you can meet us there later.

    A. but   B. and   C. or   D. then

11. [2004 春季 北京/安徽]

The shop doesn't open until 11:00 a. m. ,_____ it loses a lot of business.

    A. for   B. or   C. but   D. so

12. [2004 春季 北京/安徽]

—Do you think I should get a good guidebook?

—Yes, of course. _____ , you also need a good camera and comfortable shoes.

    A. What's more   B. In other words   C. By the way   D. All in all

13. [2004 全国 I]

I don't mind picking up your things from the store. _____ , the walk will do me good.

    A. Sooner or later   B. Still   C. In time   D. Besides

14. [2004 全国 III]

To enjoy the scenery, Irene would rather spend long hours on the train _____ travel by air.

    A. as   B. to   C. than   D. while

15. [2004 全国 III]

I hope you don't mind me asking,_____ where did you buy those shoes?

    A. so   B. and   C. yet   D. but

16. [2004 全国 III]

I do every single bit of housework _____ my husband Bob just does the dishes now and then.

    A. since   B. while   C. when   D. as

17. [2004 全国 IV]

Paul had to write a history paper,_____ he couldn't find time to do it.

    A. but   B. so   C. because   D. if

18. [2004 全国 IV]

People may have different opinions about Karen, but I admire her. _____ , she is a great musician.

    A. After all   B. As a result   C. In other words   D. As usual

19. [2004 上海]

—English has a large vocabulary, hasn't it?

—Yes. _____ more words and expressions and you will find it easier to read and communicate.

    A. Know   B. Knowing   C. To know   D. Known

20. [2004 天津]

Stand over there _____ you'll be able to see it better.

    A. or   B. while   C. but   D. and

班级_____ 姓名_____ 分数_____

1.〔2004 重庆〕

—I think George doesn't really care for TV plays.

—Right,_____ he still watches the program.

A. and   B. but   C. or   D. so

2.〔2004 辽宁〕

There are many kinds of sports,_____ my favorite is swimming.

A. as   B. then   C. so   D. but

3.〔2004 浙江〕

The winter of 1990 was extremely bad. _____,most people say it was the worst winter of their lives.

A. At last   B. In fact   C. In a word   D. As a result

4.〔2004 湖北〕

_____ straight on and you'll see a church. You won't miss it.

A. Go   B. Going   C. If you go   D. When going

5.〔2005 春季 北京〕

Lose one hour in the morning _____ you will be looking for it the rest of the day.

A. but   B. and   C. or   D. so

6.〔2005 全国 I／II〕

They wanted to charge ＄5 000 for the car,_____ we managed to bring the price down.

A. but   B. so   C. when   D. since

7.〔2005 北京〕

—Somebody wants you on the telephone.

—_____ no one knows I'm here.

A. For   B. And   C. But   D. So

8.〔2005 上海〕

At last,we found ourselves in a pleasant park with trees providing shade and _____ down to eat our picnic lunch.

A. sitting   B. having sat   C. to sit   D. sat

9.〔2005 辽宁〕

Follow your doctor's advice,_____ your cough will get worse.

A. or   B. and   C. then   D. so

10.〔2005 江苏〕

Unlike watching TV,reading is a highly active process,_____ it requires attention as well as memory and imagination.

A. until   B. but   C. unless   D. for

11. [2005 浙江]

Maggie has been fortunate to find a job she loves and, _____, she gets well paid for it.

A. sooner or later   B. what's more   C. as a result   D. more or less

12. [2005 江西]

My friend Martin was very sick with a strange fever; _____, he could neither eat nor sleep.

A. as a result   B. after all   C. any way   D. otherwise

13. [2006 全国 I]

We thought there were 35 students in the dining hall, _____, in fact, there were 40.

A. while   B. whether   C. what   D. which

14. [2006 北京]

He found it increasingly difficult to read, _____ his eyesight was beginning to fail.

A. and   B. for   C. but   D. or

15. [2006 天津]

The cost of living in Glasgow is among the lowest in Britain, _____ the quality of life is probably one of the highest.

A. since   B. when   C. as   D. while

16. [2006 辽宁]

I grew up in Africa, _____ at least I should say that I spent much of the first years of my life there.

A. and   B. or   C. so   D. but

17. [2006 浙江]

Progress so far has been very good. _____, we are sure that the project will be completed on time.

A. However   B. Otherwise   C. Therefore   D. Besides

18. [2006 江西]

The hurricane damaged many houses and business buildings; _____, it caused 20 deaths.

A. or else   B. therefore   C. after all   D. besides

19. [2006 湖北]

I'm certain David's told you his business troubles. _____, it's no secret that he owes a lot of money to the bank.

A. However   B. Anyway   C. Therefore   D. Though

20. [2006 湖南]

A man cannot smile like a child, _____ a child smiles with his eyes, while a man smiles with his lips alone.

A. so   B. but   C. and   D. for

21. [2006 四川]

Start out right away, _____ you'll miss the first train.

A. and   B. but   C. or   D. while

班级＿＿＿＿＿姓名＿＿＿＿＿分数＿＿＿＿＿

1. [1998 全国]

Why do you want a new job ＿＿＿＿＿＿ you've got such a good one already?

A. that B. where C. which D. when

2. [1998 上海]

I thought her nice and honest ＿＿＿＿＿＿ I met her.

A. first time B. for the first time

C. the first time D. by the first time

3. [1998 上海]

＿＿＿＿＿＿ journalism seems like a good profession, I would prefer to be a teacher.

A. Although B. Even C. No matter D. Now that

4. [1999 全国]

—I'm going to the post office.

—＿＿＿＿＿＿ you're there, can you get me some stamps?

A. As B. While C. Because D. If

5. [1999 全国]

＿＿＿＿＿＿ you've got a chance, you might as well make full use of it.

A. Now that B. After C. Although D. As soon as

6. [1999 上海]

＿＿＿＿＿＿ everybody knows about it, I don't want to talk any more.

A. For B. Even C. Since D. However

7. [1999 上海]

The director gave me a better offer than ＿＿＿＿＿＿.

A. that of Dick's B. Dick's C. he gave Dick D. those of Dick

8. [1999 上海]

＿＿＿＿＿＿ your composition carefully, some spelling mistakes can be avoided.

A. Having checked B. Check

C. If you check D. To check

9. [2000 春季 北京/安徽]

John may phone tonight. I don't want to go out ＿＿＿＿＿＿ he phones.

A. as long as B. in order that C. in case D. so that

10. [2000 春季 上海]

I shall stay in the hotel all day ＿＿＿＿＿＿ there is news of the missing child.

A. in case　　　　B. no matter　　　　C. in any case　　　　D. ever since

11. [2000 全国]

Someone called me up in the middle of the night, but they hung up _____ I could answer the phone.

A. as　　　　B. since　　　　C. until　　　　D. before

12. [2000 全国]

The WTO cannot live up to its name _____ it does not include a country that is home to one fifth of mankind.

A. as long as　　　　B. while　　　　C. if　　　　D. even though

13. [2001 春季 北京/安徽/内蒙古]

The men will have to wait all day _____ the doctor works faster.

A. if　　　　B. unless　　　　C. whether　　　　D. that

14. [2001 春季 北京/安徽/内蒙古]

—Did you remember to give Mary the money you owed her?

—Yes, I gave it to her _____ I saw her.

A. while　　　　B. the moment　　　　C. suddenly　　　　D. once

15. [2001 春季 上海]

You will succeed in the end _____ you give up halfway.

A. even if　　　　B. as though　　　　C. as long as　　　　D. unless

16. [2002 春季 上海]

It _____ long before we _____ the result of the experiment.

A. will not be; will know　　　　B. is; will know

C. will not be; know　　　　D. is; know

17. [2002 全国]

John shut everybody out of the kitchen _____ he could prepare his grand surprise for the party.

A. which　　　　B. when　　　　C. so that　　　　D. as if

18. [2002 上海]

He was about to tell me the secret _____ someone patted him on the shoulder.

A. as　　　　B. until　　　　C. while　　　　D. when

19. [2003 春季 安徽]

Sally worked late in the evening to finish her report _____ her boss could read it first thing next morning.

A. so that　　　　B. because　　　　C. before　　　　D. or else

20. [2003 春季 安徽]

Mr. Hall understands that _____ maths has always been easy for him, it is not easy for the students.

A. unless　　　　B. since　　　　C. although　　　　D. when

班级_____ 姓名_____ 分数_____

1. [2003 春季 北京]

—Was his father very strict with him when he was at school?

—Yes. He had never praised him _____ he became one of the top students in his grade.

A. after　　　　　B. unless　　　　　C. until　　　　　D. when

2. [2003 春季 上海]

I would appreciate it _____ you call back this afternoon for the doctor's appointment.

A. until　　　　　B. if　　　　　C. when　　　　　D. that

3. [2003 全国]

Don't be afraid of asking for help _____ it is needed.

A. since　　　　　B. unless　　　　　C. although　　　　　D. when

4. [2003 北京]

He made a mistake, but then he corrected the situation _____ it got worse.

A. until　　　　　B. when　　　　　C. before　　　　　D. as

5. [2003 北京]

_____ I know the money is safe, I shall not worry about it.

A. Even though　　　B. Unless　　　　C. As long as　　　D. While

6. [2003 上海]

—How far apart do they live?

—_____ I know, they live in the same neighbourhood.

A. As long as　　　B. As far as　　　C. As well as　　　D. As often as

7. [2003 上海]

A good storyteller must be able to hold his listeners' curiosity _____ he reaches the end of the story.

A. when　　　　　B. unless　　　　　C. after　　　　　D. until

8. [2003 上海]

—Dad, I've finished my assignment.

—Good, and _____ you play or watch TV, you mustn't disturb me.

A. whenever　　　B. whether　　　C. whatever　　　D. no matter

9. [2004 春季 北京/安徽]

We were swimming in the lake _____ suddenly the storm started.

A. when　　　　　B. while　　　　　C. until　　　　　D. before

10. [2004 春季 北京/安徽]

_____ I can see, there is only one possible way to keep away from the danger.

A. As long as　　　B. As far as　　　C. Just as　　　D. Even if

11. [2004 全国 I]

Roses need special care _____ they can live through winter.

A. because　　　　　B. so that　　　　　C. even if　　　　　D. as

12. [2004 全国 II]

_____ you call me to say you're not coming, I'll see you at the theatre.

A. Though　　　　　B. Whether　　　　　C. Until　　　　　D. Unless

13. [2004 全国 IV]

Several weeks had gone by _____ I realized the painting was missing.

A. as　　　　　B. before　　　　　C. since　　　　　D. when

14. [2004 上海]

Jasmine was holidaying with her family in a wildlife park _____ she was bitten on the leg by a lion.

A. when　　　　　B. while　　　　　C. since　　　　　D. once

15. [2004 上海]

Parents should take seriously their children's requests for sunglasses _____ eye protection is necessary in sunny weather.

A. because　　　　　B. though　　　　　C. unless　　　　　D. if

16. [2004 天津]

It was evening _____ we reached the little town of Winchester.

A. that　　　　　B. until　　　　　C. since　　　　　D. before

17. [2004 重庆]

You can eat food free in my restaurant _____ you like.

A. whenever　　　　　B. wherever　　　　　C. whatever　　　　　D. however

18. [2004 辽宁]

We were told that we should follow the main road _____ we reached the central railway station.

A. whenever　　　　　B. until　　　　　C. while　　　　　D. wherever

19. [2004 江苏]

_____ I accept that he is not perfect, I do actually like the person.

A. While　　　　　B. Since　　　　　C. Before　　　　　D. Unless

20. [2004 浙江]

—Brad was Jane's brother!

—_____ he reminded me so much of Jane.

A. No doubt　　　　　B. Above all　　　　　C. No wonder　　　　　D. Of course

21. [2004 浙江]

_____ modeling business is by no means easy to get into, the good model will always be in demand.

A. While　　　　　B. Since　　　　　C. As　　　　　D. If

班级_____ 姓名_____ 分数_____

1. [2004 福建]

Scientists say it may be five or six years _____ it is possible to test this medicine on human patients.

A. since   B. after   C. before   D. when

2. [2004 湖北]

You should try to get a good night's sleep _____ much work you have to do.

A. however   B. no matter   C. although   D. whatever

3. [2005 春季 北京]

It is almost five years _____ we saw each other last time.

A. before   B. since   C. after   D. when

4. [2005 春季 北京]

Simon thought his computer was broken _____ his little brother pointed out that he had forgotten to turn it on.

A. until   B. unless   C. after   D. because

5. [2005 春季 上海]

I am sure that Laura's latest play, _____ staged, will prove a great success.

A. since   B. unless   C. once   D. until

6. [2005 全国Ⅲ]

I always take something to read when I go to the doctor's _____ I have to wait.

A. in case   B. so that   C. in order   D. as if

7. [2005 北京]

I'd like to arrive 20 minutes early _____ I can have time for a cup of tea.

A. as soon as   B. as a result   C. in case   D. so that

8. [2005 上海]

He transplanted the little tree to the garden _____ it was the best time for it.

A. where   B. when   C. that   D. until

9. [2005 天津]

He tried his best to solve the problem, _____ difficult it was.

A. however   B. no matter   C. whatever   D. although

10. [2005 重庆]

It is known to all that _____ you exercise regularly, you won't keep good health.

A. unless   B. whenever   C. although   D. if

11. [2005 辽宁]

There was never any time for Kate to feel lonely, _____ she was an only child.

A. ever since   B. now that   C. even though   D. even as

12. [2005 山东]

It was some time _____ we realized the truth.

A. when   B. until   C. since   D. before

13. [2005 浙江]

The old tower must be saved, _____ the cost.

A. however   B. whatever   C. whichever   D. wherever

14. [2005 安徽]

You must keep on working in the evening _____ you are sure you can finish the task in time.

A. as   B. if   C. when   D. unless

15. [2005 安徽]

That was really a splendid evening. It's years _____ I enjoyed myself so much.

A. when   B. that   C. before   D. since

16. [2005 江西]

Your uncle seems to be a good driver; _____ , I wouldn't dare to travel in his car.

A. even so   B. even though   C. therefore   D. so

17. [2005 福建]

—Did Jack come back early last night?

—Yes. It was not yet eight o'clock _____ he arrived home.

A. before   B. when   C. that   D. until

18. [2005 湖南]

Allow children the space to voice their opinions, _____ they are different from your own.

A. until   B. even if   C. unless   D. as though

19. [2005 广东]

The American Civil War lasted four years _____ the North won in the end.

A. after   B. before   C. when   D. then

20. [2006 春季 上海]

_____ most of the earth's surface is covered by water, fresh water is very rare and precious.

A. As   B. Once   C. If   D. Although

21. [2006 全国Ⅱ]

_____ he has limited technical knowledge, the old worker has a lot of experience.

A. Since   B. Unless   C. As   D. Although

22. [2006 北京]

_____ you've tried it, you can't imagine how pleasant it is.

A. Unless   B. Because   C. Although   D. When

23. [2006 上海]

A dozen ideas were considered _____ the chief architect decided on the design of the building.

A. because   B. before   C. whether   D. unless

班级_____姓名_____分数_____

1. [2006 上海]

My parents were quarrelling about me _____ I could not quite tell why.

A. since　　　　　B. though　　　　　C. if　　　　　D. until

2. [2006 重庆]

In time of serious accidents, _____ we know some basic things about first aid, we can save lives.

A. whether　　　　B. until　　　　　C. if　　　　　D. unless

3. [2006 辽宁]

He was about halfway through his meal _____ a familiar voice came to his ears.

A. why　　　　　B. where　　　　　C. when　　　　　D. while

4. [2006 山东]

How can you expect to learn anything _____ you never listen?

A. in case　　　　B. even if　　　　C. unless　　　　D. when

5. [2006 江苏]

_____ environmental damage is done, it takes many years for the *ecosystem* (生态系统) to recover.

A. Even if　　　　B. If only　　　　C. While　　　　D. Once

6. [2006 浙江]

We won't keep winning games _____ we keep playing well.

A. because　　　　B. unless　　　　C. when　　　　D. while

7. [2006 江西]

In peace, too, the Red Cross is expected to send help _____ there is human suffering.

A. whoever　　　　B. however　　　　C. whatever　　　　D. wherever

8. [2006 福建]

—How long do you think it will be _____ China sends a manned spaceship to the moon?

—Perhaps two or three years.

A. when　　　　　B. until　　　　　C. that　　　　　D. before

9. [2006 湖南]

I had just stepped out of the bathroom and was busily drying myself with a towel _____ I heard the steps.

A. while　　　　　B. when　　　　　C. since　　　　　D. after

10. [2006 四川]

—Why didn't you tell him about the meeting?

—He rushed out of the room _____ I could say a word.

A. before　　　　B. until　　　　C. when　　　　D. after

11. [2006 陕西]

His plan was such a good one _____ we all agreed to accept it.

    A. as   B. that   C. so   D. and

12. [2006 陕西]

This is a very interesting book. I'll buy it, _____.

    A. no matter how it may cost   B. how may it cost

    A. how much may it cost   D. however much it may cost

13. [2007 春季 上海]

_____ there is a snowstorm or some other bad weather, the mail always comes on time.

    A. Because   B. If   C. When   D. Unless

14. [2007 全国 I]

I won't call you, _____ something unexpected happens.

    A. unless   B. whether   C. because   D. while

15. [2007 全国 II]

_____ he had not hurt his leg, John would have won the race.

    A. If   B. Since   C. Though   D. When

16. [2007 北京]

—Where's that report?

—I brought it to you _____ you were in Mr. Black's office yesterday.

    A. if   B. when   C. because   D. before

17. [2007 北京]

Leave your key with a neighbor _____ you lock yourself out one day.

    A. ever since   B. even if   C. soon after   D. in case

18. [2007 上海]

Pop music is such an important part of society _____ it has even influenced our language.

    A. as   B. that   C. which   D. where

19. [2007 上海]

Small sailboats can easily turn over in the water _____ they are not managed carefully.

    A. though   B. before   C. until   D. if

20. [2007 天津]

It is difficult for us to learn a lesson in life _____ we've actually had that lesson.

    A. until   B. after   C. since   D. when

21. [2007 重庆]

My parents live in a small village. They always keep candles in the house _____ there is a power cut.

    A. if   B. unless   C. in case   D. so that

22. [2007 辽宁]

We had to wait half an hour _____ we had already booked a table.

    A. since   B. although   C. until   D. before

历届高考题选 1（测试时间 20 分钟）

1. [**1998 上海**]

It was a matter of _____ would take the position.

A. who   B. whoever   C. whom   D. whomever

2. [**1998 上海**]

_____ caused the accident is still a complete mystery.

A. What   B. That   C. How   D. Where

3. [**1998 上海**]

I had neither a raincoat nor an umbrella. _____ I got wet through.

A. It's the reason   B. That's why   C. There's why   D. It's how

4. [**1998 上海**]

He made another wonderful discovery, _____ of great importance to science.

A. which I think is   B. which I think it is

C. which I think it   D. I think which is

5. [**1998 上海**]

He was very rude to the customs officer, _____ of course made things even worse.

A. who   B. whom   C. what   D. which

6. [**1999 全国**]

You should make it a rule to leave things _____ you can find them again.

A. when   B. where   C. then   D. there

7. [**1999 全国**]

Carol said the work would be done by October, _____ personally I doubt very much.

A. it   B. that   C. when   D. which

8. [**1999 全国**]

—I drove to Zhuhai for the air show last week.

—Is that _____ you had a few days off?

A. why   B. when   C. what   D. where

9. [**1999 上海**]

_____ is mentioned above, the number of the students in senior high schools is increasing.

A. Which   B. As   C. That   D. It

10. [**1999 上海**]

_____ has helped to save the drowning girl is worth praising.

A. Who   B. The one   C. Anyone   D. Whoever

11. [2000 春季 北京/安徽]

The result of the experiment was very good, _____ we hadn't expected.

A. when   B. that   C. which   D. what

12. [2000 春季 北京/安徽]

It was an exciting moment for these football fans this year, _____ for the first time in years their team won the World Cup.

A. that   B. while   C. which   D. when

13. [2000 春季 北京/安徽]

These wild flowers are so special that I would do _____ I can to save them.

A. whatever   B. that   C. which   D. whichever

14. [2000 春季 上海]

The gentleman _____ you told me yestereday proved to be a thief.

A. who   B. about whom   C. whom   D. with whom

15. [2000 春季 上海]

These houses are sold at such a low price _____ people expected.

A. like   B. as   C. that   D. which

16. [2000 春季 上海]

Eat _____ cake you like and leave the others for _____ comes in late.

A. any; who   B. every; whoever   C. either; whoever   D. whichever; whoever

17. [2000 全国]

Dorothy was always speaking highly of her role in the play, _____, of course, made the others unhappy.

A. who   B. which   C. this   D. what

18. [2000 上海]

_____ she couldn't understand was _____ fewer and fewer students showed interest in her lessons.

A. What; why   B. That; what   C. What; because   D. Why; that

19. [2000 上海]

Recently I bought an ancient Chinese vase, _____ was very reasonable.

A. which price   B. the price of which

C. its price   D. the price of whose

20. [2000 上海]

Someone is ringing the doorbell. Go and see _____.

A. who is he   B. who he is   C. who is it   D. who it is

21. [2000 上海]

She found her calculator _____ she lost it.

A. where   B. when   C. in which   D. that

22. [2001 春季 北京/安徽/内蒙古]

John said he'd been working in the office for an hour, _____ was ture.

A. he   B. this   C. which   D. who

班级_____ 姓名_____ 分数_____

1. [2001 春季 北京/安徽/内蒙古]

I read about it in some book or other, does it matter _____ it was?

A. where   B. what   C. how   D. which

2. [2001 春季 上海]

What the doctors really doubt is _____ my mother will recover from the serious disease soon.

A. when   B. how   C. whether   D. why

3. [2001 春季 上海]

Have you seen the film *Titanic*, _____ leading actor is world famous?

A. its   B. it's   C. whose   D. which

4. [2001 春季 上海]

Little Tommy was reluctant to tell the schoolmaster _____ he had done the day before.

A. that   B. how   C. where   D. what

5. [2001 全国]

A computer can only do _____ you have instructed it to do.

A. how   B. after   C. what   D. when

6. [2001 全国]

The film brought the hours back to me _____ I was taken good care of in that faraway village.

A. until   B. that   C. when   D. where

7. [2001 全国]

_____ is known to everybody, the moon travels round the earth once every month.

A. It   B. As   C. That   D. What

8. [2001 上海]

Information has been put forward _____ more middle school graduates will be admitted into universities.

A. while   B. that   C. when   D. as

9. [2001 上海]

He's got himself into a dangerous situation _____ he is likely to lose control over the plane.

A. where   B. which   C. while   D. why

10. [2002 春季 北京/安徽/内蒙古]

—I think it's going to be a big problem.

—Yes, it could be.

—I wonder _____ we can do about it.

A. if   B. how   C. what   D. that

11. [2002 春季 北京/安徽/内蒙古]

The famous basketball star, _____ tried to make a comeback, attracted a lot of attention.

A. where   B. when   C. which   D. who

12. [2002 春季 上海]

_____ fashion differs from country to country may reflect the cultural differences from one aspect.

A. What   B. That   C. This   D. Which

13. [2002 春季 上海]

The famous scientist grew up _____ he was born and in 1930 he came to Shanghai.

A. when   B. whenever   C. where   D. wherever

14. [2002 春季 上海]

Is this the reason _____ at the meeting for his carelessness in his work?

A. he explained   B. what he explained

C. how he explained   D. why he explained

15. [2002 春季 上海]

When you answer questions in a job interview, please remember the golden rule: Always give the monkey exactly _____ he wants.

A. what   B. which   C. when   D. that

16. [2002 北京]

We will be shown around the city: schools, museums, and some other places, _____ other visitors seldom go.

A. what   B. which   C. where   D. when

17. [2002 上海]

Alec asked the policeman _____ he worked to contact him whenever there was an accident.

A. with him   B. who   C. with whom   D. whom

18. [2002 上海]

There's a feeling in me _____ we'll never know what a UFO is—not ever.

A. that   B. which   C. of which   D. what

19. [2002 上海]

_____ be sent to work there?

A. Who do you suggest   B. Who do you suggest that should

C. Do you suggest who should   D. Do you suggest whom should

20. [2002 上海]

Perseverance is a kind of quality—and that's _____ it takes to do anything well.

A. what   B. that   C. which   D. why

21. [2003 春季 安徽]

People have heard what the President has said; they are waiting to see _____ he will do.

A. how   B. what   C. when   D. that

班级_____ 姓名_____ 分数_____

1. [2003 春季 北京]

—Are you still thinking about yesterday's game?

—Oh, that's _____.

A. what makes me feel excited   B. whatever I feel excited about

C. how I feel about it   D. when I feel excited

2. [2003 春季 北京]

We are living in an age _____ many things are done on computer.

A. which   B. that   C. whose   D. when

3. [2003 春季 上海]

_____ has been announced, we shall have our final exams next month.

A. That   B. As   C. It   D. What

4. [2003 春季 上海]

_____ made the school proud was _____ more than 90% of the students had been admitted to key universities.

A. What; because   B. What; that   C. That; what   D. That; because

5. [2003 北京]

York, _____ last year, is a nice old city.

A. that I visited   B. which I visited

C. where I visited   D. in which I visited

6. [2003 上海]

I can think of many cases _____ students obviously knew a lot of English words and expressions but couldn't write a good essay.

A. why   B. which   C. as   D. where

7. [2004 春季 北京/安徽]

Luckily, we'd brought a road map without _____ we would have lost our way.

A. it   B. that   C. this   D. which

8. [2004 春季 上海]

A fast food restaurant is the place _____, just as the name suggests, eating is performed quickly.

A. which   B. where   C. there   D. what

9. [2004 春季 上海]

The other day, my brother drove his car down the street at _____ I thought was a dangerous speed.

A. as   B. which   C. what   D. that

10. 〔2004 全国 I〕

You are saying that everyone should be equal, and this is _____ I disagree.

A. why   B. where   C. what   D. how

11. 〔2004 全国 I〕

The English play _____ my students acted at the New Year's party was a great success.

A. for which   B. at which   C. in which   D. on which

12. 〔2004 全国 II〕

There were dirty marks on her trousers _____ she had wiped her hands.

A. where   B. which   C. when   D. that

13. 〔2004 全国 III〕

The journey around the world took the old sailor nine months, _____ the sailing time was 226 days.

A. of which   B. during which   C. from which   D. for which

14. 〔2004 全国 IV〕

There are altogether eleven books on the shelf, _____ five are mine.

A. on which   B. in which   C. of which   D. from which

15. 〔2004 全国 IV〕

The road is covered with snow. I can't understand _____ they insist on going by motor-bike.

A. why   B. whether   C. when   D. how

16. 〔2004 北京〕

George Orwell, _____ was Eric Arthur, wrote many political novels and essays.

A. the real name   B. what his real name

C. his real name   D. whose real name

17. 〔2004 北京〕

We cannot figure out _____ quite a number of insects, birds, and animals are dying out.

A. that   B. as   C. why   D. when

18. 〔2004 北京〕

_____ is reported in the newspapers, talks between the two countries are making progress.

A. It   B. As   C. That   D. What

19. 〔2004 上海〕

American women usually identify their best friend as someone _____ they can talk frequently.

A. who   B. as   C. about which   D. with whom

20. 〔2004 上海〕

After Yang Liwei succeeded in circling the earth, _____ our astronauts desire to do is walk in space.

A. where   B. what   C. that   D. how

班级_____ 姓名_____ 分数_____

1. [2004 上海]

A story goes _____ Elizabeth I of England liked nothing more than being surrounded by clever and qualified noblemen at court.

A. when   B. where   C. what   D. that

2. [2004 上海]

Why! I have nothing to confess. _____ you want me to say?

A. What is it that   B. What it is that   C. How is it that   D. How it is that

3. [2004 天津]

Helen was much kinder to her youngest son than to the others, _____, of course, made the others envy him.

A. who   B. that   C. what   D. which

4. [2004 天津]

A modern city has been set up in _____ was a wasteland ten years ago.

A. what   B. which   C. that   D. where

5. [2004 辽宁]

The factory produces half a million pairs of shoes every year, 80% _____ are sold abroad.

A. of which   B. which of   C. of them   D. of that

6. [2004 江苏]

_____ is often the case, we have worked out the production plan.

A. Which   B. When   C. What   D. As

7. [2004 浙江]

Anyway, that evening, _____ I'll tell you more about later, I ended up staying at Rachel's place.

A. when   B. where   C. what   D. which

8. [2004 湖北]

There are two buildings, _____ stands nearly a hundred feet high.

A. the larger   B. the larger of them

C. the larger one that   D. the larger of which

9. [2004 湖北]

What surprised me was not what he said but _____ he said it.

A. the way   B. in the way that   C. in the way   D. the way which

10. [2004 湖南]

I work in a business _____ almost everyone is waiting for a great chance.

A. how   B. which   C. where   D. that

11. [2004 湖南]

I think Father would like to know _____ I've been up to so far, so I decide to send him a quick note.

A. which   B. why   C. what   D. how

12. [2004 广东]

I have always been honest and straightforward, and it doesn't matter _____ I'm talking to.

A. who is it   B. who it is   C. it is who   D. it is whom

13. [2004 广东]

Parents are taught to understand _____ important education is to their children's future.

A. that   B. how   C. such   D. so

14. [2005 春季 北京]

Do you still remember the chicken farm _____ we visited three months ago?

A. where   B. when   C. that   D. what

15. [2005 春季 上海]

I want to know _____ the thief was caught on the spot.

A. which   B. that   C. what   D. whether

16. [2005 春季 上海]

Don't leave the sharp knife _____ our little Jane can get it.

A. in which   B. to which   C. that   D. where

17. [2005 春季 上海]

The United States is made up of fifty states, one of _____ is separated from the others by the Pacific Ocean.

A. them   B. those   C. which   D. whose

18. [2005 全国 I / II]

Mary wrote an article on _____ the team had failed to win the game.

A. why   B. what   C. who   D. that

19. [2005 全国 I / II]

I have many friends, _____ some are businessmen.

A. of them   B. from which   C. who of   D. of whom

20. [2005 全国 III]

The poor young man is ready to accept _____ help he can get.

A. whichever   B. however   C. whatever   D. whenever

21. [2005 北京]

As soon as he comes back, I'll tell him when _____ and see him.

A. you will come   B. will you come   C. you come   D. do you come

22. [2005 北京]

—Why does she always ask you for help?

—There is no one else _____, is there?

A. who to turn to   B. she can turn to

C. for whom to turn   D. for her to turn

班级_____姓名_____分数_____

1. [2005 上海]

_____ in the regulations that you should not tell other people the password of your e-mail account.

A. What is required   B. What requires

C. It is required   D. It requires

2. [2005 上海]

If a shop has chairs _____ women can park their men, women will spend more time in the shop.

A. that   B. which   C. when   D. where

3. [2005 天津]

Elephants have their own way to tell the shape of an object and _____ it is rough or smooth.

A. /   B. whether   C. how   D. what

4. [2005 天津]

Last month, part of Southeast Asia was struck by floods, from _____ effects the people are still suffering.

A. that   B. whose   C. those   D. what

5. [2005 重庆]

Mark was a student at this university from 1999 to 2003, _____ he studied very hard and was made Chairman of the Students' Union.

A. during which time   B. for which time

C. during whose time   D. by that time

6. [2005 重庆]

The old lady's hand shook frequently. She explained to her doctor _____ this shaking had begun half a year before, and _____, only because of this, she had been forced to give up her job.

A. when; how   B. how; when   C. how; how   D. why; why

7. [2005 辽宁]

I walked in our garden, _____ Tom and Jim were tying a big sign onto one of the trees.

A. which   B. when   C. where   D. that

8. [2005 辽宁]

Do you have any idea _____ is actually going on in the classroom?

A. that   B. what   C. as   D. which

9. [2005 山东]

The shopkeeper did not want to sell for _____ he thought was not enough.

A. where   B. how   C. what   D. which

10. [**2005 江苏**]

The place _____ the bridge is supposed to be built should be _____ the cross-river traffic is the heaviest.

    A. which; where   B. at which; which

    C. at which; where   D. which; in which

11. [**2005 浙江**]

Jim passed the driving test, _____ surprised everybody in the office.

    A. which   B. that   C. this   D. it

12. [**2005 浙江**]

Danby left word with my secretary _____ he would call again in the afternoon.

    A. who   B. that   C. as   D. which

13. [**2005 浙江**]

_____ I explained on the phone, your request will be considered at the next meeting.

    A. When   B. After   C. As   D. Since

14. [**2005 安徽**]

Great changes have taken place in that school. It is no longer _____ it was 20 years ago, _____ it was so poorly equipped.

    A. what; when   B. that; which   C. what; which   D. which; that

15. [**2005 江西**]

The schools themselves admit that not all children will be successful in the jobs _____ they are being trained.

    A. in that   B. for that   C. in which   D. for which

16. [**2005 江西**]

The way he did it was different _____ we were used to.

    A. in which   B. in what   C. from what   D. from which

17. [**2005 福建**]

Mum is coming. What present _____ for your birthday?

    A. you expect she has got   B. you expect has she got

    C. do you expect she has got   D. do you expect has she got

18. [**2005 福建**]

—Is that the small town you often refer to?

—Right, just the one _____ you know I used to work for years.

    A. that   B. which   C. where   D. what

19. [**2005 湖北**]

Her sister has become a lawyer, _____ she wanted to be.

    A. who   B. that   C. what   D. which

20. [**2005 湖南**]

Frank's dream was to have his own shop _____ to produce the workings of his own hands.

    A. that   B. in which   C. by which   D. how

班级_____ 姓名_____ 分数_____

1. [2005 湖南]

I was surprised by her words, which made me recognize _____ silly mistakes I had made.

A. what　　　　B. that　　　　C. how　　　　D. which

2. [2005 广东]

Some researchers believe that there is no doubt _____ a cure for AIDS will be found.

A. which　　　　B. that　　　　C. what　　　　D. whether

3. [2005 广东]

Many people who had seen the film were afraid to go to the forest when they remembered the scenes _____ people were eaten by the tiger.

A. in which　　　　B. by which　　　　C. which　　　　D. that

4. [2006 春季 上海]

These shoes look very good . I wonder _____ .

A. how much cost they are　　　　B. how much do they cost

C. how much they cost　　　　D. how much are they cost

5. [2006 春季 上海]

Doris' success lies in the fact _____ she is co-operative and eager to learn from others.

A. which　　　　B. that　　　　C. when　　　　D. why

6. [2006 春季 上海]

You can find whatever you need at the shopping centre, _____ is always busy at the weekend.

A. that　　　　B. where　　　　C. what　　　　D. which

7. [2006 全国 I]

—What did your parents think about your decision?

—They always let me do _____ I think I should.

A. when　　　　B. that　　　　C. how　　　　D. what

8. [2006 全国 II]

See the flags on top of the building? That was _____ we did this morning.

A. when　　　　B. which　　　　C. where　　　　D. what

9. [2006 全国 II]

Please remind me _____ he said he was going. I may be in time to see him off.

A. where　　　　B. when　　　　C. how　　　　D. what

10. [2006 北京]

—Could you do me a favor?

—It depends on _____ it is.

A. which　　　　B. whichever　　　　C. what　　　　D. whatever

11. [2006 北京]

Women _____ drink more than two cups of coffee a day have a greater chance of having heart disease than those _____ don't.

A. who;/   B. /;who   C. who;who   D. /;/

12. [2006 上海]

One advantage of playing the guitar is _____ it can give you a great deal of pleasure.

A. how   B. why   C. that   D. when

13. [2006 上海]

In an hour, we can travel to places _____ would have taken our ancestors days to reach.

A. where   B. when   C. which   D. what

14. [2006 上海]

He spoke proudly of his part in the game, without mentioning _____ his teammates had done.

A. what   B. which   C. why   D. while

15. [2006 天津]

If you are traveling _____ the customs are really foreign to your own, please do as the Romans do.

A. in which   B. what   C. when   D. where

16. [2006 天津]

There is much chance _____ Bill will recover from his injury in time for the race.

A. that   B. which   C. until   D. if

17. [2006 天津]

The Beatles, _____ many of you are old enough to remember, came from Liverpool.

A. what   B. that   C. how   D. as

18. [2006 重庆]

Nobody believed his reason for being absent from the class _____ he had to meet his uncle at the airport.

A. why   B. that   C. where   D. because

19. [2006 辽宁]

I was told that there were about 50 foreign students _____ Chinese in the school, most _____ were from Germany.

A. study;of whom   B. study;of them

C. studying;of them   D. studying;of whom

20. [2006 辽宁]

_____ makes this shop different is that it offers more personal services.

A. What   B. Who   C. Whatever   D. Whoever

21. [2006 山东]

_____ team wins on Saturday will go through to the national championships.

A. No matter what   B. No matter which

C. Whatever   D. Whichever

历届高考题选 7（测试时间 20 分钟）

1. ［2006 山东］

Engines are to machines _____ hearts are to animals.

A. as 　　　　　　 B. that 　　　　　　 C. what 　　　　　　 D. which

2. ［2006 山东］

We're just trying to reach a point _____ both sides will sit down together and talk.

A. where 　　　　　 B. that 　　　　　　 C. when 　　　　　　 D. which

3. ［2006 山东］

I just wonder _____ that makes him so excited.

A. why it does 　　 B. what he does 　 C. how it is 　　　　 D. what it is

4. ［2006 江苏］

The owner of the cinema needed to make a lot of improvements and employ more people to keep it running, _____ meant spending tens of thousands of pounds.

A. who 　　　　　　 B. that 　　　　　　 C. as 　　　　　　　 D. which

5. ［2006 江苏］

We haven't settled the question of _____ it is necessary for him to study abroad.

A. if 　　　　　　　 B. where 　　　　　 C. whether 　　　　　 D. that

6. ［2006 浙江］

I was given three books on cooking, the first _____ I really enjoyed.

A. of that 　　　　 B. of which 　　　　 C. that 　　　　　　 D. which

7. ［2006 安徽］

A warm thought suddenly came to me _____ I might use the pocket money to buy some flowers for my mother's birthday.

A. if 　　　　　　　 B. when 　　　　　 C. that 　　　　　　 D. which

8. ［2006 江西］

—Do you have anything to say for yourselves?

—Yes, there's one point _____ we must insist on.

A. why 　　　　　　 B. where 　　　　　 C. how 　　　　　　 D. /

9. ［2006 福建］

Look out! Don't get too close to the house _____ roof is under repair.

A. whose 　　　　　 B. which 　　　　　 C. of which 　　　　 D. that

10. ［2006 湖南］

We saw several natives advancing towards our party, and one of them came up to us, _____ we gave some bells and glasses.

A. to which 　　　　 B. to whom 　　　　 C. with whom 　　　 D. with which

11. [2006 湖南]

With his work completed, the businessman stepped back to his seat, feeling pleased _____ he was a man of action.

A. which   B. that   C. what   D. whether

12. [2006 四川]

—Mom, what did your doctor say?

—He advised me to live _____ the air is fresher.

A. in where   B. in which   C. the place where   D. where

13. [2006 四川]

—It's thirty years since we last met.

—But I still remember the story, believe it or not, _____ we got lost on a rainy night.

A. which   B. that   C. what   D. when

14. [2006 陕西]

She was educated at Beijing University, _____ she went on to have her advanced study abroad.

A. after that   B. from that   C. from which   D. after which

15. [2007 春季 上海]

The thought of going back home was _____ kept him happy while he was working abroad.

A. that   B. all that   C. all what   D. which

16. [2007 春季 上海]

By improving reading skills, you can read faster and understand more of _____ you read.

A. that   B. what   C. which   D. whether

17. [2007 全国 I]

Some pre-school children go to a day care center, _____ they learn simple games and songs.

A. then   B. there   C. while   D. where

18. [2007 全国 II]

_____ matters most in learning English is enough practice.

A. What   B. Why   C. Where   D. Which

19. [2007 北京]

We shouldn't spend our money testing so many people, most of _____ are healthy.

A. that   B. which   C. what   D. whom

20. [2007 上海]

His movie won several awards at the film festival, _____ was beyond his wildest dream.

A. which   B. that   C. where   D. it

21. [2007 上海]

_____ he referred to in his article was unknown to the general reader.

A. That   B. What   C. Whether   D. Where

班级_____姓名_____分数_____

1. [2007 上海]

The traditional view is _____ we sleep because our brain is "programmed" to make us do so.

A. when　　　　B. why　　　　C. whether　　　　D. that

2. [2007 天津]

Those successful deaf dancers think that dancing is an activity _____ sight matters more than hearing.

A. when　　　　B. whose　　　　C. which　　　　D. where

3. [2007 天津]

The seaside here draws a lot of tourists every summer. Warm sunshine and soft sands make it _____ it is.

A. what　　　　B. which　　　　C. how　　　　D. where

4. [2007 重庆]

Human facial expressions differ from those of animals in the degree _____ they can be controlled on purpose.

A. with which　　　　B. to which　　　　C. of which　　　　D. for which

5. [2007 辽宁]

Eric received training in computer for one year, after _____ he found a job in a big company.

A. that　　　　B. which　　　　C. it　　　　D. this

6. [2007 山东]

Could I speak to _____ is in charge of International Sales, please?

A. anyone　　　　B. someone　　　　C. whoever　　　　D. no matter who

7. [2007 山东]

The book was written in 1946, _____ the education system has witnessed great changes.

A. when　　　　B. during which　　　　C. since then　　　　D. since when

8. [2007 江苏]

He was educated at the local high school, _____ he went on to Beijing University.

A. after which　　　　B. after that　　　　C. in which　　　　D. in that

9. [2007 江苏]

Choosing the right dictionary depends on _____ you want to use it for.

A. what　　　　B. why　　　　C. how　　　　D. whether

10. [2007 浙江]

Why not try your luck downtown, Bob? That's _____ the best jobs are.

A. where　　　　B. what　　　　C. when　　　　D. why

11. [2007 浙江]

Chan's restaurant on Baker Street, _____ used to be poorly run, is now a successful business.

    A. that   B. which   C. who   D. where

12. [2007 安徽]

You can only be sure of _____ you have at present; you cannot be sure of something _____ you might get in the future.

    A. that; what   B. what; /   C. which; that   D. /; that

13. [2007 安徽]

Last week, only two people came to look at the house, _____ wanted to buy it.

    A. none of them   B. both of them   C. none of whom   D. neither of whom

14. [2007 江西]

After graduation she reached a point in her career _____ she needed to decide what to do.

    A. that   B. what   C. which   D. where

15. [2007 福建]

The village has developed a lot _____ we learned farming two years ago.

    A. when   B. which   C. that   D. where

16. [2007 福建]

It's none of your business _____ other people think about you. Believe yourself.

    A. how   B. what   C. which   D. when

17. [2007 湖南]

Having checked the doors were closed, and _____ all the lights were off, the boy opened the door to his bedroom.

    A. why   B. that   C. when   D. where

18. [2007 湖南]

By serving others, a person focuses on someone other than himself or herself, _____ can be very eye-opening and rewarding.

    A. who   B. which   C. what   D. that

19. [2007 四川]

It is reported that two schools, _____ are being built in my hometown, will open next year.

    A. they both   B. which both   C. both of them   D. both of which

20. [2007 陕西]

_____ parents say and do has a life-long effect on their children.

    A. That   B. Which   C. What   D. As

21. [2007 陕西]

Today, we'll discuss a number of cases _____ beginners of English fail to use the language properly.

    A. which   B. as   C. why   D. where

第十六章 交际用语和谚语警句

班级_____姓名_____分数_____

1. [2000 上海]

—I don't have any change with me. Will you pay the fare for me?

—_____.

A. That's fine

B. Nothing serious

C. Never mind

D. No problem

2. [2000 上海]

—I didn't know this was a one-way street, officer.

—_____

A. That's all right.

B. I don't believe you.

C. How dare you say that?

D. Sorry, but that's no excuse.

3. [2001 春季 上海]

—Let's go swimming, shall we?

—_____

A. It's my pleasure

B. It doesn't matter

C. Yes, let's go

D. I agree with you

4. [2001 春季 上海]

—I enjoyed the food very much.

—I'm glad you like it. Please drop in any time you like.

—_____

A. Is it all right?

B. I'm afraid I won't be free.

C. Yes, I will.

D. That's great.

5. [2001 春季 上海]

—I'm afraid I can't finish the book within this week.

—_____.

A. Please go ahead

B. That's right

C. Not at all

D. Take your time

6. [2001 春季 上海]

—Hello, may I have an appointment with the doctor?

—_____

A. Sorry, he is busy at the moment.

B. Why didn't you call earlier?

C. Certainly. May I know your name?

D. Sorry, he doesn't want to see you.

7. [2001 春季 上海]

—Do you think our basketballers played very well yesterday?

—_____.

A. They were not nervous at all B. They were still young

C. They played naturally D. They couldn't have done better

8. [2001 全国]

—Good morning, Grand Hotel.

—Hello, I'd like to book a room for the nights of the 18th and 19th.

—_____

A. What can I do for you? B. Just a minute, please.

C. What's the matter? D. At your service.

9. [2002 春季 北京/安徽/内蒙古]

—I've got your invitation.

—Oh, good. _____.

A. Can you come? B. Thanks a lot. C. I'll take it. D. May I help you?

10. [2002 全国]

—I'm taking my driving test tomorrow.

—_____!

A. Cheers B. Good luck C. Come on D. Congratulations

11. [2002 北京]

—It's been a wonderful evening. Thank you very much.

—_____.

A. My pleasure B. I'm glad to hear that

C. No, thanks D. It's OK

12. [2003 春季 安徽]

—Thanks for the lovely party and the delicious food.

—_____.

A. No thanks B. Never mind C. All right D. My pleasure

13. [2003 春季 北京]

—I'm sorry I'm calling you so late.

—_____ okay.

A. This is B. You're C. That's D. I'm

14. [2003 全国]

—I think you should phone Jenny and say sorry to her.

—_____. It was her fault.

A. No way B. Not possible C. No chance D. Not at all

15. [2004 全国 I]

—It's getting late. I'm afraid I must be going now.

—OK. _____.

A. Take it easy B. Go slowly C. Stay longer D. See you

班级_____姓名_____分数_____

1. [2004 全国 I]

—Susan, will you please go and empty that drawer?

—_____?

A. What for   B. What is it   C. How is it   D. How come

2. [2004 全国 II]

—Can I look at the menu for a few more minutes before I decide?

—Of course. _____, Sir.

A. Make yourself at home   B. Enjoy yourself

C. It doesn't matter   D. Take your time

3. [2004 全国 III]

—I'd like to take a week's holiday.

—_____, we're too busy.

A. Don't worry   B. Don't mention it

C. Forget it   D. Pardon me

4. [2004 全国 IV]

—Could I ask you a rather personal question?

—_____.

A. Yes, don't worry   B. Of course, go ahead

C. Yes, help yourself   D. Of course, why not

5. [2004 天津]

—How often do you eat out?

—_____, but usually once a week.

A. Have no idea   B. It depends

C. As usual   D. Generally speaking

6. [2004 重庆]

—Let's go and have a good drink tonight.

—_____ Have you got the first prize in the competition?

A. What for?   B. Thanks a lot

C. Yes, I'd like to.   D. Why not?

7. [2004 辽宁]

—Guess what! I came across an old friend at the party last night.

—_____ I'm sure you had a wonderful time.

A. Sounds good!   B. Very well.   C. How nice!   D. All right.

8. [2004 辽宁]

—_____ I didn't hear you clearly. It's too noisy here.

—I was saying that the party was great.

A. Repeat.   B. Once again.   C. Sorry?   D. So what?

9. [2004 江苏]

—How long are you staying?

—I don't know. _____.

A. That's OK   B. Never mind

C. It depends   D. It doesn't matter

10. [2004 浙江]

—What do you want to do next? We have half an hour until the basketball game.

—_____. Whatever you want to do is fine with me.

A. It just depends   B. It's up to you

C. All right   D. Glad to hear that

11. [2004 福建]

—Go for a picnic this weekend, OK?

—_____. I love getting close to nature.

A. I couldn't agree more   B. I'm afraid not

C. I believe not   D. I don't think so

12. [2004 湖南]

—Now, where is my purse?

—_____! We'll be late for the picnic.

A. Take your time   B. Don't worry   C. Come on   D. Take it easy

13. [2004 广东]

—No, I'm afraid he isn't in. This is his secretary speaking. Can I help you?

—_____

A. Oh, you will.   B. Oh, that's a pity.

C. I should think so.   D. Well, I look forward to hearing from you.

14. [2004 广东]

—Do you mind if I open the window?

—_____ I feel a bit cold.

A. Of course not.   B. I'd rather you didn't.

C. Go ahead.   D. Why not?

15. [2005 全国 I / II]

—Can I speak to Mr. Wang, please?

—_____

A. Who are you?   B. I'm Wang.

C. Speaking.   D. Are you John?

16. [2005 全国 I / II]

—Oh dear! I've just broken a window.

—_____. It can't be helped.

A. Never mind   B. All right   C. That's fine   D. Not at all

班级_____姓名_____分数_____

1. [2005 全国Ⅲ]

—Would you like some more tea?

—_____,please.

A. No more   B. Just a little   C. I've had enough   D. Yes,I would

2. [2005 天津]

—It'll take at least 2 hours to do this!

—Oh,_____! I could do it in 30 minutes.

A. come on   B. pardon me   C. you are right   D. don't mention it

3. [2005 重庆]

—My family usually goes skating for vacation. I like skating,but I want to try something different this year.

—_____

A. Let's go.   B. Cheer up.   C. Like what?   D. Take care.

4. [2005 重庆]

—We missed you at this morning's meeting,Diana.

—_____,but if I hadn't had to meet a friend,I would have been there.

A. Me,too   B. I'm sorry   C. Never mind   D. Thank you

5. [2005 辽宁]

—We'd like you to start work tomorrow if possible.

—I'm sorry,but I can't possibly start until Monday. _____?

A. Do you agree with me   B. Is that a good idea

C. Do you think I'm right   D. Will that be all right

6. [2005 山东]

—Could you do me a favor and take these books to my office?

—Yes,_____.

A. for pleasure   B. I could   C. my pleasure   D. with pleasure

7. [2005 山东]

—Let's go to a movie after work,OK?

—_____

A. Not at all.   B. Why not?   C. Never mind.   D. What of it?

8. [2005 江苏]

—How about putting some pictures into the report?

—_____ A picture is worth a thousand words.

A. No way.   B. Why not?   C. All right?   D. No matter.

9 [2005 浙江]

—Do you think I could borrow your bicycle?

—_____

A. How come?　　　　B. Take your time.　　C. Yes,go on.　　D. Yes,help yourself.

10. [2005 浙江]

—People should stop using their cars and start using public transport.

—_____. The roads are too crowded as it is.

A. All right　　　　B. Exactly　　　　C. Go ahead　　　　D. Fine

11. [2005 浙江]

—I'm afraid Mr. Wood can't see you until 4 o'clock.

—Oh,_____ I won't wait.

A. no doubt　　　B. after all　　　　C. in that case　　　D. in this way

12. [2005 安徽]

—Shall we go to the art exhibition right away?

—_____.

A. It's your opinion　　　　　　　B. I don't mind

C. It's all up to you　　　　　　　D. That's your decision

13. [2005 安徽]

—I'm terribly sorry I broke your glass.

—_____.

A. That's right　　B. Bad luck　　　C. Sorry　　　D. You can forget it

14. [2005 江西]

—Shall I give you a ride as you live so far away?

—Thank you. _____.

A. It couldn't be better　　　　　B. Of course you can

C. If you like　　　　　　　　　D. It's up to you

15. [2005 江西]

—Hello,Mr. Smith. This is Larry Jackson. I am afraid I won't be able to arrive on time for the meeting in your office.

—_____. We'll wait for you.

A. Hurry up　　　B. No doubt　　　C. Cheer up　　　D. That's all right

16. [2005 福建]

—James,I am sorry I used your computer when you were away this morning.

—_____.

A. That's all right　　　　　　　B. It's a pleasure

C. You are welcome　　　　　　　D. Don't mention it

17. [2005 湖北]

—Would you mind my coming over and having a look at your new garden? My little son's curious about those roses you grow.

—_____. You're welcome.

A. Yes,I do　　　B. Never mind　　　C. Yes,please　　　D. Not at all

历届高考题选 4（测试时间 20 分钟）

班级_____ 姓名_____ 分数_____

1. [2005 湖南]

—It's cloudy outside. Please take an umbrella.

—_____.

  A. Yes, take it easy   B. Well, it just depends

  C. OK, just in case   D. All right, you're welcome

2. [2005 广东]

—Mike, our team will play against the Rockets this weekend. I'm sure we will win.

—_____!

  A. Congratulations   B. Cheers   C. Best wishes   D. Good luck

3. [2006 全国 II]

—Excuse me, can you tell me where the nearest bank is, please?

—_____ Oh yes! It's past the post office, next to a big market.

  A. Mm, let me think.   B. Oh, I beg your pardon?

  C. You're welcome.   D. What do you mean?

4. [2006 全国 II]

—I wonder if I could possibly use your car for tonight.

—_____. I'm not using it anyhow.

  A. Sure, go ahead   B. I don't know

  C. Yes, indeed   D. I don't care

5. [2006 天津]

—I'm thinking of the test tomorrow. I'm afraid I can't pass this time.

—_____! I'm sure you'll make it.

  A. Go ahead   B. Good luck   C. No problem   D. Cheer up

6. [2006 重庆]

—Would you like some more soup?

—_____. It is delicious, but I've had enough.

  A. Yes, please   B. No, thank you   C. Nothing more   D. I'd like some

7. [2006 重庆]

—How about seeing the new movie at the theatre tonight?

—_____, but I've got to go over my notes for tomorrow's exam.

  A. All right   B. Sounds great   C. I can't   D. No, I am terribly sorry

8. [2006 辽宁]

—These books are too heavy for me to carry.

—_____.

  A. You may ask for help   B. I'll give you a hand

C. I'll do you a favor   D. I'd come to help

9. [2006 辽宁]

—I'm sorry I'm late, I got held up in the traffic on my way here.

—_____.

A. Don't be late next time   B. You should be blamed

C. It doesn't matter. I'm also late   D. Never mind. Come and sit down.

10. [2006 山东]

—How did you find your visit to Qingdao, Joanna?

—_____.

A. Oh, wonderful indeed   B. I went there alone

C. First by train and then by ship   D. A guide showed me the way

11. [2006 江苏]

—It took me ten years to build up my business, and it almost killed me.

—Well, you know what they say. _____.

A. There is no smoke without fire   B. Practice makes perfect

C. All roads lead to Rome   D. No pains, no gains

12. [2006 浙江]

—Would you take this along to the office for me?

—_____.

A. With pleasure   B. That's right   C. Never mind   D. Don't mention it

13. [2006 安徽]

—How are you getting on with your cleaning? Do you need my help?

—_____, but I think I'm all right.

A. No, thanks   B. That's OK

C. You are helpful   D. That's very kind of you

14. [2006 安徽]

—It's been raining for a whole week. I think it'll get fine soon.

—_____. We are getting into the rainy season now.

A. Yes, it will   B. Of course not

C. It's possible   D. It's hard to say

15. [2006 江西]

—I'm dead tired. I can't walk any farther, Jenny.

—_____, Tommy. You can do it!

A. No problem   B. No hurry   C. Come on   D. That's OK

16. [2006 江西]

—Michael was late for Mr. Smith's oral class this morning.

—_____? As far as I know, he never came late to class.

A. How come   B. So what   C. Why not   D. What for

班级_____ 姓名_____ 分数_____

1. [2006 湖北]

—You know who came yesterday?

—Yao Ming? We had a basketball match.

—_____ He came and watched the game.

A. You guessed it!   B. How did you know that?

C. Well done!   D. That was good news!

2. [2006 四川]

—What a beautiful picture you've drawn!

—_____.

A. Not at all   B. Thank you   C. You're great   D. I'm proud of you

3. [2006 四川]

—Do you mind my smoking here?

—_____.

A. No, thanks   B. No. Good idea   C. Yes, please   D. Yes. Better not

4. [2006 陕西]

—I'm terribly sorry that I made your table cloth dirty.

—_____.

A. Sorry   B. Never mind   C. Don't mention it   D. That's right

5. [2007 全国 I]

—Can you read the sign, sir? No smoking allowed in the lift!

—_____.

A. Never mind   B. Don't mention it

C. Sure, I don't smoke   D. Pardon me

6. [2007 全国 II]

—We have booked a room for today and tomorrow.

—_____, sir.

A. I'm sure   B. My pleasure   C. It's all right   D. I'll check

7. [2007 全国 II]

—I'm sorry to have kept you waiting.

—_____, Bill.

A. You're welcome   B. Go ahead   C. Don't mention it   D. No problem

8. [2007 天津]

—Could you turn the TV down a little bit?

—_____. Is it disturbing you?

A. Take it easy   B. I'm sorry

C. Not a bit   D. It depends

9. [2007 天津]

—I apologize for not being able to join you for dinner.

—_____. We'll get together later.

A. Go ahead   B. Not to worry   C. That's right   D. Don't mention it

10. [2007 重庆]

—Now let's move on to another topic. Do you follow me?

—_____,Professor.

A. No,I am not   B. Yes,I will   C. No,I haven't   D. Yes,perfectly

11. [2007 重庆]

—I've studied growing plants as one of my interests. Could I make some suggestions?

—_____.

A. You will make it   B. Go right ahead

C. Don't mention it   D. Take it easy

12. [2007 辽宁]

—Excuse me,could you tell me the way to the British Museum?

—Sorry,I'm a stranger here.

—_____.

A. Thanks,anyway   B. It doesn't matter

C. Never mind   D. No problem

13. [2007 辽宁]

—Tony said he could fix my bicycle,but I really doubt it.

—_____. He's very good at this sort of thing.

A. Don't worry   B. I couldn't agree more

C. Of course   D. A piece of cake

14. [2007 山东]

—Have you been wasting time on computer games again?

—_____. I've been studying a lot and I need a break.

A. No way   B. Not really   C. I don't agree   D. I couldn't agree more

15. [2007 江苏]

You may not have played very well today,but at least you've got through to the next round and _____.

A. tomorrow never comes   B. tomorrow is another day

C. never put off till tomorrow   D. there is no tomorrow

16. [2007 浙江]

—You should apologize to her,Barry.

—_____,but it's not going to be easy.

A. I suppose so   B. I feel so   C. I prefer to   D. I like to

第十七章 名词辨析

班级_____姓名_____分数_____

1. [1998 上海]

You can take as many as you like because they are free of _____.

A. fare   B. charge   C. money   D. pay

2. [1998 上海]

A _____ will be offered for information leading to the arrest of the bank robber.

A. price   B. fund   C. reward   D. profit

3. [1998 上海]

Do you know the _____ of the saying I just quoted?

A. source   B. resource   C. course   D. cause

4. [1999 上海]

We all know that _____ speak louder than words.

A. movements   B. performances   C. operations   D. actions

5. [1999 上海]

My parents always let me have my own _____ of living.

A. way   B. method   C. manner   D. fashion

6. [1999 上海]

The new law will come into _____ on the day it is passed.

A. effect   B. use   C. service   D. existence

7. [1999 上海]

_____ with foreign countries can bring us much information about the world.

A. Contrast   B. Competition   C. Contact   D. Combination

8. [2000 春季 上海]

Some of the passengers spoke to reporters about their _____ in the burning train.

A. details   B. trips   C. events   D. experiences

9. [2000 春季 上海]

Everybody believes he will be the winner of the 100-metre _____.

A. match   B. competition   C. contest   D. race

10. [2000 春季 上海]

The rescue team made every _____ to find the missing mountain climber.

A. force   B. energy   C. effort   D. possibility

11. [2000 上海]

The lion is considered the king of the forest as it is a(n) _____ of courage and power.

A. example   B. sign   C. mark   D. symbol

12. [2000 上海]

We volunteered to collect money to help the _____ of the earthquake.

A. victims   B. folks   C. fellows   D. villagers

13. [2000 上海]

If you don't take away all your things from the desk, there won't be enough _____ for my stationery.

A. area   B. place   C. room   D. surface

14. [2000 上海]

It is widely accepted that young babies learn to do things because certain acts lead to _____.

A. rewards   B. prizes   C. awards   D. results

15. [2000 上海]

I wrote him a letter to show my _____ of his thoughtfulness.

A. achievement   B. agreement   C. attention   D. appreciation

16. [2000 上海]

One of the advantages of living on the top floor of a highrise is that you can get a good _____.

A. sight   B. scene   C. view   D. look

17. [2001 春季 上海]

This is not a match. We're playing chess just for _____.

A. habit   B. hobby   C. fun   D. game

18. [2001 春季 上海]

No matter what you do, you should put your _____ into it.

A. mind   B. heart   C. brain   D. thought

19. [2001 春季 上海]

There are usually at least two _____ of looking at every question.

A. means   B. directions   C. views   D. ways

20. [2001 上海]

In the botanic garden we can find a(n) _____ of plants that range from tall trees to small flowers.

A. species   B. group   C. amount   D. variety

21. [2001 上海]

—Can you shoot that bird at the top of the tree?

—No, it's out of _____.

A. range   B. reach   C. control   D. distance

22. [2001 上海]

The life of London is made up of many different _____.

A. elements   B. sections   C. materials   D. realities

历届高考题选 2（测试时间 20 分钟）

班级_____姓名_____分数_____

1. [2002 春季 上海]

For the sake of her daughter's health, she decided to move to a warm _____.

A. weather   B. temperature   C. season   D. climate

2. [2002 春季 上海]

I saw Bob play the piano at John's party and on that _____ he was simply brilliant.

A. scene   B. circumstance   C. occasion   D. situation

3. [2002 春季 上海]

It can't be a(n) _____ that four jewelry stores were robbed in one night.

A. coincidence   B. accident   C. incident   D. chance

4. [2002 上海]

To regain their _____ after an exhausting game, the players lay in the grass.

A. force   B. energy   C. power   D. health

5. [2002 上海]

According to the recent research, heavy coffee drinking and heart attack is not necessarily _____ and effect.

A. reason   B. impact   C. fact   D. cause

6. [2002 上海]

Every new _____ has the possibility of making or losing money.

A. event   B. venture   C. adventure   D. expectation

7. [2003 春季 安徽]

If you're driving to the airport, can you give me a _____?

A. hand   B. seat   C. drive   D. lift

8. [2003 春季 安徽]

Perhaps we need to clear away these books to make _____ for our new students.

A. place   B. area   C. space   D. room

9. [2003 春季 北京]

The manager has got a good business _____ so the company is doing well.

A. idea   B. sense   C. thought   D. thinking

10. [2003 春季 上海]

The collapse of the World Trade Centre has put US economy in a difficult _____.

A. occasion   B. case   C. situation   D. background

11. [2003 春季 上海]

More and more people choose to shop in a supermarket as it offers a great _____ of goods.

A. variety   B. mixture   C. extension   D. combination

12. [**2003 北京**]

—I'm sorry I stepped outside for a smoke. I was very tired.

—There is no _____ for this while you are on duty.

A. reason   B. excuse   C. cause   D. explanation

13. [**2003 上海**]

"I don't think it's my _____ that the TV blew up. I just turned it on, that's all," said the boy.

A. error   B. mistake   C. fault   D. duty

14. [**2003 上海**]

One of the consequences of our planet's being warming up is a(n) _____ in the number of natural disasters.

A. result   B. account   C. reason   D. increase

15. [**2003 上海**]

Life is tough in the city. In order to lose their _____, some people drink alcohol.

A. temper   B. mood   C. consciousness   D. pressures

16. [**2004 春季 上海**]

I have read the material several times but it doesn't make any _____ to me.

A. meaning   B. importance   C. sense   D. significance

17. [**2004 春季 上海**]

Usually a child's behaviour is a _____ of his family environment.

A. recognition   B. reflection   C. return   D. record

18. [**2004 春季 上海**]

We need to consider what _____ we will be using for language training.

A. abilities   B. appliances   C. facilities   D. qualities

19. [**2004 全国 IV**]

The faces of four famous American presidents on Mount Rushmore can be seen from a _____ of 60 miles.

A. length   B. distance   C. way   D. space

20. [**2004 上海**]

The environmentalists said wild goats' _____ on the vast grasslands was a good indication of the better environment.

A. escape   B. absence   C. attendance   D. appearance

21. [**2004 上海**]

In dealing with public relations, we should make every effort to prevent the _____ in personality.

A. contact   B. contrast   C. connection   D. conflict

22. [**2004 上海**]

Chinese arts have won the _____ of a lot of people outside China.

A. enjoyment   B. appreciation   C. entertainment   D. reputation

班级_____姓名_____分数_____

1. [2004 湖北]

   Don't leave matches or cigarettes on the table within _____ of little children.

   A. hand   B. reach   C. space   D. distance

2. [2005 春季 上海]

   You will find this map of great _____ in helping you to get around the city.

   A. source   B. sense   C. favour   D. value

3. [2005 春季 上海]

   Do you have any _____ of what life would be like if we lived on other planets?

   A. plan   B. idea   C. impression   D. imagination

4. [2005 春季 上海]

   Beginners are expected to be familiar with the _____ of the reading material before they come to the class.

   A. condition   B. concept   C. contest   D. content

5. [2005 上海]

   He proved himself a true gentleman and the beauty of his _____ was seen as its best when he worked with others.

   A. temper   B. appearance   C. talent   D. character

6. [2005 天津]

   Bill was doing a lot of physical exercise to build up his _____.

   A. ability   B. force   C. strength   D. mind

7. [2005 辽宁]

   The head office of the bank is in Beijing, but it has _____ all over the country.

   A. companies   B. branches   C. organizations D. businesses

8. [2005 浙江]

   I am sure David will be able to find the library—he has a pretty good _____ of direction.

   A. idea   B. feeling   C. experience   D. sense

9. [2005 安徽]

   My _____ of this weekend's activity is going out with some good friends.

   A. idea   B. opinion   C. mind   D. thought

10. [2005 湖北]

    He hasn't slept at all for three days. _____ he is tired out.

    A. There is no point   B. There is no need

    C. It is no wonder   D. It is no way

11. [2006 春季 上海]

    Put the _____ of your tongue against your upper teeth when you produce the sound.

A. tip   B. top   C. peak   D. pole

12. [2006 全国 I]

It is no _____ arguing with Bill because he will never change his mind.

A. use   B. help   C. time   D. way

13. [2006 上海]

When Jane began to take swimming lessons, her main _____ was the fear of water.

A. evidence   B. crisis   C. obstacle   D. danger

14. [2006 天津]

Finding information in today's world is easy. The _____ is how you can tell if the information

you get is useful or not.

A. ability   B. competition   C. challenge   D. knowledge

15. [2006 辽宁]

School children must be taught how to deal with dangerous _____.

A. states   B. conditions   C. situations   D. positions

16. [2006 浙江]

—If you like I can do some shopping for you.

—That's a very kind _____.

A. offer   B. service   C. point   D. suggestion

17. [2006 江西]

It is said that dogs will keep you _____ for as long as you want when you are feeling lonely.

A. safety   B. company   C. house   D. friend

18. [2006 湖北]

To make members of a team perform better, the trainer first of all has to know their _____

and weaknesses.

A. strengths   B. benefits   C. techniques   D. values

19. [2006 湖北]

The _____ on his face told me that he was angry.

A. impression   B. sight   C. appearance   D. expression

20. [2006 湖北]

At the meeting they discussed three different _____ to the study of mathematics.

A. approaches   B. means   C. methods   D. ways

21. [2006 福建]

Always read the _____ on the bottle carefully and take the right amount of medicine.

A. explanations   B. instructions   C. descriptions   D. introductions

22. [2007 春季 上海]

AIDS control and prevention is a _____ to China as well as the whole world.

A. surprise   B. challenge   C. reaction   D. threat

第十八章　形容词和副词辨析

班级_____姓名_____分数_____

1. ［**1998 上海**］

Some of the houses on the hillside are _____ to cars.

A. inaccessible　　　B. impossible　　　C. inconvenient　　　D. inadequate

2. ［**1998 上海**］

Don't be too _____ about things you are not supposed to know.

A. strange　　　B. amusing　　　C. curious　　　D. conscious

3. ［**1998 上海**］

The new research team was led by the _____ enigineer.

A. main　　　B. major　　　C. chief　　　D. primary

4. ［**1999 上海**］

It is a good way for us to memorize new words by seeing them _____.

A. properly　　　B. repeatedly　　　C. clearly　　　D. usually

5. ［**1999 上海**］

Those T-shirts are usually ＄35 each, but today they have a _____ price of ＄19 in the Shopping Center.

A. regular　　　B. special　　　C. cheap　　　D. particular

6. ［**2000 春季 上海**］

A person's _____ body temperature is about 37℃.

A. ordinary　　　B. normal　　　C. common　　　D. usual

7. ［**2000 春季 上海**］

—Will Miss Wang attend our meeting tomorrow?

—It will not be _____ so.

A. commonly　　　B. necessarily　　　C. usually　　　D. extremely

8. ［**2000 春季 上海**］

His laziness at work made him _____ with his workmates.

A. distrusted　　　B. disliked　　　C. unpopular　　　D. unwelcome

9. ［**2000 全国**］

It's always difficult being in a foreign country, _____ if you don't speak the language.

A. extremely　　　B. naturally　　　C. basically　　　D. especially

10. ［**2000 上海**］

What he has done is far from _____.

A. satisfactory　　　B. satisfied　　　C. satisfaction　　　D. satisfy

11. [2000 上海]

After the president made an official announcement, she expressed her _____ opinion.

    A. personal   B. private   C. single   D. individual

12. [2000 上海]

Alice laid her baby on the sofa _____ and wrapped it with a blanket.

    A. silently   B. tenderly   C. friendly   D. comfortably

13. [2000 上海]

Fred is second to none in maths in our class, but believe it or not, he _____ passed the last exam.

    A. easily   B. hardly   C. actually   D. successfully

14. [2000 上海]

Our bodies are strengthened by taking exercise. _____, our minds are developed by learning.

    A. Probably   B. Likely   C. Similarly   D. Generally

15. [2001 春季 北京/安徽/内蒙古]

I am surprised that you should have been fooled by such a(an) _____ trick.

    A. ordinary   B. easy   C. smart   D. simple

16. [2001 春季 上海]

I would be very _____ if you could give me an early reply.

    A. pleasant   B. grateful   C. satisfied   D. helpful

17. [2001 春季 上海]

The lessons given by Mr. Smith are always _____ and interesting.

    A. lovingly   B. lovely   C. lively   D. vividly

18. [2001 春季 上海]

He left in such a hurry that I _____ had time to thank him.

    A. almost   B. even   C. hardly   D. nearly

19. [2001 春季 上海]

While a person is asleep, a part of his brain is still _____.

    A. active   B. alive   C. awake   D. aware

20. [2001 春季 上海]

When you turn on the TV set, clear pictures will _____ appear on the screen.

    A. rapidly   B. hurriedly   C. lately   D. immediately

21. [2001 上海]

When climbing the hill John was knocked unconscious by an _____ rolling stone.

    A. untouched   B. unexpected   C. unfamiliar   D. unbelievable

22. [2001 上海]

Her son, to whom she was so _____, went abroad ten years ago.

    A. loved   B. cared   C. devoted   D. affected

班级_____ 姓名_____ 分数_____

1. [2001 上海]

I don't think Peter is too young to take care of the peg dog _____.

A. correctly   B. properly   C. exactly   D. actively

2. [2001 上海]

According to the new research gardening is a more _____ exercise for older women than jogging or swimming.

A. mental   B. physical   C. effective   D. efficient

3. [2002 春季 北京/安徽/内蒙古]

Two middle-aged passengers fell into the sea. _____, neither of them could swim.

A. In fact   B. Luckily   C. Unfortunately   D. Naturally

4. [2002 春季 上海]

The magazine is a(n) _____ number. You can take it out of the reading-room.

A. back   B. past   C. old   D. former

5. [2002 春季 上海]

It is good for elderly people to be _____ involved in community service.

A. honestly   B. patiently   C. eagerly   D. actively

6. [2002 北京]

All the people _____ at the party were his supporters.

A. present   B. thankful   C. interested   D. important

7. [2002 上海]

Sugar is not an important element in bread, but flour is _____.

A. unique   B. essential   C. natural   D. adequate

8. [2002 上海]

The secret of his success is that he does everything _____.

A. efficiently   B. curiously   C. anxiously   D. sufficiently

9. [2002 上海]

The shopkeeper gave us _____ weight: we got 9 kilos instead of 10 kilos.

A. scarce   B. short   C. light   D. slight

10. [2003 春季 北京]

—You don't look very _____. Are you ill?

—No, I'm just a bit tired.

A. good   B. well   C. strong   D. healthy

11. [2003 春季 上海]

In _____, the northerners are keen on dumplings while the southerners are fond of rice.

A. common   B. total   C. general   D. particular

12. [**2003 春季 上海**]

According to the recent survey, cancer is the leading cause of death among young adults in this area, _____ women.

A. apparently   B. especially   C. exactly   D. probably

13. [**2003 春季 上海**]

The university claims that a(n) _____ international student requires $12 000 to cover the cost of living in one academic year.

A. single   B. only   C. independent   D. unique

14. [**2003 上海**]

My grandfather is as _____ as a young man and hates sitting around doing nothing all day.

A. enthusiastic   B. energetic   C. talkative   D. sensitive

15. [**2003 上海**]

Broadly speaking, I would agree with Shirley, though not _____.

A. widely   B. thoroughly   C. entirely   D. extensively

16. [**2003 上海**]

Those who change mobile phones frequently will pay a heavy price for being _____.

A. graceful   B. fashionable   C. particular   D. feasible

17. [**2004 春季 上海**]

Although I can walk about, there is still a _____ pain in my leg.

A. weak   B. slight   C. tender   D. soft

18. [**2004 春季 上海**]

Finnish President said Finland-China relations had progressed _____ with fruitful cooperation in new and high-tech fields.

A. peacefully   B. highly   C. quietly   D. smoothly

19. [**2004 春季 上海**]

The elderly need special care in winter, as they are _____ to the sudden change of weather.

A. sensitive   B. sensible   C. flexible   D. positive

20. [**2004 全国Ⅲ**]

When we plan our vacation, mother often offers _____ suggestions.

A. careful   B. practical   C. effective   D. acceptable

21. [**2004 上海**]

In _____ Chinese culture, marriage decisions were often made by parents for their children.

A. traditional   B. historic   C. remote   D. initial

22. [**2004 上海**]

Most people on this island are recreational fishers, and _____, fishing forms an actual part of their leisure time.

A. accidentally   B. purposefully   C. obviously   D. formally

班级_____姓名_____分数_____

1. [2004 天津]

Mr. Smith used to smoke _____ but he has given it up.

A. seriously   B. heavily   C. badly   D. hardly

2. [2005 春季 上海]

That his only son was killed in the air crash was a _____ blow to the old man.

A. heavy   B. broad   C. plain   D. main

3. [2005 春季 上海]

I don't care about the good salary offered by the company. What I need is a(n) _____ post.

A. creating   B. awarding   C. challenging   D. competing

4. [2005 春季 上海]

The more frequently farmers use insecticides, the more _____ the insects will become to the chemicals.

A. resistant   B. available   C. sensitive   D. agreeable

5. [2005 春季 上海]

Studies show that many diseases such as SARS and AIDS are _____ from wildlife.

A. especially   B. originally   C. magically   D. visibly

6. [2005 上海]

There was such a long queue for coffee at the interval that we _____ gave up.

A. eventually   B. unfortunately   C. generously   D. purposefully

7. [2005 上海]

At times, worrying is a normal, _____ response to a difficult event or situation—a loved one being injured in an accident, for example.

A. effective   B. individual   C. inevitable   D. unfavorable

8. [2005 天津]

If it is quite _____ to you, I will visit you next Tuesday.

A. convenient   B. fair   C. easy   D. comfortable

9. [2005 浙江]

My mother always gets a bit _____ if we don't arrive when we say we will.

A. anxious   B. ashamed   C. weak   D. patient

10. [2006 春季 上海]

Small cars are _____ of fuel, so they have more appeal for consumers.

A. free   B. short   C. typical   D. economical

11. [2006 春季 上海]

The performer was waving his stick in the street and it _____ missed the child standing nearby.

A. narrowly   B. nearly   C. hardly   D. closely

12. [2006 上海]

You can see the stars on a clear night, but in the daytime they are _____.

A. unavoidable   B. invisible   C. inaccessible   D. unavailable

13. [2006 上海]

I hope I will not be called on in class as I'm not yet _____ prepared.

A. attentively   B. readily   C. actively   D. adequately

14. [2006 天津]

Fitness is important in sport, but of at least _____ importance are skills.

A. fair   B. reasonable   C. equal   D. proper

15. [2006 江苏]

The committee is discussing the problem right now. It will _____ have been solved by the end of next week.

A. eagerly   B. hopefully   C. immediately   D. gradually

16. [2006 浙江]

Letterboxes are much more _____ in the UK than in the US, where most people have a mailbox instead.

A. common   B. normal   C. ordinary   D. usual

17. [2006 福建]

Green products are becoming more and more popular because they are environmentally _____.

A. friendly   B. various   C. common   D. changeable

18. [2007 春季 上海]

Although the country has had political independence for over a century, _____, it needs the support of its neighbours.

A. naturally   B. economically   C. especially   D. luckily

19. [2007 春季 上海]

The study surveyed 500 families and found the main _____ problem people suffered was tiredness, followed by loneliness and anxiety.

A. domestic   B. public   C. psychological   D. biological

20. [2007 上海]

Since Tom _____ downloaded a virus into his computer, he can not open the file now.

A. readily   B. horribly   C. accidentally   D. irregularly

21. [2007 上海]

John was dismissed last week because of his _____ attitude towards his job.

A. informal   B. casual   C. determined   D. earnest

22. [2007 天津]

A new _____ bus service to Tianjin Airport started to operate two months ago.

A. normal   B. usual   C. regular   D. common

第十九章 动词和动词词组辨析

班级_____姓名_____分数_____

1. [1998 全国]

Nobody noticed the thief slip into the house because the lights happened to _____.

A. be put up   B. give in   C. be turned on   D. go out

2. [1998 全国]

They _____ the train until it disappeared in the distance.

A. saw   B. watched   C. noticed   D. observed

3. [1998 上海]

Don't _____ that all those who get good grades in the entrance examination will prove to be most successful.

A. take as granted   B. take this for granted

C. take that for granted   D. take it for granted

4. [1999 全国]

_____ him and then try to copy what he does.

A. Mind   B. Glance at   C. Stare at   D. Watch

5. [1999 全国]

—Do you think the *Stars* will beat the *Bulls*?

—Yes. They have better players, so I _____ them to win.

A. hope   B. prefer   C. expect   D. want

6. [1999 上海]

—May I speak to Mr. Thomas, please?

—I'm afraid he isn't in. Would you like to _____ a message?

A. take   B. write   C. leave   D. tell

7. [1999 上海]

The manager has _____ to improve the working conditions in the company.

A. accepted   B. allowed   C. permitted   D. agreed

8. [2000 春季 北京/安徽]

—It's a good idea. But who's going to _____ the plan?

—I think Tom and Grey will.

A. set aside   B. carry out   C. take in   D. get through

9. [2000 春季 北京/安徽]

Nick is looking for another job because he feels that nothing he does _____ his boss.

A. serves   B. satisfies   C. promises   D. supports

10. [**2000 春季 上海**]

What you said just now _____ me of that American professor.

    A. mentioned   B. informed   C. reminded   D. memorized

11. [**2000 春季 上海**]

Our English teacher _____ us buying a good English-Chinese dictionary.

    A. asked   B. ordered   C. suggested   D. required

12. [**2000 春季 上海**]

Every classroom in this modern school is _____ with a new TV set.

    A. equipped   B. installed   C. fixed   D. placed

13. [**2000 春季 上海**]

Happily for John's mother, he is working harder to _____ his lost time.

    A. make up for   B. keep up with   C. catch up with   D. make use of

14. [**2000 全国**]

Let Harry play with your toys as well, Clare—you must learn to _____.

    A. support   B. care   C. spare   D. share

15. [**2000 上海**]

—Excuse me, may I ask you some questions?

—Sorry, I'm too busy and haven't even a minute to _____.

    A. spend   B. spare   C. share   D. stop

16. [**2000 上海**]

Although the working mother is very busy, she still _____ a lot of time to her children.

    A. devotes   B. spends   C. offers   D. provides

17. [**2000 上海**]

When I opened the door, a parcel on the floor _____ my eye.

    A. met   B. caught   C. drew   D. attracted

18. [**2000 上海**]

If you had _____ your test paper carefully before handing it in, you would have made fewer mistakes.

    A. looked up   B. thought about   C. gone over   D. gone round

19. [**2001 春季 北京/安徽/内蒙古**]

Would you slow down a bit, please? I can't _____ you.

    A. keep up with   B. put up with   C. make up to   D. hold on to

20. [**2001 春季 北京/安徽/内蒙古**]

—Why haven't you bought any butter?

—I _____ to but I forgot about it.

    A. liked   B. wished   C. meant   D. expected

21. [**2001 春季 北京/安徽/内蒙古**]

Have a good rest, you need to _____ your energy for the tennis match this afternoon.

    A. leave   B. save   C. hold   D. get

班级_____姓名_____分数_____

1. [2001 春季 上海]

My chest _____ when I make a deep breath, doctor.

A. harms   B. wounds   C. hurts   D. injures

2. [2001 春季 上海]

He came to my class every week, but his attitude _____ he was not really interested in the subject.

A. expressed   B. described   C. explained   D. suggested

3. [2001 春季 上海]

The rubber plantation _____ as far as the river.

A. advances   B. extends   C. lies   D. develops

4. [2001 春季 上海]

Tom, _____ yourself. Did you forget the school rules?

A. behave   B. believe   C. perform   D. conduct

5. [2001 春季 上海]

Time will _____ whether I made the right choice or not.

A. see   B. say   C. know   D. tell

6. [2001 春季 上海]

You'd better _____ some money for special use.

A. pick up   B. set aside   C. put off   D. give away

7. [2001 春季 上海]

In order to _____ with the advanced countries, we must keep learning.

A. catch up   B. get along   C. put up   D. go on

8. [2001 全国]

We didn't plan our art exhibition like that but it _____ very well.

A. worked out   B. tried out   C. went on   D. carried on

9. [2001 上海]

I'm planning to hold a party in the open air, but I can make no guarantees because it _____ the weather.

A. links with   B. depends on   C. connects to   D. decides on

10. [2001 上海]

Alice trusts you; only you can _____ her to give up the foolish idea.

A. suggest   B. attract   C. tempt   D. persuade

11. [2001 上海]

Her brother _____ to leave her in the dark room alone when she disobeyed his order.

A. declared   B. threatened   C. warned   D. exclaimed

12. [2002 春季 北京/安徽/内蒙古]

—How are the team playing?

—They're playing well, but one of them _____ hurt.

A. got   B. gets   C. are   D. were

13. [2002 春季 北京/安徽/内蒙古]

—Smoking is bad for your health.

—Yes, I know. But I simply can't _____.

A. give it up   B. give it in   C. give it out   D. give it away

14. [2002 春季 上海]

It seems difficult to _____ "hurt" from "injure" in meaning.

A. judge   B. tell   C. divide   D. separate

15. [2002 春季 上海]

Please follow your supervisor's instructions, or you'll _____ him.

A. discourage   B. offend   C. disturb   D. bother

16. [2002 春季 上海]

After much _____, the shop owner agreed to cut down the price by 20%.

A. debating   B. talking   C. discussing   D. bargaining

17. [2002 春季 上海]

Although he has taken a lot of medicine, his health _____ poor.

A. proves   B. remains   C. maintains   D. continues

18. [2002 春季 上海]

If you _____ any problems when you arrive at the airport, give me a ring.

A. come up with B. set about   C. run into   D. put aside

19. [2002 全国]

The taxi driver often reminds passengers to _____ their belongings when they leave the car.

A. keep   B. catch   C. hold   D. take

20. [2002 全国]

We thought of selling this old furniture, but we've decided to _____ it. It might be valuable.

A. hold on to   B. keep up with C. turn to   D. look after

21. [2002 北京]

—When shall we start?

—Let's _____ it 8:30. Is that all right?

A. set   B. meet   C. make   D. take

22. [2002 北京]

Be careful when you cross this very busy street. If not, you may _____ run over by a car.

A. have   B. get   C. become   D. turn

班级_____姓名_____分数_____

1. [2002 北京]

His mother had thought it would be good for his character to _____ from home and earn some money on his own.

A. run away　　　　B. take away　　　　C. keep away　　　　D. get away

2. [2002 北京]

—Mummy, can I put the peaches in the cupboard?

—No dear. They don't _____ well. Put them in the fridge instead.

A. keep　　　　B. fit　　　　C. get　　　　D. last

3. [2002 上海]

Mary finally _____ Bruce as her life-long companion.

A. received　　　　B. accepted　　　　C. made　　　　D. honoured

4. [2002 上海]

Go and join in the party. _____ it to me to do the washing-up.

A. Get　　　　B. Remain　　　　C. Leave　　　　D. Send

5. [2002 上海]

Whatever rank you may be in, it would be wrong to _____ the law into your own hands.

A. bring　　　　B. hold　　　　C. take　　　　D. seize

6. [2002 上海]

Can you make a sentence to _____ the meaning of the phrase?

A. show off　　　　B. turn out　　　　C. bring out　　　　D. take in

7. [2003 春季 北京]

The idea puzzled me so much that I stopped for a few seconds to try to _____.

A. make it out　　　　B. make it off　　　　C. make it up　　　　D. make it over

8. [2003 春季 上海]

Papermaking began in China and from here it _____ to North Africa and Europe.

A. spread　　　　B. grew　　　　C. carried　　　　D. developed

9. [2003 春季 上海]

Project Hope aims at helping the poor children in remote areas to _____ education.

A. accept　　　　B. keep　　　　C. assist　　　　D. receive

10. [2003 春季 上海]

My brother worked all summer vacation, saving money to _____ his hobby of photography.

A. seek　　　　B. search　　　　C. hunt　　　　D. pursue

11. [2003 春季 上海]

By 1909, Picasso had _____ himself as a painter of great talent in Paris.

A. made　　　　B. recognized　　　　C. admitted　　　　D. established

12. [2003 春季 上海]

He _____ some French while he was away on a business trip in Paris.

A. made out   B. picked up   C. gave up   D. took in

13. [2003 全国]

If anybody calls, tell them I'm out, and ask them to _____ their name and address.

A. pass   B. write   C. take   D. leave

14. [2003 全国]

News reports say peace talks between the two countries _____ with no agreement reached.

A. have broken down   B. have broken out

C. have broken in   D. have broken up

15. [2003 北京]

Don't mention that at the beginning of the story, or it may _____ the shocking ending.

A. give away   B. give out   C. give up   D. give off

16. [2003 上海]

Some passengers complain that it usually _____ so long to fill in travel insurance documents.

A. costs   B. takes   C. spends   D. spares

17. [2003 上海]

Tony is _____ the guidebook, looking for information about Japan, where he will travel soon.

A. tracing   B. skipping   C. inspecting   D. scanning

18. [2003 上海]

Her talent and experience _____ her to the respect of her colleagues.

A. permitted   B. qualified   C. deserved   D. entitled

19. [2003 上海]

The engine of the ship was out of order and the bad weather _____ the helplessness of the crew at sea.

A. added to   B. resulted from   C. turned out   D. made up

20. [2004 春季 北京/安徽]

We're going to _____ with some friends for a picnic. Would you like to join us?

A. get in   B. get over   C. get along   D. get together

21. [2004 春季 北京/安徽]

He was in hospital for six months. He felt as if he was _____ from the outside world.

A. cut out   B. cut off   C. cut up   D. cut through

22. [2004 春季 上海]

The three sisters decided to hold a family party to _____ their parents' silver wedding.

A. celebrate   B. memorize   C. congratulate   D. welcome

班级_____姓名_____分数_____

1. [2004 春季 上海]

Joe Jones, the eldest of the eight children, had to _____ out of high school at the age of 16 to help his father on the farm.

A. leave   B. drop   C. fall   D. go

2. [2004 春季 上海]

Words _____ me when I wanted to express my thanks to him for having saved my son from the burning house.

A. failed   B. left   C. discouraged   D. disappointed

3. [2004 春季 上海]

It was foolish of him to _____ his notes during that important test, and as a result, he got punished.

A. stick to   B. refer to   C. keep to   D. point to

4. [2004 全国 I]

—How about eight o'clock outside the cinema?

—That _____ me fine.

A. fits   B. meets   C. satisfies   D. suits

5. [2004 全国 I]

You can take anything from the shelf and read, but please _____ the books when you've finished with them.

A. put on   B. put down   C. put back   D. put off

6. [2004 全国 II]

The evening news comes on at seven o'clock and _____ only thirty minutes.

A. keeps   B. continues   C. finishes   D. lasts

7. [2004 全国 II]

The forest guards often find campfires that have not been _____ completely.

A. turned down   B. put out   C. put away   D. turned over

8. [2004 全国 III]

In some western countries, demand for graduates from MBA courses has _____.

A. turned down   B. turned over   C. fallen down   D. fallen over

9. [2004 北京]

I don't _____ rock 'n' roll. It's much too noisy for my taste.

A. go after   B. go away with   C. go into   D. go in for

10. [2004 上海]

Hospital staff burst into cheers after doctors completed a 20-hour operation to have one-year-old twins _____ at the head.

A. isolated   B. separated   C. divided   D. removed

11. [2004 上海]

After the trainer was sure that the whale could look after itself, he _____ it into the sea.

A. transported   B. unloaded   C. released   D. handled

12. [2004 上海]

Some people like drinking coffee, for it has _____ effects.

A. promoting   B. stimulating   C. enhancing   D. encouraging

13. [2004 上海]

The teacher wrote an example on the blackboard to _____ the point.

A. illustrate   B. suggest   C. express   D. recognize

14. [2004 上海]

To keep healthy, Professor Johnson _____ cycling as a regular form of exercise after he retired.

A. took up   B. caught on   C. carried out   D. made for

15. [2004 天津]

Happy birthday, Alice! So you have _____ twenty-one already!

A. become   B. turned   C. grown   D. passed

16. [2004 天津]

It was not a serious illness, and she soon _____ it.

A. got over   B. got on with   C. got around   D. got out of

17. [2004 重庆]

Before the war broke out, many people _____ in safe places possessions they could not take with them.

A. threw away   B. put away   C. gave away   D. carried away

18. [2004 重庆]

They see you as something of a worrier, _____ problems which don't exist and crossing bridges long before you come to them.

A. settling   B. discovering   C. seeing   D. designing

19. [2004 辽宁]

The final examination is coming up soon. It's time for us to _____ our studies.

A. get down to   B. get out   C. get back for   D. get over

20. [2004 辽宁]

John was late for the business meeting because his flight had been _____ by a heavy storm.

A. kept   B. stopped   C. slowed   D. delayed

21. [2004 江苏]

It's ten years since the scientist _____ on his life's work of discovering the valuable chemical.

A. made for   B. set out   C. took off   D. turned up

班级_____ 姓名_____ 分数_____

1. [2004 江苏]

A man is being questioned in relation to the _____ murder last night.

   A. advised   B. attended   C. attempted   D. admitted

2. [2004 浙江]

We wanted to get home before dark, but it didn't quite _____ as planned.

   A. make out   B. turn out   C. go on   D. come up

3. [2004 浙江]

If you are feeling so tired, perhaps a little sleep would _____.

   A. act   B. help   C. serve   D. last

4. [2004 福建]

—How do you _____ we go to Beijing for our holidays?

—I think we'd better fly there. It's much more comfortable.

   A. insist   B. want   C. suppose   D. suggest

5. [2004 福建]

It is certain that he will _____ his business to his son when he gets old.

   A. take over   B. think over   C. hand over   D. go over

6. [2004 湖北]

On hearing the news of the accident in the coal mine, she _____ pale.

   A. got   B. changed   C. went   D. appeared

7. [2004 湖北]

We have to _____ the wheat as soon as possible because a storm is on the way.

   A. get away   B. get across   C. get through   D. get in

8. [2004 湖北]

Once a decision has been made, all of us should _____ it.

   A. direct to   B. stick to   C. lead to   D. refer to

9. [2004 湖南]

—_____ for the glass!

—It's OK. I'm wearing shoes.

   A. Look out   B. Walk out   C. Go out   D. Set out

10. [2004 湖南]

He accidentally _____ he had quarreled with his wife and that he hadn't been home for a couple of weeks.

   A. let out   B. took care   C. made sure   D. made out

11. [2004 湖南]

They've _____ us £ 150000 for the house. Shall we take it?

A. provided   B. supplied   C. shown   D. offered

12. [2004 广东]

Helen always helps her mother even though going to school _____ most of her day.

A. takes up   B. makes up   C. saves up   D. puts up

13. [2005 春季 北京]

The Internet has brought _____ big changes in the way we work.

A. about   B. out   C. back   D. up

14. [2005 春季 上海]

The way Einstein answered the question _____ his talent and sense of humour.

A. relieved   B. released   C. revealed   D. recovered

15. [2005 春季 上海]

Doctors are doing research to find out what happens physically when people _____ smoking.

A. quit   B. decline   C. depart   D. reserve

16. [2005 春季 上海]

The photographer needs to charge up the digital camera every day as the battery _____ quickly.

A. shuts up   B. ends up   C. runs out   D. turns out

17. [2005 全国Ⅲ]

Before building a house, you will have to _____ the government's permission.

A. get from   B. follow   C. receive   D. ask for

18. [2005 北京]

It's the present situation in poor areas that _____ much higher spending on education and training.

A. answers for   B. provides for   C. calls for   D. plans for

19. [2005 上海]

The company is starting a new advertising campaign to _____ new customers to its stores.

A. join   B. attract   C. stick   D. transfer

20. [2005 天津]

—Sorry to _____ you, but could I ask a quick question?

—No problem.

A. worry   B. prevent   C. trouble   D. disappoint

21. [2005 天津]

—Julia said she sent you a birthday card yesterday. Have you got it?

—Oh, really! I haven't _____ my mailbox yet.

A. examined   B. reviewed   C. tested   D. checked

22. [2005 重庆]

His idea of having weekly family meals together, which seemed difficult at first, has _____ many good changes in their lives.

A. got through   B. resulted from   C. turned into   D. brought about

1. ［2005 辽宁］

Could you please tell me where you bought the shoes you _____ yesterday?

    A. tried on   B. put on   C. had on   D. pulled on

2. ［2005 山东］

Modern plastics can _____ very high and very low temperatures.

    A. stand   B. hold   C. carry   D. support

3. ［2005 山东］

What shall we use for power when all the oil in the world has _____?

    A. given out   B. put out   C. held up   D. used up

4. ［2005 江苏］

Everybody in the village likes Jack because he is good at telling and _____ jokes.

    A. turning up   B. putting up   C. making up   D. showing up

5. ［2005 江苏］

In our childhood, we were often _____ by Grandma to pay attention to our table manners.

    A. demanded   B. reminded   C. allowed   D. hoped

6. ［2005 浙江］

The president spoke at the business meeting for nearly an hour without _____ his notes.

    A. bringing up   B. referring to   C. looking for   D. trying on

7. ［2005 浙江］

—Ow! I've burnt myself!

—How did you do that?

—I _____ a hot pot.

    A. touched   B. kept   C. felt   D. held

8. ［2005 浙江］

I couldn't _____. The line was busy.

    A. go by   B. go around   C. get in   D. get through

9. ［2005 安徽］

Kathy _____ a lot of Spanish by playing with the native boys and girls.

    A. picked up   B. took up   C. made up   D. turned up

10. ［2005 安徽］

He is such a man who is always _____ fault with other people.

    A. putting   B. seeking   C. finding   D. looking for

11. ［2005 福建］

If anyone happens to drop in while I am out, _____ him or her leave a message.

    A. have   B. get   C. ask   D. tell

12. [2005 福建]

The dictionary is being printed and it will soon _____.

    A. turn out   B. come out   C. start out   D. go out

13. [2005 江西]

Please tell me how the accident _____. I am still in the dark.

    A. came by   B. came upon   C. came to   D. came about

14. [2005 湖北]

To understand the grammar of the sentence, you must break it _____ into parts.

    A. down   B. up   C. off   D. out

15. [2005 湖北]

They started off late and got to the airport with minutes to _____.

    A. spare   B. catch   C. leave   D. make

16. [2005 湖北]

This picture was taken a long time ago. I wonder if you can _____ my father.

    A. find out   B. pick out   C. look out   D. speak out

17. [2005 湖南]

I was just talking to Margaret when Jackson _____.

    A. cut in   B. cut down   C. cut out   D. cut up

18. [2005 湖南]

We went to Canada to travel and my cousin _____ as our guide.

    A. played   B. showed   C. acted   D. performed

19. [2005 广东]

John is leaving for London tomorrow and I will _____ him _____ at the airport.

    A. send; away   B. leave; off   C. see; off   D. show; around

20. [2006 春季 上海]

Sean's strong love for his country is _____ in his recently published poems.

    A. relieved   B. reflected   C. responded   D. recovered

21. [2006 全国Ⅰ]

Mary wanted to travel around the world all by herself, but her parents did not _____ her to do so.

    A. forbid   B. allow   C. follow   D. ask

22. [2006 全国Ⅰ]

There were a lot of people standing at the door and the small girl couldn't get _____.

    A. between   B. through   C. across   D. beyond

23. [2006 全国Ⅱ]

We _____ the last bus and didn't have any money for taxi, so we had to walk home.

    A. reached   B. lost   C. missed   D. caught

24. [2006 全国Ⅱ]

Mike didn't play football yesterday because he had _____ his leg.

    A. damaged   B. hurt   C. hit   D. struck

1. [2006 上海]

Try not to start every sentence with "the". _____ the beginnings of your sentences.

A. Vary   B. Decorate   C. Form   D. Describe

2. [2006 天津]

We want to rent a bus which can _____ 40 people for our trip to Beijing.

A. load   B. hold   C. fill   D. support

3. [2006 天津]

Most of us know we should cut down on fat, but knowing such things isn't much help when it _____ shopping and eating.

A. refers to   B. speaks of   C. focuses on   D. comes to

4. [2006 天津]

Don't respond to any e-mails _____ personal information, no matter how official they look.

A. searching   B. asking   C. requesting   D. questioning

5. [2006 重庆]

—How are you managing to do your work without an assistant?

—Well, I _____ somehow.

A. get along   B. come on   C. watch out   D. set off

6. [2006 辽宁]

The computer system _____ suddenly while he was searching for information on the Internet.

A. broke down   B. broke out   C. broke up   D. broke in

7. [2006 山东]

Someone who lacks staying power and perseverance is unlikely to _____ a good researcher.

A. make   B. turn   C. get   D. grow

8. [2006 山东]

After he retired from office, Rogers _____ painting for a while, but soon lost interest.

A. took up   B. saved up   C. kept up   D. drew up

9. [2006 江苏]

—Are you going to have a holiday this year?

—I'd love to. I can't wait to leave this place _____.

A. off   B. out   C. behind   D. over

10. [2006 浙江]

We're trying to ring you back, Bryan, but we think we _____ your number incorrectly.

A. looked up   B. took down   C. worked out   D. brought about

11. [2006 浙江]

—What should I do first?

—The instructions _____ that you should mix flour with water carefully first.

A. go   B. tell   C. write   D. say

12. [2006 安徽]

It was already past midnight and only three young men _____ in the tea house.

A. left   B. remained   C. delayed   D. deserted

13. [2006 安徽]

—Four dollars a pair? I think it's a bit too much.

—If you buy three pairs, the price for each will _____ to three fifty.

A. come down   B. take down   C. turn over   D. go over

14. [2006 福建]

She _____ Japanese when she was in Japan. Now she can speak it freely.

A. picked out   B. made out   C. made up   D. picked up

15. [2006 江西]

After the earthquake, the injured were cared _____ in the local hospitals or taken by air to the hospitals in the neighboring cities.

A. of   B. for   C. after   D. with

16. [2006 江西]

For all these years I have been working for others. I'm hoping I'll _____ my own business someday.

A. turn up   B. fix up   C. set up   D. make up

17. [2006 湖北]

One of the best ways for people to keep fit is to _____ healthy eating habits.

A. grow   B. develop   C. increase   D. raise

18. [2006 湖北]

It's already 10 o'clock. I wonder how it _____ that she was two hours late on such a short trip.

A. came over   B. came out   C. came about   D. came up

19. [2006 湖北]

The building around the corner caught fire last night. The police are now _____ the matter.

A. seeing through   B. working out   C. looking into   D. watching over

20. [2006 湖北]

As I grew up in a small town at the foot of a mountain, the visit to the village _____ scenes of my childhood.

A. called up   B. called for   C. called on   D. called in

21. [2006 湖北]

Although the wind has _____, the rain remains steady, so you still need a raincoat.

A. turned up   B. gone back   C. died down   D. blown out

历届高考题选 8 (测试时间 20 分钟)

班级_____姓名_____分数_____

1. [2006 四川]

—The boss said we had only three days to finish the work.

—Don't worry. We have already _____ two thirds of it.

A. got down   B. got through   C. given in   D. given away

2. [2006 陕西]

With no one to _____ in such a frightening situation, she felt very helpless.

A. turn on   B. turn off   C. turn over   D. turn to

3. [2007 春季 上海]

If your race car isn't insured, you may _____ losing everything when it hits something solid.

A. delay   B. deny   C. avoid   D. risk

4. [2007 全国 I]

Does this meal cost $50? I _____ something far better than this!

A. prefer   B. expect   C. suggest   D. suppose

5. [2007 全国 I]

"Goodbye, then," she said, without even _____ from her book.

A. looking down   B. looking up   C. looking away   D. looking on

6. [2007 全国 II]

I have _____ all my papers but I still can't find my notes.

A. looked through   B. looked for   C. looked after   D. looked out

7. [2007 全国 II]

Why don't you just _____ your own business and leave me alone?

A. make   B. open   C. consider   D. mind

8. [2007 上海]

At minus 130℃, a living cell can be _____ for a thousand years.

A. spared   B. protected   C. preserved   D. developed

9. [2007 天津]

Hardly could he _____ this amount of work in such a short time.

A. get through   B. get off   C. get into   D. get down

10. [2007 天津]

Lucy has _____ all of the goals she set for herself in high school and is ready for new challenges at university.

A. acquired   B. finished   C. concluded   D. achieved

11. [2007 重庆]

She's having a lot of trouble with the new computer, but she doesn't know whom to _____.

A. turn to   B. look for   C. deal with   D. talk about

12. [2007 辽宁]

Don't be _____ by products promising to make you lose weight quickly.

A. taken off   B. taken out   C. taken away   D. taken in

13. [2007 山东]

It's the sort of work that _____ a high level of concentration.

A. calls for   B. makes up   C. lies in   D. stands for

14. [2007 山东]

In this seaside resort, you can _____ all the comfort and convenience of modern tourism.

A. enjoy   B. apply   C. receive   D. achieve

15. [2007 江苏]

—Have you _____ some new ideas?

—Yeah. I'll tell you later.

A. come about   B. come into   C. come up with   D. come out with

16. [2007 江苏]

—Do you think that housing price will keep _____ in the years to come?

—Sorry, I have no idea.

A. lifting up   B. going up   C. bringing up   D. growing up

17. [2007 浙江]

—Look! He's running so fast!

—Hard to _____ his legs were once broken.

A. know   B. imagine   C. realize   D. find

18. [2007 浙江]

We firmly believe that war never settles anything. It only _____ violence.

A. runs into   B. comes from   C. leads to   D. begins with

19. [2007 浙江]

Would you please _____ this form for me to see if I've filled it in right?

A. take off   B. look after   C. give up   D. go over

20. [2007 安徽]

—Didn't you have a good time at the party?

—Of course I did. As a matter of fact, I had such fun that time seemed to _____ so quickly.

A. go by   B. go away   C. go out   D. go over

21. [2007 福建]

The news of the mayor's coming to our school for a visit was _____ on the radio yesterday.

A. turned out   B. found out   C. given out   D. carried out

22. [2007 湖北]

Emergency line operators must always _____ calm and make sure that they get all the information they need to send help.

A. grow   B. appear   C. become   D. stay

班级_____姓名_____分数_____

1. The house the Smiths bought is anything _____ cheap.

   A. expect　　　　　B. expect for　　　　C. but　　　　　D. but for

2. Sometimes it is the way people say things,_____ what they actually say, that tells us whether they are serious or not.

   A. rather than　　　B. more than　　　　C. but　　　　　D. and

3. If you put your money into that business you risk _____ every penny.

   A. to miss　　　　　B. missing　　　　　C. to lose　　　　D. losing

4. Whenever the two are playing cards together, they are _____ have bitter quarrels.

   A. used to　　　　　B. inclined to　　　　C. like to　　　　D. tend to

5. The sick man's condition is grave, but with careful nursing he will still have chance to pull _____.

   A. over　　　　　　B. through　　　　　C. off　　　　　D. up

6. The young couple kept their friends _____ about their plan of marriage until the wedding day.

   A. illiterate　　　　B. in the dark　　　　C. in dark　　　　D. unknown

7. The doctor told me that the medicine would _____ my fever.

   A. bring down　　　B. settle down　　　　C. run down　　　D. get down

8. The house was *burgled*(盗窃) while the family was _____ in a card game.

   A. entertained　　　B. interested　　　　C. attracted　　　D. absorbed

9. People should be taught to _____ with difficulties from early childhood.

   A. cope　　　　　　B. get along　　　　　C. arrange　　　　D. overlook

10. No one is so _____ as the person who has no wish to learn.

    A. unwise　　　　　B. dull　　　　　　C. ignorant　　　　D. silly

11. It's high time they _____ this road.

    A. mend　　　　　　B. should mend　　　　C. mended　　　　D. will mend

12. With the help of the strong wind, the forest fire is getting _____ control.

    A. above　　　　　　B. outside　　　　　C. beyond　　　　D. under

13. You must remember to _____ all of your belongings with you when you leave this classroom today.

    A. fetch　　　　　　B. get　　　　　　C. bring　　　　　D. take

14. The new skyscraper was _____ only last year.

    A. put up　　　　　B. got up　　　　　C. raised　　　　D. arisen

15. They lifted their heads to _____ in the fresh, clean air.

    A. breath   B. breathe   C. blast   D. absorb

16. He wrote his name _____ and carefully at the top of the paper.

    A. absolutely   B. attentively   C. obviously   D. constantly

17. I'll agree _____ your proposal if you lower the price.

    A. with   B. to   C. on   D. about

18. Jack speaks four languages although he is only of _____ intelligence.

    A. average   B. common   C. middle   D. minor

19. The reason _____ the flood was that heavy rain.

    A. to   B. about   C. for   D. of

20. —What is that building?

    —_____ the garden equipment is stored.

    A. There's a room in which   B. That's the building

    C. It is that   D. That's where

21. Why are you so _____? You never smile or look cheerful.

    A. miserable   B. merry   C. merciful   D. mysterious

22. The flat we have rented is very _____, for it is near the underground station.

    A. suitable   B. convenient   C. comfortable   D. close

23. The plane is _____ take off at 9:30, so we must be at the airport by 8:30.

    A. arranged to   B. due to   C. likely to   D. about to

24. Does Betty object _____ her every night?

    A. you to call   B. for you to call C. to your calling D. your calling

25. The brakes need _____.

    A. adjusted   B. adjustment   C. to adjust   D. adjusting

26. _____ he could not persuade the other members of the committee, he gave in.

    A. To see that   B. That   C. While   D. Seeing that

27. In _____ the room looks like the letter L.

    A. form   B. pattern   C. shape   D. figure

28. _____ he knew nobody in his class, but now he has many friends.

    A. At first   B. First   C. In the first place   D. Firstly

29. The one who murdered Mr. Black was _____ Mrs. Black.

    A. no one than   B. nobody than

    C. none other than   D. no more than

30. The policeman looked me _____ several times and obviously disliked what he saw.

    A. inside out   B. up and down   C. from side to side   D. in and out

1. Though the long-term _____ cannot be predicted, the project has been approved by the committee.

    A. result   B. defect   C. effect   D. affect

2. _____, John is an amateur athlete, but he is well paid for playing football in many countries.

    A. Generally speaking   B. Technically speaking

    C. Biologically speaking   D. Strictly speaking

3. The boy held _____ from social activities because he felt embarrassed with people.

    A. back   B. out   C. down   D. on

4. The earthquake victims are in _____ need of medical supplies.

    A. insistent   B. imminent   C. important   D. urgent

5. It's impossible for a seven-year-old to _____ the solution to such difficult problems.

    A. puzzle over   B. point out   C. figure out   D. single out

6. —I heard that Bod was robbed in the street last night.

    —Well, he _____. He was with me the whole night.

    A. shouldn't be   B. shouldn't have been

    C. couldn't be   D. couldn't have been

7. _____ halfway through the experiment, there was a power failure and the teacher told us to stop.

    A. When only   B. While only

    C. When we were only   D. While we were only

8. Mary Smith decided to give up her job for the _____ of her children.

    A. care   B. sake   C. reason   D. concern

9. From the _____ on his face, I could tell he was surprised.

    A. expression   B. sight   C. appearance   D. view

10. The fact is that I just cannot _____ this dreadful cough.

    A. get out of   B. get rid of   C. get down to   D. get round to

11. The old lady managed to turn _____ at the party despite the awful weather.

    A. up   B. in   C. back   D. round

12. The committee has elected a new _____.

    A. chief   B. principal   C. head   D. chairman

13. The terrible storm did little _____ to the crops.

    A. destruction   B. ruin   C. damage   D. disaster

14. M. Vallee used to be my _____ singer.

    A. famous   B. favorite   C. favorable   D. popular

15. His father forbids _____ at home.

    A. him smoke   B. him to smoke   C. him smoking   D. that he smokes

16. Mary had only a one-week vacation this year _____ her colleagues had more time off.

    A. in spite that   B. except

    C. despite the fact that   D. despite

17. Can you _____ me to the post office?

    A. direct   B. point   C. explain   D. indicate

18. Whenever you go to a new country, you must _____ yourself to new customs.

    A. adapt   B. adopt   C. offer   D. turn

19. Nowadays a large number of people buy _____ Christmas trees instead of real ones.

    A. fake   B. unreal   C. artificial   D. pretended

20. The young teacher is becoming more and more popular among the students because of his _____ of humor.

    A. skill   B. feelings   C. principle   D. sense

21. The bear fell into the _____ the hunters had set for it.

    A. trail   B. trap   C. trick   D. trip

22. I can't _____ him from his brother, for they look very much alike.

    A. keep   B. separate   C. divide   D. distinguish

23. He was at the _____ of his career when he was killed in an accident.

    A. cnd   B. peak   C. best   D. extreme

24. I just didn't know how to deal with the problem and then suddenly a new idea _____ me.

    A. occurred to   B. happened to   C. hit at   D. appeared to

25. I don't think the students are short of paper. But I'll leave some to them _____ they are.

    A. unless   B. until   C. provided   D. in case

26. If you want to know more about our new product, please _____ at the office.

    A. acquire   B. request   C. inquire   D. require

27. The culture and customs of America are more like _____ of England than of any other countries.

    A. these   B. those   C. that   D. one

28. The police finally ran _____ the thief as he was about to escape.

    A. for   B. off   C. after   D. down

29. Please allow me to offer my _____ apologies for my rudeness.

    A. sincere   B. earnest   C. real   D. kind

30. _____, he must be totally exhausted after a two weeks' trip by bus.

    A. As he is strong   B. Strong as he is

    C. Being very strong   D. As a strong man

班级_____姓名_____分数_____

1. The weather is changeable these days, but _____ we'll set off tomorrow because we have to.

   A. in no case   B. in any case   C. in case   D. in that case

2. The students have got to come back before dark, _____?

   A. don't they   B. do they   C. have they   D. haven't they

3. A lot of modern hospital _____ imported from abroad.

   A. equipment has

   C. equipment has been

   B. equipments have

   D. equipments have been

4. People such as government officials, scientists and teachers earn _____.

   A. pay   B. wages   C. income   D. salaries

5. They _____ for ten minutes in a traffic jam.

   A. held up   B. were held up   C. held out   D. were held out

6. She said she would like to _____ next Sunday.

   A. call on my house

   C. call on me

   B. call to my house

   D. call to me

7. Here is a passage _____ from a news item in *China Daily*。

   A. adopted   B. accepted   C. derived   D. adapted

8. I felt it rather difficult to take a stand _____ the opinion of the majority.

   A. to   B. by   C. in   D. against

9. The car the Smiths bought is anything _____ cheap.

   A. but   B. except   C. except for   D. but for

10. _____ the letter, John hurried to the post office to have it mailed.

    A. As he was about to finish writing

    C. As he was writing

    B. Having finished writing

    D. To have finished writing

11. Every means _____ tried out but never with success, as far as I know.

    A. have been   B. has been   C. are   D. is

12. At any time we should combine theory _____ practice.

    A. with   B. into   C. of   D. at

13. If my legs had not been broken, I _____ in bed for days.

    A. would not have lain

    C. would not lay

    B. would not have laid

    D. would not lie

14. _____ for pickpockets when you are shopping in those big crowded stores.

    A. Make out   B. Check out   C. Look out   D. Carry out

15. We were required to _____ the text in one paragraph.

    A. sum up   B. pick up   C. pack up   D. step up

16. Plain clothes _____ the policeman to look into the case thoroughly.

    A. engaged   B. encouraged   C. entitled   D. enabled

17. The Olympic Games to be held in Sydney in the year of 2000 will be televised _____ across the globe.

    A. lively   B. live   C. living   D. alive

18. The old man built a _____ on the slope of the mountain.

    A. wooden small house   B. wooden little house

    C. small wooden house   D. little house wooden

19. Dr. James was last seen in public _____ his daughter's wedding.

    A. on the occasion of   B. on occasion of

    C. in the event of   D. on the chance of

20. If you come across some new words while reading, you may _____ a dictionary.

    A. inquire   B. find   C. search for   D. consult

21. Prof. Li published a _____ book on the history of her motherland.

    A. three-volumes   B. three-volume   C. three-volume's   D. three-volumes'

22. Petrol is manufactured from the _____ oil we take out of the ground.

    A. crude   B. rough   C. raw   D. tough

23. I _____ him to be careful because the road was dangerous.

    A. suggested   B. considered   C. imagined   D. urged

24.   Did you send Mary a present on her birthday?

    —Oh, I _____ but I didn't, for I've been too busy these days.

    A. must have   B. ought to   C. should have   D. have got to

25. _____ in 1943 that the harmful smog made its appearance in Los Angeles.

    A. It is   B. That is   C. It was   D. That was

26. Although the teacher warned him on several occasions, yet he never took any _____ of what she said.

    A. notice   B. notes   C. attention   D. observation

27. Human beings are superior to animals _____ they can use language as a tool to communicate.

    A. in which   B. for which   C. in that   D. for that

28. We had just sat down in the theater when the _____ went up and the play began.

    A. screen   B. curtain   C. sheet   D. cover

29. A circle is a different _____ from a square.

    A. style   B. sign   C. number   D. shape

30. He should like to rent a house, modern, comfortable and, _____, in a quiet environment.

    A. after all   B. in all   C. above all   D. first of all

班级＿＿＿＿＿ 姓名＿＿＿＿＿ 分数＿＿＿＿＿

1. As soon as I get to New York, I'll _____ Jones and get his reaction.

   A. contact   B. contract   C. touch   D. connect

2. He was _____ for words to express his disappointment.

   A. at his best   B. in search   C. on the point   D. at a loss

3. The teacher looked about as if he wanted to _____ everything in the classroom on himself.

   A. express   B. press   C. suppress   D. impress

4. The game was _____ on account of rain.

   A. called for   B. called off   C. called on   D. called up

5. Can you describe the _____ by which paper is made from wood?

   A. process   B. measure   C. procession   D. production

6. Bad treatment _____ her dislike to hate.

   A. increased   B. promoted   C. made   D. fanned

7. She was not aware of his _____ the meeting until he began to speak to the audience.

   A. presence at   B. present at   C. absence from   D. absent from

8. The Chinese government takes _____ towards the population problem.

   A. effective measures   B. decisive measures

   C. a firm attitude   D. a hostile attitude

9. There seems to be no easy _____ to the pollution problem.

   A. answer   B. key   C. solution   D. remedy

10. The thick trees _____ the city from the north spring wind and the sandstorm.

    A. prevent   B. protect   C. defend   D. save

11. She quickly washed the milk off her skirt so that it would not leave a _____.

    A. color   B. shadow   C. dirt   D. stain

12. The plate fell to the ground and _____.

    A. smashed   B. flattened   C. ruined   D. spoiled

13. Our task was to _____ a number of these monkeys alive.

    A. arrest   B. capture   C. seize   D. grasp

14. Any student who _____ his homework is unlikely to pass his examination.

    A. ignores   B. neglects   C. forgets   D. overlooks

15. In my opinion, he's _____ the most imaginative of all the contemporary poets.

    A. by and by   B. as far as   C. by far   D. by then

16. I was not _____ by his many arguments, so finally we agreed to differ.

    A. convicted   B. confirmed   C. convinced   D. concerned

17. Steam-powered trains _____ electricity-driven trains soon after the war.

 A. stood in the way of   B. got out of the way of

 C. gave way to   D. made its way for

18. Most people _____ a television set as an essential piece of furniture.

 A. look at   B. look for   C. look down   D. look upon

19. His explanation has thrown _____ the puzzling problem.

 A. a strange idea of   B. a new light on

 C. a good solution to   D. an easy approach to

20. The police _____ the spy to his house and arrested him.

 A. tracked down   B. traced back   C. traded on   D. trailed behind

21. The child was so interested in the painting that he _____ at it for minutes.

 A. glared   B. watched   C. viewed   D. stared

22. As the snow is still going on, _____ no point in sweeping the road.

 A. that's   B. it is   C. there's   D. we have

23. You _____ your neighbours for help when the robbery took place, but you didn't.

 A. may ask   B. might ask   C. must have asked   D. might have asked

24. A woman and three children are said _____ in the traffic accident.

 A. to be injured   B. to have been injured

 C. having been injured   D. being injured

25. The police are always ready to give a hand to _____ needs help.

 A. who   B. whoever   C. whomever   D. whom

26. Does _____ surprise you to know that the wonderful invention was made by a twelve-year-old schoolboy?

 A. he   B. that   C. this   D. it

27. Liberty does not mean _____ can do what he pleases.

 A. anyone   B. someone   C. everyone   D. man

28. This possibility to raise production _____.

 A. was hardly ever made   B. was hardly ever made use

 C. was hardly ever made use of   D. was hardly ever of use

29. The notice was written in several languages _____ foreign tourists should misunderstand it.

 A. so that   B. lest   C. if   D. otherwise

30. The boy speaks English more fluently that _____ in his class.

 A. any other student   B. any student

 C. all students   D. all the students

班级_____姓名_____分数_____

1. At school they always tried to _____ Bill from me because we were considered troublemakers.
   A. distinguish   B. separate   C. divide   D. tell

2. None of our _____ at contacting Professor Jones was successful.
   A. trials   B. desires   C. attempts   D. requests

3. The boy has _____ for music, but he needs training to be a good singer.
   A. materials   B. potential   C. resources   D. possession

4. The child had gone into the park. _____ his mother was searching for him in the street.
   A. Otherwise   B. Moreover   C. Therefore   D. Meanwhile

5. Many new devices have been designed to make the best possible use of the energy _____ by the sun.
   A. released   B. sent   C. relieved   D. thrown

6. The doctor _____ that an apple a day is the minimum requirement for the sick child to improve his appetite.
   A. maintains   B. retains   C. persists   D. advises

7. Our professor believes that vocabulary is the biggest problem in our English study and all the other professors think _____: they are of similar opinion.
   A. otherwise   B. differently   C. likewise   D. alike

8. At the break between the two classes, our teacher gave us a brief but very interesting _____ of her trip to Hong Kong.
   A. account   B. story   C. introduction   D. counting

9. Scientists have _____ people that the greenhouse effect would bring about very dangerous environment changes.
   A. mentioned   B. warned   C. pointed out   D. urged

10. No western foods were _____ at the dinner party: everything was Chinese.
    A. presented   B. cooked   C. given   D. served

11. It is important that we _____ advantage of what we can find to develop our economy.
    A. take   B. use   C. make   D. get

12. It was so dark in the room that I could _____ read by the window.
    A. fairly   B. barely   C. subtly   D. vaguely

13. Technical schools prepare their students for the _____ of practical skills they learn in class to their work.
    A. study   B. attendance   C. training   D. application

14. I can't see there's any _____ in memorizing large numbers of English words without knowing how to use them.
    A. sense   B. goal   C. purpose   D. meaning

15. When questioned, the students _____ that they had cheated in the test.

    A. indicated   B. realized   C. admitted   D. advocated

16. He is so _____ that he is not only interested in whats, whys and hows, but also able to find

    the answers to all these questions.

    A. diligent   B.. absorbed   C. determined   D. intelligent

17. If you take this task, you must be ready to _____ hardships.

    A. endure   B. undertake   C. experience   D. meet

18. His classmates have _____ a total of 12 400 *yuan* for the student who had a major operation

    last week.

    A. devoted   B. dedicated   C. contributed   D. concentrated

19. Mary's voice _____ with anger as she told about the brutal deeds of the enemy in the village.

    A. turned down   B. turned up   C. troubled   D. trembled

20. My grandfather likes to read in a _____ corner near the fireplace in winter days.

    A. calm   B. cozy   C. casual   D. coarse

21. In the _____ of the concert, the audience strolled and chatted in the hall near the entrance.

    A. pause   B. interruption   C. interval   D. rest

22. In 1920, the writer was born in Fenyang, which was _____ to be on the map.

    A. a town too samll   B. a very small town

    C. a too small town   D. a town very small

23. One and a half hours _____ since we arrived. No one has come to meet us.

    A. was passed   B. have passed   C. has passed   D. pass

24. _____ is the most qualified should be given the job.

    A. Anyone   B. Everyone   C. No matter who   D. Whoever

25. The students are allowed to borrow any books from this library, _____ they can produce the

    library card at the counter and promise to return the books in due time.

    A. provide   B. providing   C. provides   D. to provide

26. _____ the unexpected trouble, we could have fulfilled the task ahead of time.

    A. But for   B. Because of   C. Except   D. Except for

27. The mother kept an extra key to her son's room, _____ the careless boy loses his.

    A. even if   B. lest   C. because   D. in case

28. _____ at the news, their commander kept calm: he knew it might not be true.

    A. As the soldiers were excited   B. Excited as the soldiers were

    C. Excited were the soldiers   D. As excited as the soldiers were

29. The meeting will be held next month, but _____ no telling about its exact date.

    A. it is   B. that is   C. there's   D. we have

30. Parents complained that their children in the kindergarten _____.

    A. were hardly taken good care   B. were hardly taken good care of

    C. had hardly taken good care   D. had hardly taken good care of

班级_____姓名_____分数_____

1. Thousands of people _____ to see the National Day parade.

   A. turned off　　　 B. turned out　　　 C. turned up　　　 D. turned over

2. It was their lack of confidence in their abilities that _____ the failure.

   A. made of　　　 B. brought into　　　 C. resulted from　　　 D. led to

3. Recently the newspapers have reported several _____ on the boundaries of India and Pakistan.

   A. accidents　　　 B. incidents　　　 C. events　　　 D. happenings

4. The actual cost of the building was much higher that our _____.

   A. consideration　　　 B. judgement　　　 C. estimate　　　 D. plan

5. The boy looked very much _____ when he was caught stealing in the supermarket.

   A. discouraged　　　 B. encouraged　　　 C. disappointed　　　 D. embarrassed

6. At the beginning of this term, our professor _____ a list of books for us to read.

   A. passed on　　　 B. fished out　　　 C. made out　　　 D. handed in

7. Only John and Mark were _____ for the difficult job, for they were the most skillful workers here.

   A. singled out　　　 B. worked out　　　 C. taken out　　　 D. picked out

8. Jane's dress is similar in design _____ her sister's.

   A. with　　　 B. like　　　 C. to　　　 D. as

9. The manager _____ the request of the wokers and decided to better the working conditions.

   A. replied to　　　 B. responded to　　　 C. answered　　　 D. reacted to

10. On hearing about the death of her beloved daughter, the old woman tried hard to _____ her emotions.

    A. check　　　 B. get back　　　 C. hold back　　　 D. delay

11. It was the people's courage that _____ the hard time during the war.

    A. brought them through　　　　　　 B. led them through

    C. led them out of　　　　　　 D. brought them out of

12. Let him have his own way. What's the _____ of forcing him to do what he is reluctant to?

    A. aim　　　 B. idea　　　 C. meaning　　　 D. point

13. Whether right or wrong, he has some new ideas about how the experiment should be _____.

    A. operated　　　 B. conducted　　　 C. performed　　　 D. carried

14. _____ giving a general introduction to digital computers, the course also provides practical experience.

    A. In addition to　　　 B. In support of　　　 C. Owing to　　　 D. Because of

15. He accepted his friend's _____ to swim across the river in the depths of winter.

A. offer   B. order   C. charge   D. challenge

16. In order to start the business he had to obtain a large _____ from the bank.

A. loan   B. finance   C. capital   D. debt

17. Mary was _____ the top prize in the sports meet for her excellent performance.

A. rewarded   B. praised   C. awarded   D. shown

18. Only those who are aged sixty or over are _____ to a retirement pension.

A. required   B. compelled   C. entailed   D. entitled

19. A violent crime was _____ every two weeks in this area of the city last year.

A. committed   B. done   C. acted   D. offended

20. It is not considered _____ to smoke in the library.

A. respectful   B. respectable   C. respective   D. respected

21. We were wet all over, for we found no shelter _____ the rain anywhere.

A. of   B. in   C. from   D. against

22. Consumers should do _____ than simply complain about the poor quality of goods.

A. much less   B. far more   C. some more   D. far less

23. It was because the applicant was too conceited _____ she failed in the interview.

A. so that   B. so   C. therefore   D. that

24. Despite all the difficulties, they fulfilled the quota ten days ahead of schedule, _____ was what we had not expected.

A. which   B. that   C. this   D. it

25. The drowning child _____ saved without the soldier's help.

A. could be   B. could have been   C. could not be   D. could not have been

26. He complained that the desks had not been delivered yet, and _____.

A. neither the chairs had been   B. the chairs too

C. the chairs weren't either   D. neither had the chairs

27. _____ you've found, you must give it back to the person it belongs to.

A. That it is   B. What it is   C. Whatever it is   D. However it is

28. I had not even a vague idea _____ was going to happen.

A. in which   B. of what   C. of which   D. in what

29. _____ has been reported in the newspaper, a new TV tower will be built in this city next year.

A. As   B. That   C. It   D. Which

30. The old lady requested that her neighbors _____ at midnight.

A. wouldn't play music loudly   B. don't play music loudly

C. not play music loudly   D. didn't play music loudly

班级_____ 姓名_____ 分数_____

1. Medical care reform has become this city's most important public health _____.
   A. matter   B. question   C. stuff   D. issue

2. When we study a branch of science or technology, the first thing we have to do is to understand the concepts _____.
   A. involved   B. connected   C. concluded   D. evolved

3. During the next few years, old buildings in this city that are _____ repair will be blown up to make room for the new ones.
   A. out of   B. in   C. beyond   D. under

4. Nutritious food, fresh air and enough exercise all _____ to good health.
   A. attribute   B. benefit   C. contribute   D. distribute

5. You'll have nothing to _____ if you refuse to listen to our advice.
   A. grasp   B. gain   C. seize   D. gear

6. The best way to deal with an impolite person is to _____ him.
   A. omit   B. ignore   C. overlook   D. neglect

7. The boy _____ his father's offer of help, for he was trying to be independent.
   A. turned down   B. turned away   C. turned off   D. turned up

8. Free medical treatment in this area covers mental disorder as well as _____ sicknesses.
   A. average   B. normal   C. regular   D. ordinary

9. It is virtually impossible to _____ the mumber of people in the world who have acquired an adequate working knowledge of English in addition to their own languages.
   A. assess   B. appraise   C. estimate   D. evaluate

10. There is little chance that old people over 80 would _____ the dreadful disease.
    A. survive   B. endure   C. maintain   D. retain

11. The old man eventually had a happy family reunion after forty _____ years living in Taiwan.
    A. alone   B. lonely   C. sole   D. single

12. Many new _____ will be opened up in the future for those with a university education.
    A. responsibilities   B. probabilities   C. capabilities   D. opportunities

13. In preparing scientific reports of laboratory experiments, a student should _____ his findings in logical order and clear language.
    A. present   B. preserve   C. propose   D. proceed

14. Many shoes nowadays are made of plastic or similar _____.
    A. objects   B. staff   C. stuff   D. items

15. We cannot _____ the house unless we get a very well-paid job.
    A. deliver   B. offer   C. provide   D. afford

16. We always argued for the _____ of argument and never reached a practical conclusion.

A. sake   B. aim   C. purpose   D. goal

17. As he read more and more widely, he gradually _____ a good habit of making detailed notes on what he was reading.

     A. learned   B. develped   C. acquired   D. raised

18. The young mother was too careless even to _____ that her child was running a fever until the poor boy got so ill that she had to take him to the hospital.

     A. mind   B. note   C. notice   D. recognise

19. The figures _____ that our economy was changing for the better as a result of the open policy.

     A. declared   B. explained   C. discovered   D. indicated

20. There is nothing special about Jane. She is just an _____ student in our class.

     A. average   B. attractive   C. efficient   D. honest

21. Nobody knows what she is going to do because she is _____ changing her mind.

     A. extremely   B. definitely   C. actively   D. constantly

22. _____ person with a little common sense should be able to answer the question.

     A. Either   B. Each   C. Any   D. One

23. The peasants, _____ had been damaged by the flood, were given help by the government.

     A. all of which homes   B. all of whose homes

     C. all of their homes   D. all homes of theirs

24. I went to the concert but it was not such good performance _____ you had told me about.

     A. as   B. what   C. that   D. which

25. New Year's Day is around the corner. It's high time that we _____ preparations for the celebrations.

     A. should make   B. make   C. made   D. must make

26. I would rather _____ at the meeting on such a controversial problem.

     A. you won't speak   B. your not speaking   C. you not speak   D. you didn't speak

27. This poem by Joe Hill _____ into Chinese.

     A. has said to have been translated   B. is said to have been translated

     C. has said having been translated   D. is said having been translated

28. Some of the roads were flooded, _____ made our journey very difficult.

     A. that   B. what   C. which   D. it

29. What a silly mistake it is! We must avoid _____ that again.

     A. doing   B. to do   C. having done   D. to be doing

30. You saw him watching the film? That was impossible. With all his work on hand, he _____ to the cinema last night.

     A. must not go   B. couldn't have gone

     C. wouldn't have gone   D. could not go

班级_____姓名_____分数_____

1. Although the pay is not good, people usually find social work _____ in other ways.

   A. grateful   B. rewarding   C. respectful   D. demanding

2. I am in no _____ this evening to listen to popular music.

   A. feeling   B. attitude   C. mood   D. tendency

3. Athough this is my first time to speak to so many people, I think I'll _____ my nervousness once I stand in front of the audience.

   A. get over   B. get away   C. get off   D. get through

4. I did not know what to do when the computer broke down, but then an idea suddenly _____ to me: Why not ask John for help?

   A. happened   B. turned out   C. came up   D. occurred

5. A _____ from every person, no matter how small, will help the Hope Project to reach its goal of ￥100,000 as the fund to set up a school in the village.

   A. contribution   B. consideration   C. construction   D. conception

6. The Americans and the British not only speak the same language but also _____ a large number of social customs.

   A. take   B. share   C. enjoy   D. have

7. Sixty percent of television viewers chose Mr. Liu as their _____ actor.

   A. perferred   B. preferable   C. favorite   D. famous

8. Every _____ has been made to prevent further pollution of the environment in this area.

   A. attempt   B. job   C. trial   D. effort

9. The news from the reporter at the front has yet to be _____.

   A. affirmed   B. confirmed   C. reformed   D. informed

10. The painter is extremly conscious of the high artistic _____ of his paintings.

    A. price   B. amount   C. value   D. taste

11. It is a nurse's job to _____ the surgeon in the operation room.

    A. assist   B. resist   C. insist   D. persist

12. You will make _____ by selling; if you wait, the price may fall.

    A. gains   B. a benefit   C. interests   D. a profit

13. What she has said so far doesn't make _____.

    A. sure   B. sense   C. money   D. room

14. The foolish parents _____ their son by giving him too much pocket money.

    A. damaged   B. harmed   C. ruined   D. spoiled

15. The play was so touching that the audience could hardly _____ their tears.

    A. hold on   B. hold back   C. hold up   D. hold on to

16. First-aid is the help given to a sick or hurt person before _____ medical treatment from the

doctor.

    A. usual   B. regular   C. original   D. normal

17. Very few of us passed the test, for it was _____ difficult even for top students in our class.

    A. totally   B. completely   C. extremely   D. extensively

18. The driver was _____ by the police that he might be arrested if he was caught speeding on Route No. 521.

    A. warned   B. charged   C. advised   D. instructed

19. There has been no decrease in production; _____ both production and sales have been doubled in the last two years.

    A. on the whole   B. by contrast   C. on the contrary   D. by comparison

20. Wealthy people are not _____ happy; money doesn't mean everything.

    A. certainly   B. naturally   C. undoubtedly   D. necessarily

21. Mary received many postcards from her former students _____ for the kind help she had given to them.

    A. in reply   B. in turn   C. in return   D. in answer

22. Mary certainly talks too much. She is never interested in what _____ has to say.

    A. someone else   B. anyone else   C. somebody   D. anybody

23. The great use of a school education is not so much to teach you things _____ teach you the art of learning.

    A. as to   B. than   C. rather than   D. as for

24. The two brothers have little in common _____ they share the same interest in football.

    A. except   B. except for   C. except that   D. except when

25. A lot of evidence has been found _____ the careless driver was responsible for the road accident.

    A. by which   B. at which   C. where   D. that

26. The shy boy did not have the courage to put his hat on with Mary _____ him.

    A. watching   B. watched   C. to watch   D. watches

27. I failed to pass the exam though my beloved teacher _____ .

    A. was expected me to   B. expected of me

    C. is expected of me   D. expected me to

28. _____ his social position is, it is necessary that he remember to work whole-heartedly for the people.

    A. However   B. Whenever   C. Whatever   D. Wherever

29. The tourist was unable to make himself _____ because of his poor English.

    A. understood   B. be understanding C. understand   D. be understood

30. _____ the traffic jam, he wouldn't have been late for class.

    A. As to   B. But for   C. Despite   D. Because of

参考答案

第一章　冠词

历届高考题选1　1. C　2. D　3. C　4. B　5. A　6. B　7. B　8. C　9. B　10. C
11. C　12. C　13. C　14. A　15. A　16. B　17. C　18. B　19. A　20. A

历届高考题选2　1. C　2. A　3. B　4. A　5. C　6. D　7. B　8. D　9. B　10. B
11. B　12. A　13. A　14. B　15. A　16. C　17. B　18. D　19. C　20. B

历届高考题选3　1. B　2. D　3. D　4. B　5. B　6. C　7. D　8. B　9. A　10. C
11. A　12. B　13. B　14. D　15. C　16. D　17. B　18. C　19. C　20. A

第二章　名词和数词

历届高考题选　1. D　2. A　3. D　4. C　5. B　6. D　7. B　8. A　9. D　10. A
11. D　12. D　13. D　14. D　15. A　16. D　17. C　18. A

第三章　代词

历届高考题选1　1. B　2. A　3. B　4. C　5. A　6. C　7. B　8. A　9. C　10. C
11. C　12. C　13. C　14. A　15. D　16. D　17. B　18. A　19. C

历届高考题选2　1. A　2. B　3. B　4. A　5. B　6. D　7. A　8. A　9. B　10. C
11. B　12. A　13. A　14. D　15. C　16. B　17. A　18. B　19. A　20. B　21. C

历届高考题选3　1. C　2. B　3. D　4. B　5. A　6. C　7. B　8. A　9. B　10. C
11. A　12. B　13. C　14. C　15. A　16. A　17. B　18. C　19. D　20. C　21. D

历届高考题选4　1. B　2. D　3. A　4. B　5. A　6. D　7. D　8. C　9. C　10. A
11. D　12. D　13. A　14. B　15. A　16. A　17. A　18. A

第四章　介词

历届高考题选1　1. D　2. A　3. A　4. A　5. B　6. A　7. B　8. C　9. C　10. B
11. C　12. A　13. D　14. A　15. D　16. A　17. D　18. D　19. B　20. B　21. C

历届高考题选2　1. D　2. A　3. B　4. C　5. B　6. B　7. D　8. C　9. C　10. B
11. D　12. D　13. A　14. B　15. A　16. D　17. B　18. D　19. D　20. D　21. D

历届高考题选3　1. C　2. C　3. B　4. C　5. D　6. A　7. A　8. C　9. A　10. B
11. C　12. A　13. D　14. C　15. A　16. D　17. D　18. C　19. A　20. D　21. A
22. A

第五章　形容词和副词

历届高考题选1　1. A　2. C　3. A　4. C　5. D　6. C　7. B　8. D　9. A　10. B
11. D　12. C　13. A　14. D　15. B　16. A　17. B　18. D　19. A

历届高考题选2　1. D　2. A　3. A　4. B　5. B　6. D　7. D　8. B　9. A　10. A

11. B　**12.** B　**13.** D　**14.** C　**15.** B　**16.** A　**17.** A　**18.** A　**19.** C

　　历届高考题选3　**1.** D　**2.** B　**3.** D　**4.** B　**5.** D　**6.** C　**7.** A　**8.** A　**9.** B　**10.** B

11. A　**12.** D　**13.** B　**14.** D　**15.** A　**16.** B　**17.** B　**18.** C　**19.** C　**20.** A

　　历届高考题选4　**1.** D　**2.** B　**3.** A　**4.** A　**5.** C　**6.** C　**7.** A　**8.** B　**9.** A　**10.** C

11. C　**12.** A　**13.** C　**14.** B　**15.** C　**16.** B　**17.** D　**18.** B　**19.** C　**20.** B　**21.** B

第六章　情态动词和虚拟语气

　　历届高考题选1　**1.** B　**2.** A　**3.** C　**4.** B　**5.** D　**6.** A　**7.** B　**8.** D　**9.** A　**10.** C

11. A　**12.** D　**13.** B　**14.** C　**15.** C　**16.** B　**17.** C　**18.** B　**19.** D

　　历届高考题选2　**1.** C　**2.** D　**3.** B　**4.** C　**5.** B　**6.** C　**7.** C　**8.** B　**9.** A　**10.** C

11. A　**12.** C　**13.** A　**14.** A　**15.** D　**16.** A　**17.** C　**18.** D　**19.** A

　　历届高考题选3　**1.** D　**2.** A　**3.** D　**4.** A　**5.** A　**6.** B　**7.** B　**8.** A　**9.** B　**10.** C

11. B　**12.** B　**13.** D　**14.** A　**15.** B　**16.** B　**17.** D　**18.** C　**19.** D

　　历届高考题选4　**1.** B　**2.** C　**3.** B　**4.** C　**5.** D　**6.** A　**7.** C　**8.** D　**9.** A　**10.** A

11. A　**12.** B　**13.** D　**14.** D　**15.** B　**16.** C　**17.** C　**18.** A　**19.** C　**20.** A

　　历届高考题选5　**1.** C　**2.** C　**3.** C　**4.** C　**5.** A　**6.** B　**7.** C　**8.** C　**9.** D　**10.** D

11. A　**12.** B　**13.** C　**14.** D

第七章　动词的时态和语态

　　历届高考题选1　**1.** B　**2.** D　**3.** C　**4.** C　**5.** B　**6.** D　**7.** A　**8.** C　**9.** D　**10.** B

11. D　**12.** A　**13.** D　**14.** A　**15.** B　**16.** B　**17.** A　**18.** D　**19.** B

　　历届高考题选2　**1.** A　**2.** D　**3.** D　**4.** B　**5.** D　**6.** C　**7.** C　**8.** D　**9.** A　**10.** B

11. B　**12.** C　**13.** A　**14.** B　**15.** D　**16.** D　**17.** B　**18.** A

　　历届高考题选3　**1.** D　**2.** C　**3.** B　**4.** B　**5.** C　**6.** A　**7.** C　**8.** C　**9.** A　**10.** C

11. C　**12.** C　**13.** A　**14.** B　**15.** C　**16.** C　**17.** A　**18.** A　**19.** D

　　历届高考题选4　**1.** D　**2.** C　**3.** B　**4.** B　**5.** D　**6.** C　**7.** D　**8.** D　**9.** C　**10.** D

11. D　**12.** D　**13.** B　**14.** D　**15.** C　**16.** A　**17.** A　**18.** C　**19.** C

　　历届高考题选5　**1.** A　**2.** D　**3.** B　**4.** D　**5.** B　**6.** A　**7.** C　**8.** C　**9.** D　**10.** A

11. C　**12.** C　**13.** B　**14.** D　**15.** C　**16.** D　**17.** B　**18.** C　**19.** D　**20.** C

　　历届高考题选6　**1.** A　**2.** C　**3.** B　**4.** A　**5.** C　**6.** B　**7.** B　**8.** D　**9.** D　**10.** A

11. B　**12.** B　**13.** B　**14.** B　**15.** C　**16.** C　**17.** D　**18.** D　**19.** C

　　历届高考题选7　**1.** D　**2.** A　**3.** B　**4.** D　**5.** D　**6.** C　**7.** B　**8.** C　**9.** B　**10.** A

11. D　**12.** D　**13.** A　**14.** B　**15.** B　**16.** C　**17.** D　**18.** C　**19.** A

　　历届高考题选8　**1.** B　**2.** D　**3.** C　**4.** A　**5.** C　**6.** A　**7.** A　**8.** B　**9.** A　**10.** D

11. C　**12.** C　**13.** B　**14.** C　**15.** D　**16.** A　**17.** C　**18.** A　**19.** D　**20.** D

　　历届高考题选9　**1.** D　**2.** B　**3.** C　**4.** C　**5.** A　**6.** B　**7.** B　**8.** A　**9.** B　**10.** B

11. B　**12.** C　**13.** D　**14.** D　**15.** C　**16.** B　**17.** D　**18.** B

第八章　非谓语动词

　　历届高考题选1　**1.** C　**2.** A　**3.** B　**4.** B　**5.** D　**6.** B　**7.** C　**8.** A　**9.** B　**10.** D

11. A **12.** C **13.** B **14.** D **15.** B **16.** B **17.** A **18.** A **19.** A

历届高考题选2 **1.** D **2.** B **3.** C **4.** B **5.** B **6.** C **7.** A **8.** D **9.** A **10.** B

11. A **12.** B **13.** D **14.** C **15.** A **16.** D **17.** D **18.** B **19.** A **20.** D

历届高考题选3 **1.** B **2.** A **3.** A **4.** D **5.** C **6.** B **7.** C **8.** D **9.** B **10.** A

11. C **12.** D **13.** C **14.** A **15.** A **16.** D **17.** A **18.** A **19.** D **20.** A

历届高考题选4 **1.** B **2.** B **3.** D **4.** D **5.** C **6.** B **7.** A **8.** A **9.** D **10.** B

11. C **12.** C **13.** B **14.** D **15.** A **16.** B **17.** A **18.** D **19.** C **20.** C **21.** D

历届高考题选5 **1.** D **2.** C **3.** C **4.** C **5.** B **6.** A **7.** B **8.** B **9.** A **10.** D

11. B **12.** C **13.** D **14.** B **15.** A **16.** B **17.** D **18.** D **19.** B **20.** C **21.** C **22.** A

历届高考题选6 **1.** A **2.** B **3.** C **4.** D **5.** C **6.** D **7.** C **8.** B **9.** A **10.** B

11. A **12.** C **13.** A **14.** D **15.** A **16.** D **17.** C **18.** B **19.** A **20.** B **21.** A

历届高考题选7 **1.** C **2.** C **3.** B **4.** B **5.** D **6.** B **7.** C **8.** A **9.** C **10.** A

11. C **12.** C **13.** C **14.** B **15.** A **16.** B **17.** A **18.** B **19.** D **20.** C **21.** B

历届高考题选8 **1.** B **2.** B **3.** A **4.** A **5.** A **6.** D **7.** C **8.** A **9.** C **10.** C

11. B **12.** B **13.** A **14.** C **15.** D **16.** B **17.** B **18.** D **19.** C **20.** A

历届高考题选9 **1.** D **2.** B **3.** D **4.** A **5.** C **6.** A **7.** D **8.** B **9.** A **10.** D

11. A **12.** C **13.** A **14.** C **15.** A **16.** B **17.** A **18.** D **19.** C **20.** B

历届高考题选10 **1.** B **2.** C **3.** D **4.** D **5.** B **6.** D **7.** A **8.** D **9.** A **10.** A

11. D **12.** A **13.** C **14.** D **15.** A **16.** B **17.** B **18.** A **19.** C **20.** B

第九章　主谓一致

历届高考题选 **1.** A **2.** A **3.** C **4.** C **5.** B **6.** D **7.** D **8.** A **9.** A **10.** D

11. A **12.** A **13.** C **14.** C **15.** D **16.** B **17.** C **18.** C **19.** A **20.** D **21.** B

第十章　反意疑问句　祈使句和感叹句

历届高考题选 **1.** D **2.** D **3.** B **4.** C **5.** D **6.** C **7.** D **8.** C **9.** C **10.** D

11. D **12.** A **13.** D **14.** C **15.** A **16.** C **17.** A **18.** A **19.** B **20.** C **21.** C **22.** A

第十一章　it 用法和强调句　there be 句型

历届高考题选1 **1.** A **2.** B **3.** B **4.** B **5.** A **6.** B **7.** B **8.** B **9.** A **10.** B

11. D **12.** B **13.** D **14.** B **15.** C **16.** B **17.** C **18.** D **19.** D **20.** D **21.** C

历届高考题选2 **1.** D **2.** B **3.** D **4.** B **5.** A **6.** A **7.** C **8.** A **9.** D **10.** C

11. A **12.** B **13.** D **14.** D **15.** C **16.** A **17.** C **18.** C **19.** C **20.** D **21.** D **22.** D

第十二章　省略和倒装

历届高考题选1 **1.** B **2.** C **3.** D **4.** D **5.** B **6.** C **7.** C **8.** A **9.** C **10.** D

11. D **12.** B **13.** D **14.** C **15.** C **16.** D **17.** B **18.** B

历届高考题选2 **1.** D **2.** A **3.** A **4.** C **5.** C **6.** A **7.** D **8.** A **9.** D **10.** B

11. A **12.** B **13.** B **14.** D **15.** C **16.** C **17.** A **18.** B **19.** B

历届高考题选3 **1.** A **2.** D **3.** B **4.** B **5.** A **6.** A **7.** B **8.** B **9.** C **10.** A

11. D　**12.** B　**13.** B　**14.** B　**15.** B　**16.** D　**17.** A　**18.** C

第十三章　并列句

历届高考题选1　**1.** D　**2.** C　**3.** C　**4.** D　**5.** D　**6.** D　**7.** C　**8.** D　**9.** D　**10.** C
11. D　**12.** A　**13.** D　**14.** C　**15.** D　**16.** B　**17.** A　**18.** A　**19.** A　**20.** D
历届高考题选2　**1.** B　**2.** D　**3.** B　**4.** A　**5.** D　**6.** A　**7.** C　**8.** D　**9.** A　**10.** D
11. B　**12.** A　**13.** A　**14.** B　**15.** D　**16.** B　**17.** C　**18.** D　**19.** B　**20.** D　**21.** C

第十四章　状语从句

历届高考题选1　**1.** D　**2.** C　**3.** A　**4.** B　**5.** A　**6.** C　**7.** C　**8.** C　**9.** C　**10.** A
11. D　**12.** C　**13.** B　**14.** B　**15.** B　**16.** C　**17.** C　**18.** D　**19.** A　**20.** C
历届高考题选2　**1.** C　**2.** B　**3.** D　**4.** C　**5.** C　**6.** B　**7.** D　**8.** B　**9.** A　**10.** B
11. B　**12.** D　**13.** B　**14.** A　**15.** A　**16.** D　**17.** A　**18.** D　**19.** A　**20.** C　**21.** A
历届高考题选3　**1.** C　**2.** A　**3.** B　**4.** A　**5.** A　**6.** C　**7.** D　**8.** B　**9.** A　**10.** A
11. C　**12.** D　**13.** B　**14.** D　**15.** D　**16.** A　**17.** B　**18.** B　**19.** B·**20.** D　**21.** D　**22.** A
23. B
历届高考题选4　**1.** B　**2.** C　**3.** C　**4.** D　**5.** D　**6.** B　**7.** D　**8.** D　**9.** B　**10.** A
11. B　**12.** D　**13.** D　**14.** A　**15.** A　**16.** B　**17.** D　**18.** B　**19.** D　**20.** A　**21.** C　**22.** B

第十五章　名词性从句和定语从句

历届高考题选1　**1.** A　**2.** A　**3.** B　**4.** A　**5.** D　**6.** B　**7.** D　**8.** A　**9.** B　**10.** D
11. C　**12.** D　**13.** A　**14.** B　**15.** B　**16.** B　**17.** B　**18.** A　**19.** B　**20.** D　**21.** A　**22.** C
历届高考题选2　**1.** D　**2.** C　**3.** C　**4.** D　**5.** C　**6.** C　**7.** B　**8.** B　**9.** A　**10.** C
11. D　**12.** B　**13.** C　**14.** A　**15.** A　**16.** C　**17.** C　**18.** A　**19.** A　**20.** A　**21.** B
历届高考题选3　**1.** A　**2.** D　**3.** B　**4.** B　**5.** B　**6.** D　**7.** D　**8.** D　**9.** C　**10.** B
11. C　**12.** A　**13.** A　**14.** C　**15.** A　**16.** B　**17.** C　**18.** D　**19.** B　**20.** B
历届高考题选4　**1.** D　**2.** A　**3.** D　**4.** A　**5.** A　**6.** D　**7.** D　**8.** D　**9.** A　**10.** C
11. C　**12.** B　**13.** B　**14.** C　**15.** D　**16.** D　**17.** C　**18.** A　**19.** C　**20.** C　**21.** A　**22.** B
历届高考题选5　**1.** C　**2.** D　**3.** B　**4.** B　**5.** A　**6.** C　**7.** C　**8.** B　**9.** C　**10.** C
11. A　**12.** B　**13.** C　**14.** C　**15.** A　**16.** C　**17.** C　**18.** C　**19.** C　**20.** B
历届高考题选6　**1.** A　**2.** B　**3.** A　**4.** C　**5.** B　**6.** D　**7.** D　**8.** D　**9.** B　**10.** C
11. C　**12.** C　**13.** C　**14.** C　**15.** A　**16.** A　**17.** B　**18.** B　**19.** B　**20.** A　**21.** D
历届高考题选7　**1.** C　**2.** A　**3.** D　**4.** D　**5.** C　**6.** D　**7.** C　**8.** D　**9.** A　**10.** B
11. B　**12.** D　**13.** C　**14.** B　**15.** B　**16.** B　**17.** D　**18.** A　**19.** D　**20.** C　**21.** B
历届高考题选8　**1.** D　**2.** D　**3.** A　**4.** B　**5.** A　**6.** C　**7.** D　**8.** A　**9.** A　**10.** A
11. B　**12.** D　**13.** D　**14.** D　**15.** D　**16.** B　**17.** D　**18.** A　**19.** D　**20.** C　**21.** D

第十六章　交际用语和谚语警句

历届高考题选1　**1.** D　**2.** D　**3.** C　**4.** C　**5.** D　**6.** C　**7.** D　**8.** B　**9.** A　**10.** B
11. A　**12.** D　**13.** C　**14.** A　**15.** D

历届高考题选2　1. A　2. D　3. C　4. B　5. B　6. A　7. C　8. C　9. C　10. B
11. A　12. C　13. C　14. B　15. C　16. A

历届高考题选3　1. B　2. A　3. C　4. B　5. D　6. D　7. B　8. B　9. D　10. B
11. C　12. C　13. D　14. A　15. D　16. A　17. D

历届高考题选4　1. C　2. D　3. A　4. A　5. D　6. B　7. B　8. B　9. D　10. A
11. D　12. A　13. D　14. D　15. C　16. A

历届高考题选5　1. A　2. B　3. D　4. B　5. D　6. D　7. D　8. B　9. B　10. D
11. B　12. A　13. A　14. B　15. B　16. A

第十七章　名词辨析

历届高考题选1　1. B　2. C　3. A　4. D　5. A　6. A　7. C　8. D　9. D　10. C
11. D　12. A　13. C　14. A　15. D　16. C　17. C　18. B　19. D　20. D　21. A
22. A

历届高考题选2　1. D　2. C　3. A　4. B　5. D　6. B　7. D　8. D　9. B　10. C
11. A　12. B　13. C　14. D　15. D　16. C　17. B　18. C　19. B　20. D　21. D　22. B

历届高考题选3　1. B　2. D　3. B　4. D　5. D　6. C　7. B　8. D　9. A　10. C
11. A　12. A　13. C　14. C　15. C　16. A　17. B　18. A　19. D　20. A　21. B　22. B

第十八章　形容词和副词辨析

历届高考题选1　1. A　2. C　3. C　4. B　5. B　6. B　7. B　8. C　9. D　10. A
11. A　12. B　13. B　14. C　15. D　16. B　17. C　18. C　19. A　20. D　21. B　22. C

历届高考题选2　1. B　2. C　3. C　4. A　5. D　6. A　7. B　8. A　9. B　10. B
11. C　12. B　13. A　14. B　15. C　16. B　17. B　18. D　19. A　20. B　21. A　22. C

历届高考题选3　1. B　2. A　3. C　4. A　5. B　6. A　7. C　8. A　9. A　10. D
11. A　12. B　13. D　14. C　15. B　16. A　17. A　18. B　19. C　20. C　21. B　22. C

第十九章　动词和动词词组辨析

历届高考题选1　1. D　2. B　3. D　4. D　5. C　6. C　7. D　8. B　9. B　10. C
11. C　12. A　13. A　14. D　15. B　16. A　17. B　18. C　19. A　20. C　21. B

历届高考题选2　1. C　2. D　3. B　4. A　5. D　6. B　7. A　8. A　9. B　10. D
11. B　12. A　13. A　14. B　15. B　16. D　17. B　18. C　19. D　20. A　21. C　22. B

历届高考题选3　1. D　2. A　3. B　4. C　5. C　6. C　7. A　8. A　9. D　10. D
11. D　12. B　13. D　14. A　15. A　16. B　17. D　18. D　19. A　20. D　21. B
22. A

历届高考题选4　1. B　2. A　3. B　4. D　5. C　6. D　7. B　8. C　9. D　10. B
11. C　12. B　13. A　14. A　15. D　16. A　17. B　18. C　19. A　20. D　21. B

历届高考题选5　1. C　2. B　3. B　4. D　5. C　6. C　7. D　8. B　9. A　10. A
11. D　12. A　13. A　14. C　15. A　16. C　17. D　18. C　19. B　20. C　21. D　22. D

历届高考题选6　1. C　2. A　3. A　4. C　5. B　6. B　7. A　8. D　9. A　10. C
11. A　12. B　13. D　14. A　15. A　16. B　17. A　18. C　19. C　20. B　21. B　22. B

23. C **24.** B

历届高考题选7 **1.** A **2.** B **3.** D **4.** C **5.** A **6.** A **7.** A **8.** A **9.** C **10.** B
11. D **12.** B **13.** A **14.** D **15.** B **16.** C **17.** A **18.** C **19.** C **20.** A **21.** C

历届高考题选8 **1.** B **2.** D **3.** D **4.** B **5.** B **6.** A **7.** D **8.** C **9.** A **10.** D
11. A **12.** D **13.** A **14.** A **15.** C **16.** C **17.** B **18.** C **19.** B **20.** A **21.** C **22.** D

第二十章 综合提高训练

综合提高训练1 **1.** C **2.** A **3.** D **4.** B **5.** B **6.** B **7.** A **8.** D **9.** A **10.** C
11. C **12.** C **13.** D **14.** A **15.** B **16.** B **17.** B **18.** A **19.** C **20.** D **21.** A
22. B **23.** B **24.** C **25.** D **26.** D **27.** C **28.** A **29.** C **30.** B

要点精讲

第1题 anything but"一点儿都不,根本不,决不",如:She is anything but a good nurse. 她根本不是个好护士。B项 expect"等待,期待",一般指预计某事将会发生,因而有心理准备,如:We put an extra plate on the table as we are expecting John to come for dinner. D项 but for"要不是,如果没有",只和虚拟语气的动词形式连用。如:But for your help, he would have failed. (等于 If it were not for your help, he would...)

第2题 rather than "而不是",连接词,可连接名词、代词、形容词、动名词、不定式等,用于肯定前者,否定后者。如:He is a reporter rather than a writer. 他是个记者而不是作家。B项 more than"多于",如:By then he was more than fifty years of age.

第3题 risk 后面要接动名词作宾语,不能接动词不定式。B项 miss"错过,漏掉",如:We missed the film when it was shown at the local cinema. 本市影院上映这部影片时,我们没能看上。lose"失去,丢失,丧失",lose every penny"丧失掉(投资进去的)每一个便士",即血本无归。

第4题 be inclined to do sth. "倾向于,易于做某事",如:Many language teachers are inclined to talk too much in class. 许多教语言的老师总是在课堂上喋喋不休。D项 tend to"倾向于,易于",只用于主动语态中。如:He tends to pitch the ball too high. 他往往会把球掷得过高。

第5题 pull through"恢复健康,渡过危机"。如:We had a rough time but we managed to pull through. 我们曾受过苦难,但是我们设法渡过了难关。A项 pull over"把(车)开到路边",如:The policeman made me pull my car over. 警察让我把车开到边上。C项 pull off"成功地完成了(一项困难的)工作",如:They managed to pull off the programme despite the lack of funds. 尽管缺乏资金,他们还是设法实现了计划。D项 pull up"使(车)停下来",如:The driver pulled up his car at the sight of the red light. 司机一看见红灯就把汽车停了下来。

第6题 keep sb. in the dark"对某人保密,不让某人知道"。in the dark 指黑暗无光的状态,引申为对某事毫不知情。dark 前一定有定冠词 the。A项 illiterate"文盲的,无知的"。D项 unknown"不为人所知,不出名的"。

第7题 A项 bring down"降低,使落下",与 fever 形成搭配。B项 settle down"安居,定居",C项 run down"贬低,筋疲力尽",D项 get down"写下",都与句子表达的意思不吻合。

第8题 be absorbed in... "全神贯注于……",如:She was absorbed in the novel. 她读小说入了神。A项 entertained"招待,款待"。C项 attracted"被……所吸引",后面常接介词 to,如:The visitors are attracted to the scenery of the west. 来访者为西部的景色所吸引。

第 **9** 题　cope with"克服,应付",如:We know how to cope with the complicated situation. 我们知道如何应付这复杂的局势。B 项 get along"进展",C 项 arrange"安排",D 项 overlook"漏看",都与句意不吻合。

第 **10** 题　ignorant"无知的",主要指对一般常识或一门学问无知,也可以指对具体事物无知。如:I am ignorant of the French language. 我对法语一无所知。A 项 unwise"不明智的"。B 项 dull"迟钝的"。

第 **11** 题　mended,动词过去式,是用在 It is high(about) time + that-clause 结构里从句的谓语动词形式。如:It is high time we went to bed. 我们该睡觉了。It is about time we summed up our results. 该总结一下我们的成绩了。

第 **12** 题　beyond control"无法控制",如:These boys are beyond control. 这些孩子无法管理。D 项 under control"受到控制,在控制之下"。通常的搭配是 get sth. under control,如:He cautioned that it took time to get budgets under control. 他警告说要使预算得到控制是需要时间的。A 项 above 和 B 项 outside 不能与 control 搭配。

第 **13** 题　略。

第 **14** 题　put up"建立,建起"。B 项 get up"起床"。C 项 raise"抬起,举起"。D 项 arise "出现"。

第 **15** 题　breathe"呼吸",用作动词。A 项 breath"呼吸",用作名词。C 项 blast"爆炸,冲击"。D 项 absorb"吸收(水、热、光等)"。

第 **16** 题　attentively"聚精会神地,专心地",如:They listened attentively to the teacher. 他们专心地听老师讲话。A 项 absolutely"绝对地"。C 项 obviously"明显地"。D 项 constantly"一贯地"。

第 **17** 题　agree"同意,赞成",可接不同的介词构成短语并与特定的名词搭配。agree to + 提案或建议(plan,proposal),如本题的句子,意思是"我同意你的建议"。A 项 agree with + sb. 表示同某人的意见一致,如:I quite agree with you on that point. 在这一点上,我完全同意你的看法。C 项 agree on 后要接确定的一件事,就某事达成协议或取得一致意见,如:The two sides have agreed on all the terms. 双方就所有的条款达成了一致意见。D 项 agree about 与 agree on 同义,如:The two governments don't agree about human rights. 两国政府在人权问题上意见不同。

第 **18** 题　average"平均的,一般水平的"。B 项 common"普通的,平常的"。C 项 middle "中间的,中部的"。D 项 minor"次要的,二流的"。

第 **19** 题　reason 后面只能接 for 表示"……的理由(原因)"。

第 **20** 题　That's 后面是 where 引导的表语从句,表示地点。又如:That is where I want to go. 这就是我要去的地方。第一句话问那所建筑是做什么用的,只有填入 D 项才能成为有意义的回答。

第 **21** 题　miserable"(心情)悲惨的,悲哀的",如:The old man felt very miserable when he learnt that his son was killed in the accident. B 项 merry"快活的",C 项 merciful"仁慈的",D 项 mysterious"神秘的",都与第二句的意思不吻合。

第 **22** 题　convenient"便捷的,方便的",住房离地铁站不远,出行方便,因此 B 项正确。A 项 suitable"合适的,适宜的"。C 项 comfortable"舒适的",住房离地铁近应该是"方便"而不是"舒适"。D 项 close 接介词 to 表示"接近的"。

第 **23** 题　be due to do sth. 表示"预定(于某时)做某事",如:He is due to meet us tomorrow morning. 他预定明天上午会见我们。A 项 arrange 表示"安排"时,它的搭配是(sb.) arrange sth. for...或 sth. is arranged for...,如:The Tourist Bureau has arranged everything for our journey to Rome. 旅游局为我们的罗马之行安排好了一切。I have arranged to meet her at 10 o'clock. 我定好 10 点与她见面。D 项 be about to 表示即将做某事,飞机航班是定点的,这些选项都不合适。

第 24 题　to your calling her 中 to 是介词,与不及物动词 object"反对"搭配,介词 to 之后用动名词 calling 作宾语,物主代词 your 是 calling 的逻辑主语。词组 object to doing sth. 表示"反对做某事"。

第 25 题　adjusting 是动名词,作 need 的宾语,need doing 等于 need to be done,在动词 need 之后作宾语用的动名词,主动形式表示被动意义。类似的动词还有:want, require, deserve, bear 等,如:The book deserves mentioning. 等于 The book deserves to be mentioned. 这本书值得一提。

第 26 题　seeing that"由于,因为",引导原因状语从句。A 项 to see that 不能起连接作用,B 项 that 连接主语从句,C 项 while 可连接时间或让步状语从句,它们用在这里都不符合句子意思。

第 27 题　shape"形状",A 项 form"形式",B 项 pattern"模式",D 项 figure"体形",只有 C 项符合题意。

第 28 题　at first"起初",符合题意,其他三个均表示"首先,第一"。

第 29 题　none other than"不是别人,正是",如:The tall man that I saw was none other than Xiao Li. 我看见的那个高个男人不是别人正是小李。D 项 no more than"不过,仅仅",表示量的含义,如:We have designed no more than six kinds of lathes. 我们仅仅设计了六种车床。

第 30 题　look sb. up and down"上下打量某人"。

综合提高训练 2　1. C　2. D　3. A　4. D　5. C　6. D　7. C　8. B　9. A　10. B　11. A　12. D　13. C　14. B　15. B　16. C　17. A　18. A　19. C　20. D　21. B　22. D　23. B　24. A　25. D　26. C　27. B　28. D　29. A　30. B

要点精讲

第 1 题　effect"效果,影响,作用",作名词;用作动词时意思是"实现,使生效"。D 项 affect 是动词,意思是"影响"。A 项 result"结果"。B 项 defect"缺点"。

第 2 题　D 项 Strictly speaking"严格地说",A 项 Generally speaking"一般地说",B 项 Technically speaking"从技术角度上讲",C 项 Biologically speaking"从生物学角度讲"。

第 3 题　hold back"踌躇,退缩不前",B 项 hold out"坚持,维持"。C 项 hold down"压制"。D 项 hold on"继续,(电话)不挂线"。

第 4 题　urgent"紧急的",in urgent need of"急需"。A 项 insistent(指行为)"坚持的,迫切的",B 项 imminent"逼近的,危急的",C 项 important"重要的",都不与 need 构成搭配。

第 5 题　figure out"想出,解出"。A 项 puzzle over"对……感到迷惑不解"。B 项 point out"指出"。D 项 single out"挑出来"。

第 6 题　couldn't have been robbed 表示"(过去)当时不可能遭劫"。B 项 shouldn't have been robbed 表示"(过去)当时不应该遭劫"。A 项 shouldn't 和 C 项 couldn't 都不指过去。

第 7 题　主句与从句的主语不一致时,从句中的主语不能省略;while 指一段时间,when 指一点时间,所以应选 C 项。

第 **8** 题　for the sake of"由于……的缘故",如:He is ready to take all risks for the sake of his country. 他甘愿为祖国冒一切危险。

第 **9** 题　B 项 sight"视觉,视力",C 项 appearance"外观,外貌",D 项 view"视野,看法",它们与后面的 on his face 相连都不表达任何意思,而且句子中的 be surprised 只能是表情。只有 A 项 expression"表情,神情"正确。

第 **10** 题　get rid of"去掉,摆脱,处理掉"。A 项 get out of"逃脱,从……中得到"。C 项 get down to"开始认真对待",D 项 get around to"花时间和精力去做"。试比较:If you don't want to go,I suppose I can get rid of the tickets. 如果你不想去,我应该能够把票处理掉。You can't get out of paying your debts. 你逃避不了还债。I'll get down to my studies as soon as the holidays are over. 假期一结束我就要认真学习了。I finally got around to the job again. 我终于有机会又做那件工作了。

第 **11** 题　turn up"出现,到来",如:None of us expected the chairman to turn up at the party. We thought he was still in hospital. 我们谁也没有料到主席会在聚会上露面。我们都以为他还在住院。B 项 turn in"上交"。C 项 turn back"折回,往回走"。D 项 turn round"转身,转交"。

第 **12** 题　"委员会"这个词要求选择 D 项 chairman"主席"。A 项 chief"首领"。B 项 principal"校长"。C 项 head"首脑,首长"。

第 **13** 题　damage"损害,损坏",不用于人,如:A great deal of damage was done to the fruit trees last year. 去年果树受害很大。A 项 destruction"毁坏",如:Dishonesty was his destruction. 他的不老实把他毁了。B 项 ruin"毁坏,崩溃",多指建筑物的毁坏,还表示人的感情方面的崩溃,如:His arrogance brought about his ruin. 他的骄傲自大导致他身败名裂。D 项 disaster"灾难,灾害",如:A natural disaster occurred. 发生了自然灾害。

第 **14** 题　C 项 favorite"最喜欢的,偏爱的"。C 项 favorable"赞成的,有帮助的,有利的",如:The weather is favorable to the sowing of wheat. 气候有利于播种小麦。D 项 popular"受欢迎的,流行的",如:The writer is very popular among the workers. 这位作家很受工人的欢迎。

第 **15** 题　forbid sb. to do sth. 是动词 forbid 要求的搭配句型.

第 **16** 题　介词 despite"尽管"后面可以接名词、动名词,但不能接从句。"Despite the fact that..."中,fact 是名词,其后是同位语从句。

第 **17** 题　direct"指引"。direct sb. to some place 为某人指明去某地的方向。B 项 point 后不接表示人的名词,point sth. to 或 point sth. at 的意思是,"把……指向",如:The policeman pointed his gun to the robber. 警察把枪指向劫匪。C 项 explain"解释"。D 项 indicate"指出,表明",如:The snow indicates the coming of winter. 这场雪表明冬天来临。

第 **18** 题　adapt oneself to"使自己适应……",如:He adapted himself to the new job. 他使自己适应新的工作。B 项 adopt"收养,采纳,采用",如:They decided to adopt the new technique. 他们决定采用这项新技术。C 项 offer"提供"。D 项 turn"转,翻转"。

第 **19** 题　artificial"假的,人工的,人造的(以区别于天然的)",如:artificial flowers 人造花,artificial light 人造光,artificial pearls 人造珍珠。A 项 fake"伪造的,假冒的",如:a fake painting 赝品绘画,a fake doctor 假医生。B 项 unreal(指经历)"不真实,虚构的",如:The whole story seemed strangely unreal. 整个故事似乎都非常离奇。D 项 pretended"假装的"。

第 **20** 题　sense of humor"幽默感",类似的搭配还有 sense of history"历史感",sense of responsibility"责任感",sense of discipline"纪律性"等。

第**21**题　trap"陷阱"。fell into the trap 掉入陷阱。A 项 trail"行踪",C 项 trick"诡计"。

第**22**题　distinguish sb. from sb. else"把某人与另一个人区别开来",如:The twins were so much alike that it was impossible to distinguish one from the other. 这对双胞胎像得使人无法分辨。A 项 keep from (doing sth.) 表示"阻止,防止(做某事)",如:Keep your little brother from playing on the road. 别让你的小弟弟在马路上玩。B 项 separate from 表示"使分离,使分开",如:England is separated from France by the English Channel. 英法两国被英吉利海峡隔开。C 项 divide into 表示"分成":The machine can be divided into three parts. 这台机器可分为三部分。

第**23**题　peak"顶峰,最高点"。

第**24**题　sth. occurred to sb. "某人突然想起某事"。B 项 sth. happened to sb. "某事发生在某人身上",如:She hoped nothing bad would happen to her son. 她希望不要有什么坏事发生在她儿子身上。另外 happen to do sth. 是"碰巧发生(做)了某事",如:She happened to be out. 她碰巧不在家。C 项 hit at"碰撞"。D 项 appear to 等于 seem to,如:He appears to have finished the job. 他好像把活干完了。

第**25**题　in case"万一,假使",如:Let's take our raincoat in case it rains. 咱们带上雨衣以防万一下雨。C 项 provided"只要",如:I'll come provided I get well enough. 只要我身体好我一定来。

第**26**题　inquire"询问,查询"。A 项 acquire"获得,得到"。B 项 request"要求,请求"。C 项 require"需要,要求"。

第**27**题　指代上文的名词要用 that 或 those,根据指代名词的数来决定。这里上文的 culture and customs 为复数,答案应是 B 项 those。

第**28**题　A 项 run for..."为(某职位)竞选",如:Bush was running for President. 布什当时在竞选总统。B 项 run off"逃走"是不及物动词。C 项 run after"追逐"可以和 the thief 形成搭配,但与后半句...was about to escape 不吻合。D 项 run down"追查到,捕获到"与全句意思吻合。

第**29**题　sincere"衷心的,真诚的",与 apologies 组成正确搭配。B 项 earnest"热心的,认真的"。

第**30**题　Strong as he is 等于 Although he is strong. A 项 As he is strong 等于 Since he is strong,C 项 Being very strong 和 D 项 As a strong man 都与后半句意思不吻合。

综合提高训练3　**1**. B　**2**. D　**3**. C　**4**. D　**5**. B　**6**. C　**7**. D　**8**. D　**9**. A　**10**. B　**11**. B　**12**. A　**13**. A　**14**. C　**15**. A　**16**. D　**17**. B　**18**. C　**19**. A　**20**. D　**21**. B　**22**. A　**23**. D　**24**. C　**25**. C　**26**. A　**27**. C　**28**. B　**29**. D　**30**. C

要点精讲

第**1**题　in any case"无论如何,不管怎样",A 项 in no case"决不,在任何情况下都不",如:In no case should we give up. 我们决不应放弃。C 项 in case"以防万一"。D 项 in that case"在那种情况下"。

第**2**题　反意疑问句前一部分的谓语动词为肯定形式,后一部分就是否定形式;前面是否定形式,后面就是肯定形式,因此 B 项和 C 项是错误的。have to 和 have got to 相当于一个情态动词,含有 have to 的反意疑问句后面表示疑问部分的动词要使用 do(does, did)。如:We have to wait for the bus, don't we? 含有 have got to 的反意疑问句后面表示疑问部分的动词一般要用 have(has, had),如:The student hasn't got to answer all the questions, has he?

第**3**题 equipment"设备"是不可数名词,谓语动词用单数形式。设备要由人来进口,应使用被动语态。

第**4**题 B项 wages 和 D项 salary 都是劳动报酬,分别是"工资"和"薪金"的意思。wages 指支付给工人或仆役的工资,通常按周计算,有时也指临时工的工钱。salary 指有专门技能的人员、脑力劳动者、企业管理人员或经理人员的劳动所得,一般按月计或按年计算。A项 pay 可以兼指两者,不过发给海陆空军事人员的工资通常被称做 pay,如:The officer was rewarded with an increase in pay. 那位军官受到了加薪的奖赏。C项 income"收入",指某一段时间中所得,包括薪金、工资、商业收益、投资利润等。income tax 是"所得税"。

第**5**题 A项 held up"阻挡,耽搁"。C项 held out"坚持,不屈服"。此句应用被动语态,所以只有 B项 were held up 是正确的。

第**6**题 call on"访问,拜访",后面接被访问的人。

第**7**题 题干中有 from,只有 C项 derived 和 D项 adapted 可以与 from 构成搭配,adapt from"由……改编",如:This TV play is adapted from a novel of the same title. 这部电视剧是由同名小说改编的。A项 adopted"采用,收养"。B项 accept"接受"。C项 derived from"由……派生出来,起源于……",如:Many English words are derived from Latin. 很多英文单词起源于拉丁文。

第**8**题 题干中 take a stand 意思是"采取立场",后接 D项 against,表示"对……持反对立场",如:take a strong stand against international terrorism 强烈反对国际恐怖主义。

第**9**题 同"综合提高训练**1**"第**1**题。D项 but for"要不是"与虚拟语气的动词连用,如:But for your help, I wouldn't have been able to make such great progress. 要不是你给我帮助,我是不能有如此巨大进步的。

第**10**题 把 B项 Having finished writing 填入句中的空白,全句的意思是"John 写完信就匆匆赶到邮局发寄"。A项 As he was about to finish writing (the letter)"他就要把信写完的时候",C项 As he was writing (the letter)"他正写信的时候",在这两种情况下 John 都不会赶去邮局寄信。

第**11**题 means"方法,手段",单数与复数同形,作主语时,谓语动词用单数和复数都可以,如:There is(are) no means of getting there. 没有办法到那儿。句中有 every 修饰 means,因此谓语动词要用单数,所以 B项 has been 是正确答案。

第**12**题 combine with"使与……相结合",如:The important thing is that films should combine education with recreation. 重要的是影片应把教育同娱乐结合起来。

第**13**题 表示与过去事实相反的虚拟语气动词形式,在 If 从句中用动词过去完成时,在主句中用 would(should, could, might) + have done。lie 的过去分词是 lain,不是 B项中的 laid。

第**14**题 look out (for)"当心,注意",如:Look out for the fire. 当心炉火。B项 check out "结账后离开",如:We checked out of the hotel three days later. 三天后我们结账离去。A项 make out"辨认出",如:I made out a village in the distance. 我看见远处有个村庄。D项 carry out "执行,贯彻",如:It is easier to make a plan than to carry it out. 制订计划比执行计划容易得多。

第**15**题 sum up"总结"。It is necessary for us to sum up experience. 我们有必要总结一下经验。B项 pick up"拣起,拾起",C项 pack up"打包,收拾行装",D项 step up"促进,增进"都不能与 text 搭配。

第**16**题 enable sb. to do sth. "使某人能够做某事"。题干句子的意思是"便装使警察能够彻底调查案情"。如:Flying enables us to go from China to America in one day. 坐飞机可以使我们在一天内从中国到美国。A 项 engaged sb. to do sth. ,B 项 encouraged sb. to do sth,C 项 entitled sb. to do sth. 分别是"安置"、"鼓励"某人做某事,和"使(某人)有资格作某事",都与句意不合。

第 **17** 题 live 在本题的句子中作副词,也可以作形容词,意思是"实时地(的)"。To televise live 是"进行实况电视播放"。A 项 lively"活泼的,充满生机的"。C 项 living"有生命的,活着的"。D 项 alive 也是"活着的,有活力的",但只能用作表语。试比较:The concert will be broadcast live. 将现场直播这场音乐会。He told a lively story about his life in Africa. 他生动地讲述了在非洲的经历。Language is a living and continually changing thing. 语言是活的并且是不断变化的。These earthquake survivors are still alive. 这些地震幸存者仍然活着。

第 **18** 题 几个形容词修饰某一个名词,须按一定的顺序排列。一般说,意义较具体的或与名词关系较密切的形容词更靠近被修饰的名词,常见的排列顺序是:限定词 + 一般描绘性形容词 + 表示大小、形状的形容词 + 表示年龄、新旧的形容词 + 表示色彩的形容词 + 表示国籍、地区、出处的形容词 + 表示物质、材料的形容词 + 表示用途、类别的形容词或名词 + 被修饰的名词。如:A gloomy-looking grey wooden house 一间阴森森的灰色木屋。

第 **19** 题 on the occasion of"在……场合,在……的时候"。B 项 on occasion of 缺少定冠词是错误的。但是 on occasion 是"偶然"的意思。C 项 in the event of"如果,万一",作短语介词用。D 项 on the chance of"期待,指望",如:I went to the teacher's office on the chance of seeing him.

第 **20** 题 consult"咨询,求教,寻求信息",在它后面的搭配词可以是 lawyer,teacher,expert,doctor,dictionary,telephone book 等,如:consult dictionary"查字典"。A 项 inquire"询问,打听",不与 dictionary 搭配。C 项 search for"搜寻"。

第 **21** 题 由"数词 + 连字符 + 名词"组成的合成形容词,连字符后的名词一律用单数形式,如:a twenty-pound note 一张面值20镑的钞票。a five-year plan 一个五年计划。an eighteen-storey building 一座18层的大楼。

第 **22** 题 crude"天然的,未提炼过的",crude oil"原油"。B 项 rough"粗糙的",强调表面不平,不与 oil 搭配。C 项 raw"未经加工的,生的,未煮熟的",raw material"原材料",raw vegetables"生的蔬菜"。D 项 tough"粗壮的,坚韧的",不与 oil 搭配。

第 **23** 题 urge"极力主张,迫切要求",常用在句型 urge sb. to do sth. 中,如:The shopkeeper urged me to buy a hat. A 项 suggested"建议"常用句型 to suggest doing sth. 和 suggest + that 从句。B 项 considered"认为",C 项 imagined"想象",这两个动词后面都可以接 sb. to be...,在本题中与句子意思不吻合。

第 **24** 题 should have 是 should have sent her a present 的省略。B 项 ought to 也表示"应该",但其后缺少 have。A 项 must have 是表示揣测,D 项 have got to"必须"都与句意不吻合。

第 **25** 题 It is(was) + that 从句是强调句型。本题的句子强调的是时间状语,A 项 It is 的时态不对。

第 **26** 题 take notice of 意思是"注意"。B 项 take notes 是"记笔记",其他两个选项都没有此用法。

第 **27** 题 in that 等于 because"因为,在于",作连接词用,如:Liquids are like solids in that they have a definite volume. 液体和固体一样有着固定的体积。

第 **28** 题　curtain"大幕，窗帘"。A 项 screen"屏幕，银幕"。C 项 sheet"被单，纸张"。D 项 cover"罩"。

第 **29** 题　句中的 circle"圆形"和 square"正方形"都属于 shape"形状"。

第 **30** 题　above all"最重要的是"，A 项 after all"毕竟"。B 项 in all"全部，合计"。如：How much is it in all? 总共多少钱? D 项 first of all"首先"。

综合提高训练 4　**1**. A　**2**. D　**3**. D　**4**. B　**5**. A　**6**. D　**7**. A　**8**. C　**9**. C　**10**. B　**11**. D　**12**. A　**13**. B　**14**. B　**15**. C　**16**. C　**17**. C　**18**. D　**19**. B　**20**. A　**21**. D　**22**. C　**23**. D　**24**. B　**25**. B　**26**. D　**27**. A　**28**. C　**29**. B　**30**. A

要点精讲

第 **1** 题　contact"与……取得联系"，如：He contacted his dentist by telephone. 他打电话与他的牙医联系。B 项 contract"订合同"，如：He has contracted to build the bridge. 他已签约承建这座大桥。C 项 touch，用作名词时可表示"联系"：get in touch with sb. "与某人取得联系"，或 keep in touch with sb. "与某人保持联系"。D 项 connect"连接，联想"，如：He is connected with the affair. 他与这事有关。Many people connect Germany with beer. 许多人把德国与啤酒联想在一起。

第 **2** 题　at a loss"困惑，不知所措"，如：When asked about who is responsible for the accident, the driver found himself at a loss for an answer. 当问及谁应该为车祸承担责任时，司机茫然不知如何回答。A 项 at one's best"处于最佳状态"，如：He was at his best when he acted the part of John. 他扮演约翰时演得最好。B 项 in search (of)，"寻找"，如：The young mother walked thhrough the streets in search of her missing child. 那位年轻的母亲穿街步行寻找她丢失的孩子。C 项 on the point (of)，"正要……的时候"，如：I was on the point of leaving when you called. 你打电话时我正要走。

第 **3** 题　impress sth. on sb. "使某人对某事留下深刻印象"，如：This lesson is impressed on my mind. 这课书深深地印在我的脑海里。A 项 express"表达，表示"，如：No words can express my gratitude to you. 我对你的感激是无法用语言表达的。C 项 suppress"压抑"，B 项 press...on sb. "强加……于某人"，如：He tried to press his opinions on me. 他要把他的看法强加于我。

第 **4** 题　call off"取消"。A 项 call for"要求"，C 项 call on"号召，拜访"，D 项 call up"打电话给某人"。

第 **5** 题　process"（工艺）程序，制法"，如：Television sets are now manufactured by a highly automatic process. 电视机目前是以高度自动化的工序制造的。C 项 procession"行进，队列"，如：The students marched in procession. 考生列队前进。

第 **6** 题　fanned"激起，煽动"，由名词 fan"扇子"转化而来，常与表示感情的名词搭配，如：Her tender care fanned his love. 她温柔体贴的关怀唤起了他的爱意。A 项 increased，B 项 promoted 和 C 项 made 一般不与这样的名词搭配。

第 **7** 题　B 项 present (at)，"出席，存在"。C 项 absence (from)，D 项 absent (from)"缺席，未到场"。A 项、C 项是名词，B 项、D 项是形容词。A 项、B 项与介词 at 搭配，C 项、D 项与介词 from 搭配。

第 **8** 题　take a...attitude towards...和 take...measures against...都是正确的英语搭配。题干中有了介词 towards。A 项 effective measures"有效措施"和 B 项 decisive measures"果断措施"都不宜填入题干中的空白。对待污染问题应持 C 项 a firm attitude"坚定态度"，而不是 D

项 a hostile attitude"敌对态度"。

第9题 A项 answer to a question"问题的回答";B项 key to exercises or test items"练习或考试题的答案";C项 solution to a problem"解决问题的办法";D项 remedy for a fault"错误的补救措施"。

第10题 protect"保护"。A项 prevent"防止"。C项 defend"防御"。D项 save"挽救,拯救"。

第11题 stain"污点,污渍"。B项 shadow"阴影"和C项 dirt"污物",它们都不符合题意。

第12题 smash"粉碎,摔成碎片"。B项 flatten"弄平,使变平",如:Can you flatten a piece of metal by hammering it? 你能将一块金属打扁锤平吗? C项 ruined"毁坏",如:Heavy smoking ruined his health. 过量吸烟毁了他的健康。D项 spoiled"变坏,弄坏",如:Fish and meat spoil easily in heated rooms. 鱼和肉在热烘烘的房间里容易变质。

第13题 capture"捕获",如:The police have captured the criminal. 警方已将罪犯捕获。C项 seize"抓住,抓紧",指突然用力抓住,如:The policeman seized the pickpocket by the collar. 那警察抓住扒手的衣领。A项 arrest"逮捕,拘捕(人)"。D项 grasp"抓紧",如:He grasped my hand and shook it. 他紧抓住我的手握了握。

第14题 neglect"疏忽,忘记",后面可以接名词,如本题的例子,也可以接动词不定式或动名词短语,如:Don't neglect to lock the door when you leave. 离开时请不要忘记把门锁上。A项 ignore"忽视,不理睬",如:She saw him coming but ignored him. 她看见他走过来但没理睬他。

第15题 by far"……得多,在很大程度上",用来修饰比较级和最高级。如:He is by far the best man for this job. 他最适合做这项工作。This is by far the longest bridge over this river. 这无疑是这条河上最长的一座桥。A项 by and by"渐渐地"。B项 as far as,短语连接词,常用在 as far as I know"就我所知",as far as I am concerned"就我而言"等表达式中。D项 by then"到那时"。

第16题 convince"使确信,使信服",着重指理智上的信服,如:I am convinced of his innocence. 我相信他无罪。B项 confirm"确定,进一步证实",如:The hotel confirmed our reservation by telegram. 旅馆打电报来确认我们预定的房间。A项 convict"证明……有罪"和D项 concern"关心"。

第17题 give way to"让路,让位"。B项 get out of the way(去掉选项中后面的 of),表示"让开路"。A项 stood in the way of"挡住……的去路"。D项 made its way for"朝(向)……走去"。

第18题 look upon"看待,看作",如:The students looked upon their football team's victory as an honor to their school. 学生把他们足球队的胜利看成是全校的光荣。A项 look at"注视",B项 look for"寻找",C项 look down on(upon)"轻视,看不起"。

第19题 throw light on"给人启发,给出线索"。C项 a good solution to 和 D项 an easy approach to 与后面的 problem 构成搭配,但不能与 throw 构成搭配。

第20题 track down"跟踪,追捕,追查",如:He tracked down every suspicious item in the expense account. 他抓住每一笔可疑的开支账目进行追查。B项 trace back"追溯",如:The origin of sericulture can be traced back to 2640 B.C. 养蚕技术的起源可以追溯到公元前2640年。C项 trade on"利用",如:I know he is trading on my lack of experience to gain his end. 我知道他是在利用我缺乏经验来达到他的目的。D项 trail behind"跟在后面"。

第 **21** 题　stare at"凝视",强调目不转睛地看。A 项 glare at"怒视",如:The two men glared at each other. 这两个人怒目相视。B 项 watch 和 C 项 view 不能与 at 连用。

第 **22** 题　There is no point(in)doing sth."做某事毫无意义",类似的结构还有:There's difficulty(in)doing sth."做某事有困难"。

第 **23** 题　"might have + 动词过去分词"表示"本来可以做,可能已做了"是对过去行为的推测。如:They know the city so well that I guess they might have been there before. 他们那么熟悉那个城市,我猜想他们以前可能到过那儿。C 项"must have + 动词过去分词"表示"一定是,准是",是对过去的行为做肯定的推测。如:It must have rained last night. The ground is wet. 昨晚一定下雨了。地上湿乎乎的。

第 **24** 题　to have been injured,不定式的完成时,常与 to be said, to be reported, to be known, to be understood, to be found, to be supposed 等等连用,表示这个动作或状态发生在句中谓语动词动作之前。如:Mrs. Brown is supposed to have left for Italy last week. 布朗夫人上周就该动身去意大利。

第 **25** 题　whoever 引导一个名词性从句,等同于 anyone who,并在从句中作主语。本题中 whoever 作 needs 的主语,同时又作主句中介词 to 的宾语。

第 **26** 题　先行词 it 是形式主语,实际主语是后面的动词不定式短语。句中的形式主语或形式宾语只能用 it,不能用 this 或 that。

第 **27** 题　不定代词 anyone 常出现在否定句和疑问句中。

第 **28** 题　谓语动词应用被动态,短语动词 make use of 中的"of"也不能省略,这句话改成主动态应是:We hardly ever made use of this possibility to raise production.

第 **29** 题　lest"以免,以防",从属连词,引导目的状语从句。从句中的谓语动词一般是"should + 原形动词",其他三个词不能引导目的状语从句。类似的连词还有:in case, for fear that,如:Batteries must be kept in dry places in case(lest, for fear that)electricity should leak away. 电池应放在干燥的地方,以免漏电。

第 **30** 题　any other student 在这里指的是班里除他以外任何别的考生,等同于 anyone else(in his class)。

综合提高训练 5　1. B　2. C　3. B　4. D　5. A　6. A　7. C　8. A　9. B　10. D 11. A　12. B　13. D　14. A　15. C　16. D　17. A　18. C　19. D　20. B　21. C 22. A　23. C　24. D　25. B　26. A　27. B　28. B　29. C　30. B

要点精讲

第 **1** 题　参照"综合提高训练 **2**"第 **22** 题。只有 separate 和 distinguish 可以和 from 搭配。其中 separate"分开",主要指把原来结合在一起或混在一起的人或物分离开来。A 项 distinguish"辨别,区分"和 tell 一样,着重于用感官去发现事物的差别,但 distinguish 更正式。

第 **2** 题　attempt"企图,尝试",后面接 at(doing)sth。如:My first attempt at photography failed. 我第一次摄影尝试失败了。B 项 desire"愿望,欲望",如:I'm filled with desire to go back there some day. 我渴望有朝一日能够旧地重游。A 项 trial 是动词 try 的名词形式,如:She succeeded in the GRE test on her third trial. 她第三次参加 GRE 考试时取得成功。D 项 request "请求,要求",如:The opportunity was granted him at his request. 这个机会是根据他自己的请求给他的。

第 **3** 题　potential"潜在的能力"。C 项 resource"资源"。A 项 material"题材,资料"。D 项

possession"所有,拥有",如:Who is in possession of the property? 谁拥有那些财产?

第4题　meanwhile"与此同时"。A项 otherwise"否则"。B项 moreover"而且,此外",如:The price is too high,and moreover,the house isn't in a suitable position. 这房价太高,而且地点也不合适。C项 therefore"因此,所以"。

第5题　release"释放"。B项 send 与 out 搭配,才表示"发射,发出"的意思,如:The sun sends out light and heat. 太阳散发光和热。C项 relieve"减轻",relieve 后面接表示病痛、紧张情绪等的词,如:What medicine will relieve a headache?

第6题　maintain"主张,强调",后面接 that 引导的名词性从句。B项 retain"保留,记住",如:I still retain clear memories of my childhood. 我对自己的童年时代仍然保留着清晰记忆。C项 persists"坚持",表示不顾外界的阻力把某事持续地做下去,后面接 in doing sth. ,如:Despite his poor health,he persists in working late at night every day. 尽管身体不好,他坚持每天工作到深夜。

第7题　likewise"同样地,照样地",等同于 similarly,in the same way,如:They went on foot and I did likewise. 他们步行去,我也步行去。A项 otherwise 或 B项 differently 与 think 相连表示"另有看法"或"有不同看法",与句中冒号后面半句话的意思矛盾。D项 alike"相似的",形容词,而且只能用作表语。

第8题　account"叙述,描述",后接 of,前面与动词 give 搭配。B项 story"故事",C项 introduction"介绍",与 story 搭配的动词是 tell,与 introduction 搭配的介词是 to。

第9题　warn"警告"。A项 mention"提及,说起",但不能省略 to。C项 point out"指出"。D项 urge"催促,迫切要求",如:The shopkeeper urged me to buy a hat. 那店主力劝我买一顶帽子。urge 后面不接 that 引导的从句。

第10题　serve"招待,上(菜)"。A项 present"提出,呈交"。C项 give"交给,托付"。表示上菜不用这两个动词。B项 cook"烹调",是在厨房里进行的工作。

第11题　take advantage of"利用",如:You should take full advantage of this opportunity to practise your oral English. 你应该充分利用这个机会练习说英语。其他三个选项均不能与 advantage 搭配。

第12题　barely"仅仅地,勉强地"。A项 fairly"相当,完全"。C项 subtly"细微地,巧妙地"。D项 vaguely"含糊地,模糊地"。

第13题　application"运用,实施",和它搭配的介词是 of 和 to,如:That is a case of the application of Marxism to the practice of the Chinese revolution. 这是把马克思主义运用到中国革命实践中的一个例子。C项 training"锻炼,培养",A项 study"研究",B项 attendance"出席,照料",这三个词与句尾的 to their work 连接起来都没有意义。

第14题　sense"价值,效用,意义",There's no sense in doing sth. "做某事毫无意义"。D项 meaning 可做"意义"解,但没有"价值,效用"的意思,不能代替 There's no sense in doing sth. 中的 sense。类似这样的结构还有 There is no use in doing sth. 和 There is no point in doing sth. 等。

第15题　admit"承认(事实、错误等)"。A项 indicated"表明,显示"。D项 advocated"拥护,主张"。

第16题　intelligent"聪明的,明智的"。A项 diligent"勤奋的"。B项 absorbed"全神贯注的"。C项 determined"下定决心的"。

第**17**题　endure"忍受",后面接表示痛苦意思的名词如 pain,hardships 等。B 项 undertake"从事,承担",它后面接表示任务和责任等词,如:The group decided to undertake investigations into the case. 这个小组决定对此案进行调查。

第**18**题　contribute"捐助,捐献",和介词 to 搭配。D 项 concentrate"集中于,全神贯注于",与介词 on 搭配。A 项 devote"奉献,贡献"。B 项 dedicate"奉献,把……用在",如:He dedicated the book to his wife. 他把此书献给他的妻子。

第**19**题　tremble"颤抖,抖动"。tremble with 表示颤抖的原因,如:The two girls trembled with fear when they heard footsteps approaching. 这两个女孩子听见越来越近的脚步声而吓得发抖。A 项 turned down"拒绝"。B 项 turn up"出现,到来"。

第**20**题　cozy"暖和的,舒适的"。C 项 casual"随便的,偶然的"。D 项 coarse"粗糙的,粗鲁的"。

第**21**题　interval 指"(时间的)间隔,间歇,幕间休息",如:There is a two-hour interval to the next train. 下一班火车还要过两小时。A 项 pause"停顿,暂停"。B 项 interruption"打断"。

第**22**题　a town too small to be on the map,其中 too small to be on the map 是修饰 a town 的后置定语。C 项 a too small town 如与后面成分相连,语序不对。B 项 a very small town 和 D 项 a town very small 与后面成分相连不能表达"太小以至于……"的意思。

第**23**题　has passed 与句子主语在人称上保持一致。当主语是表示时间、金钱的时候,强调一定量的总和,是单数概念,另外句子中的时间状语是 since 引导的从句,因此要用现在完成时。

第**24**题　参见"综合提高训练4"第25题。C 项 no matter who"无论是谁",引导让步状语从句,试比较:Those who break the law will be punished no matter who they are. 那些违法者都将受到惩罚,不管他们是谁。Whoever breaks the law will be punished. 违法者都要受惩罚。

第**25**题　providing"只要,假如",是引导的条件状语从句的连接词。A 项 provide,C 项 provides 和 D 项 to provide 是动词 provide"供给,提供"的不同形式。另外 provided 也有同样的意思和句法功能,如:I'll lend you the money,providing you pay it back in two weeks. 只要你在两周内把钱还回来,我就借给你。The apartment house can be built within three months provided that the supply of materials is sufficient and timely. 只要材料供应充足、及时,公寓可在三个月建成。

第**26**题　参见"综合提高训练1"第1题。

第**27**题　参见"综合提高训练4"第29题。in case 后面从句里说的是应该预防的情况,指以后可能发生的事,谓语动词要用一般现在时,也可以用"should + 原形动词",表示事情发生的可能性小。B 项 lest"唯恐,免得",从句中的动词常常是"should + 原形动词",如:Be quiet lest you should wake the baby.

第**28**题　as 引导一个部分倒装的让步状语从句:形容词(副词) + as + 主语 + 谓语,如:Young as she is,she has seen much of the world. 她虽然年轻,但却见过很多世面。A 项 As the soldiers were excited"由于士兵听到这消息都很激动",与后半句相连意思不通。

第**29**题　There is no telling...."难说,不清楚",如:There is no telling when he will be back. 说不清他什么时候会回来。

第**30**题　were hardly taken good care of 是被动语态,不能省略 of。

综合提高训练6　**1**. B　**2**. D　**3**. B　**4**. C　**5**. D　**6**. C　**7**. A　**8**. C　**9**. B　**10**. C

11. A **12**. D **13**. B **14**. A **15**. D **16**. A **17**. C **18**. D **19**. A **20**. B **21**. C
22. B **23**. D **24**. A **25**. D **26**. D **27**. C **28**. B **29**. A **30**. C

要点精讲

第**1**题　turn out"出来",全句意思"成千上万的人都出来看国庆节游行。"A项 turned off
"切断,关闭(煤气、自来水、电灯等)",如:Please turn off the ignition of a motor. 请关掉汽车的点
火装置。C项 turned up"出现,来到"。如:We thought he had been killed,but he turned up safe
and sound. 我们以为他已遇害,但他却安然无恙地出现了。D项 turned over"移交,考虑". 如:
to turn a matter over and over in one' mind 再三考虑一件事情。

第**2**题　本句是强调句。D项 led to"导致"。

第**3**题　incidents 多指政治性事件,如:As the result of the incident, the diplomatic ties
between the two countries were severed. 这起事件直接导致两国外交关系紧张。A项 accidents 指
有损失或伤亡的意外事故。如:There was a motor-car accident yesterday. 昨天有一起车祸。C
项 events 指重大事件。如:The discovery of America was a great event. 发现美洲是重大事件。D
项 happenings 指意外事件。如:The unfortunate happenings must now be described more fully. 这
些不幸事件现在肯定被描述得更详细一些了。

第**4**题　estimate"估计"。A项 consideration"考虑",名词。

第**5**题　embarrassed"窘迫的,为难的"。A项 discouraged"失去勇气的,灰心的",与B项
encouraged"受到鼓励的"互为反义词。

第**6**题　made out"书写,开列"。A项 passed on"传下去"。如:The veteran workers are
doing their best to pass on their technical knowledge to the younger generation. 老工人尽力把技术
传授给青年工人。B项 fished out"拖出,拉出"。D项 handed in"上交,递交"。

第**7**题　single out"挑选出"。如:The teacher singled me out for praise. 老师把我挑选出来
给予表扬。B项 work out"想出,制订出"。如:to work out a scheme for the whole project 为整个
工程设计出一个精密的计划。C项 take out"拿出,去除"。如:to have a tooth taken out 拔掉一
颗牙齿。D项 pick out"挑出,选出"。

第**8**题　similar to 是固定搭配。

第**9**题　responded to"对……作出回应(响应)"。A项 replied to"对……作答复",用于较
正式的文体中或表示较正式而且经考虑的答复。C项 answered"回答"使用场合广泛,可指口
头或书面的回答。D项 reacted to"对……作出反应",如:The audience reacted readily to his
speech. 听众对他的演说立即起了反应。

第**10**题　hold back"克制",如:Though very angry,I held back from telling him exactly what
I thought. 我虽然很生气,但仍然克制住没有将我的想法告诉他。B项 get back"回来,取回"。
D项 delay"延期,耽搁"。

第**11**题　bring sb. (sth.) through"使……渡过困难",如:to bring all the newly transplanted
seedlings through 使新移植的秧苗都能存活。

第**12**题　参见"综合提高训练5"第**14**题。

第**13**题　conduct"进行",如:to conduct an investigation 进行调查。A项 oprated"操作,开
动"。C项 performed"执行,表演",如:You should always perform what you promise. 你应永远履
行所承诺的事。

第**14**题　in addition to"除……之外",如:In addition to English,he has to study a second foreign language. 除了英语之外，他还要学习第二外国语。B 项 in support of "支持，援助"，如：He spoke in support of the plan. 他发言支持这项计划。C 项 owing to "因为，由于"，如：We couldn't get here in time owing to an accident. 由于一件意外事故，我们没能及时到达这里。

第 15 题　challenge "挑战，要求"。如：give(accept) a challenge 挑战(应战)。A 项 offer 意为"(主动提出来的)帮助，建议，赠予"等，如：refuse an offer of help 拒绝(别人提供的)帮助。B 项 order "命令"。C 项 charge "职责"，如：He resigned his charge at the university. 他辞去了在大学的职位。

第 16 题　loan "贷款"，如：The organization was authorized to make loans upon farm commodities. 该机构受权代理农产品贷款。B 项 finance "财力"，用复数形式。C 项 capital "资本"。D 项 debt "债务"。

第 17 题　award "授予，给予"，award a prize to sb. "授奖给某人"。全句意思是"由于玛丽在运动会上的出色表现她被授予最高奖项"。A 项 rewarded "答谢，报答"，如：His efforts were rewarded by success. 他的努力获得了成功。

第 18 题　be entitled to "被给予了……权利(资格)"。本题全句意思为"只有那些 60 岁或 60 岁以上的人有资格享受退休养老金"。如：This ticket entitles you to a free lunch. 你凭此券可以享受免费午餐一次。B 项 compelled "强迫，迫使屈服"。如：Circumstance compelled him to be desperate. 环境迫使他不顾一切。C 项 entailed "需要，必需"。如：The work entails precision. 这工作需要精确性。

第 19 题　commit "犯(错误，罪行)，干(坏事，傻事)"，常和 crime、suicide 这样的名词搭配使用。D 项 offended "冒犯，违犯"，如：offend against law 犯法。

第 20 题　respectable "可敬的，文雅的"，有被动含义。全句意思是"在图书馆吸烟被认为是不文雅的。"A 项 respectful "恭敬的，尊敬人的"，有主动尊敬他人的意思。C 项 respective "各自的，各个的"，如：They were chosen according to their respective merits. 他们是根据他们各自的优点被选拔出来的。D 项 respected "受尊敬的"，指年长的人或具有权威性的人。

第 21 题　find shelter from "获得……的保护"。

第 22 题　far more than "比……多得多"。句中把 do 和 complain 做比较，than 是比较连接词，全句的意思是"消费者所应该做的远不只是单单抱怨商品的低劣质量"。

第 23 题　that 是用于强调句型 It is(was)...that-clause 中的连词。

第 24 题　which 是关系代词，引导非限定性定语从句。

第 25 题　could not have been saved 是虚似语气动词形式。

第 26 题　由 neither 或 nor 打头的句子或从句用倒装语序。

第 27 题　whatever it is，"无论它是什么"，让步状语从句。D 项 However it is "不管它怎么样"。

第 28 题　of what was going to happen 是修饰 idea 的介词短语结构，介词要用 of。have some idea of sth. 对某事有一点了解。

第 29 题　略。

第 30 题　在表示愿望、建议、命令、要求等动词后的宾语从句中，从句的谓语动词形式一般是"should + 原形动词"，但是 should 可以省略。这类动词有 request "请求"，decide "决定"，propose "提议"，order "命令"，insist "坚持"等。

综合提高训练 7　**1.** D　**2.** A　**3.** C　**4.** C　**5.** B　**6.** B　**7.** A　**8.** D　**9.** C　**10.** A

11．B　**12**．D　**13**．A　**14**．C　**15**．D　**16**．A　**17**．B　**18**．C　**19**．D　**20**．A　**21**．D　**22**．C　**23**．B　**24**．A　**25**．C　**26**．D　**27**．B　**28**．C　**29**．A　**30**．B

要点精讲

第1题　issue"争论,争论点,问题",全句意思是"医疗改革已成为该城市最重要的公众健康问题。"A项 matter"事件,问题",如:It is a matter of habit. 这是习惯问题。C项 stuff"东西,材料",如:Many shoes nowadays are made of plastic or similar stuff. 现在许多鞋子都是用塑料或类似的材料做成的。

第2题　involved"所涉及的,有关的",过去分词作后置定语。B项 connected"有关联的,连接的",与介词 with 连用。C项 concluded"下结论的,推断的"。D项 evolved"发展的,引申的,推断的"。

第3题　beyond repair"无法修补的"。后半句的意思是"……无法修理的旧建筑物应该炸掉,为新建筑物腾出地方。"A项 out of repair"失修的,已损坏的"。B项 in repair"维修良好的"。D项 under repair"正在修补中的"。

第4题　contribute"有助于,为……作出贡献",与介词 to 搭配。B项 benefit"有益于,获益",与介词 from 搭配,如:He will benefit from the new way of doing business. 他会从经营业务的新方法中获益。A项 attribute"归于,属于",也与介词 to 搭配,如:They attributed their failure to poor judgment. 他们把自己的失败归咎于判断失误。D项 distribute"分配,分发",如:The teacher distributed the exam papers to the class. 老师把试卷分发给全班。

第5题　gain"获取,获得",全句意思是"你不听我们的劝告,将一事无成。"D项 gear"开动,以齿轮连接"。

第6题　ignore"不理睬,忽视",有故意不予理会的意思。D项 neglect"疏忽,忘记做"。neglect 有由于轻视而不认真做或不认真对待的意思,如:It seems to me that he has been neglecting his duty. 看来他一直在玩忽职守。A项 omit"遗漏,忽略",如:omit a letter in a word 在一个词中漏掉了一个字母。C项 overlook"漏看,未注意",如:to overlook a printer's error 看漏一个印刷错误。

第7题　turned down"拒绝",B项 turn away"(把某人)赶走,不许(某人)进入",如:Large crowds of people were turned away from the theatres. 大批人被拒之于剧院大门以外。C项 turned off"辞退"。D项 turned up"出现"。

第8题　ordinary"一般的,普通的"。全句意思是"这个地区的免费医疗包括精神病和一般的疾病。"B项 normal"正常的",如:A normal heart beats around seventy-six times a minute. 正常的心脏每分钟跳76次。A项 average"平常的、普通的",如:Take a sheet of paper of average thickness. 取一张普通厚度的纸。C项 regular"通常的,常规的",如:Do you want the regular size or this big one? 你要一般尺寸的,还是这个大号的?

第9题　estimate"估计",全句意思是"实际上不可能估计出世界上有多少人除了掌握自己的母语以外,还掌握了起码的英语。"A项 assess"评定"。B项 appraise"鉴定"。D项 evaluate"评价"。

第10题　survive"(经历灾难、危险等之后)仍然活着"。B项 endure"忍受"。C项 maintain"保持,维持",如:Be careful to maintain your reputation. 要小心维护你的名誉。D项 retain"保留,留住",如:Carbon dioxide catches and retains some of the sunlight's energy as heat. 二氧化碳以热的形式吸收并保留了一部分阳光中的能量。

第 **11** 题　lonely "孤独的,寂寞的",是形容词,指人精神、心理方面的孤独与寂寞。D 项 single "单一的,单个的",与 sole 同义,如:A single red rose stood in a glass on the table. 桌上的玻璃杯中只有一支红玫瑰。A 项 alone "单独的",形容词,可以作表语或宾语补足语,也可以当作副词作状语,如:These facts alone show that he's not to be trusted. 仅仅这些事实就足以说明他是不可信赖的。C 项 sole "唯一的,仅有的",如:My sole purpose is to make the information more widely available. 我唯一的目的是让更多的人能获得这些信息。

第 **12** 题　opportunities "机会,机遇"。全句意思是"将来受过高等教育的人会有很多新的机会。" open up opportunity for... "为……提供机会"。C 项 capabilities "能力,可能性"。A 项 responsibilities "责任,负担"。B 项 probabilities "可能发生的事,可能的结果"。

第 **13** 题　present "陈述,提出(观点,看法等)"。B 项 preserve "保存",如:Ice helps to preserve food. 冰有助于保存食物。C 项 propose "建议,提议",如:It was proposed that this matter be considered at the next meeting. 有人建议这个问题在下次会上讨论。D 项 proceed "(停止后)继续进行,进展",如:Proceed with what you were doing. 继续做你原来在做的事。

第 **14** 题　stuff "材料,素材,东西"。B 项 staff "全体职员",如:He is on the regular staff. 他是正式职员。A 项 objects "物体",如:Please tell me the names of the objects in this room. 请告诉我这屋里各个物件的名称。D 项 items "条目,一条新闻",如:Are there any interesting items in the paper this morning? 今天早晨报纸上有什么有趣的新闻吗?

第 **15** 题　afford "付得起,花得起",常与 can,could 或 be able to 连用。

第 **16** 题　sake "原因,缘故"。for the sake of "为了……的缘故,因为",是一个固定搭配,如:For the sake of our old friendship,do not leave me now. 为了我们多年的友谊,你现在不要离开我。B、C、D 三项不能这样搭配。

第 **17** 题　develop a habit "养成某种习惯"。C 项 acquired "习得,获得",不能和 habit 搭配。

第 **18** 题　notice "注意到",如:I noticed a big difference. 我注意到一大差别。

第 **19** 题　indicate "显示,表示"。A 项 declare "公告,宣布"。

第 **20** 题　average "平常的,普通的"。B 项 attractive "有吸引力的"。C 项 efficient "有效率的"。

第 **21** 题　constantly "经常地,不断地",如:He is constantly tearing up what he has already written and beginning over again. 他不断地撕了再写。A 项 extremely "极端地,过分地",如:It is extremely kind of you to invite me. 承蒙你邀请我,实在太客气了。

第 **22** 题　略。

第 **23** 题　all of whose homes,引导两个逗号之间的非限定性定语从句,定语从句修饰主语 the peasants,全句意思是"那些房屋全部被洪水毁坏的农民得到了政府的救济。"A 项 all of which homes 中的 which 不是所有格的关系代词,因此不能放在 homes 之前表示"他们的家园"。

第 **24** 题　as 是关系代词,引导句尾的定语从句,并在其中作 had told 的直接宾语。such... as 表示"像……那样的"。

第 **25** 题　句型"It's about(high) time + that-clause"里从句中的谓语动词要用过去式表示虚拟语气形式。A 项"should make + 原形动词"用在"It is(was) necessary(essential,insisted,suggested) + that-clause"结构中,两者不可混淆。

第 **26** 题　you didn't speak 是动词过去形式的名词性从句,用在 would rather 之后,是一种虚拟语气形式,表示说话人的愿望,如:I'd rather you didn't make any comment on the issue for the time being. 我宁愿你暂时不要对此事发表评论。C 项 you not speak 是 you should not speak 省去 should 的用法,可以用在"It is(was) necessary(essential,insisted,suggested) + that-clause"的结构中。

第 **27** 题　be said to have been translated 是复合谓语,全句的意思是"据说 Joe Hill 写的这首诗已译成汉语了。"句中不定式中的动词 translate 表示的动作发生在主句谓语动词 say 表示的动作之前,所以不定式须用完成形式。这个句子等同于 It is said the poem by Joe Hill has been translated into Chinese. 属于同类结构的句子还可以举出另一个例子,如:This method of printing is known to have been used as far back as the Song Dynasty. 众所周知,这种印刷方法早在宋代就已经使用了。

第 **28** 题　略。

第 **29** 题　avoid 要求动名词作宾语。

第 **30** 题　"couldn't + 动词完成时"表示对过去事实的否定推测。

综合提高训练 8　1. B　2. C　3. A　4. D　5. A　6. B　7. C　8. D　9. B　10. C
11. A　12. D　13. B　14. D　15. B　16. B　17. C　18. A　19. C　20. D　21. C
22. B　23. A　24. C　25. D　26. A　27. D　28. C　29. A　30. B

要点精讲

第 **1** 题　rewarding"有益的,有报酬的"。C 项 respectful"表示尊敬的,有礼貌的",如:He is always respectful to older people. 他对年龄大的人总是彬彬有礼。A 项 grateful"感激的,感谢的"。如:We were grateful for all you did. 我们对你所做的一切深表感激。D 项 demanding"费力的,苛求的",如:Language teaching is a demanding job. 语言教学是一项要求很高的工作。

第 **2** 题　全句意思是"今晚我没心情听流行音乐。"词组 be in the(no) mood to do sth. "有(没有)……的心情",如:My father seemed to be in no mood to look at my school report. 我父亲看起来没心思看我的成绩单。

第 **3** 题　get over"克服,战胜"。B 项 get away"离开,躲开",如:Don't ask him how he is because if he starts talking about his health you'll never get away from him. 千万别问他身体怎么样,要是他谈起来,你就甭走了。C 项 get off"跳下来,逃脱惩罚",如:Considering his record, he was lucky to get off with a six month sentence. 看看他的犯罪记录,判 6 个月刑已经够幸运的了。D 项 get through"完成,通过",如:I'll be with you as soon as I get through this work. 我完成这件工作后立即与你相会。

第 **4** 题　参见"综合提高训练 2"第 24 题。

第 **5** 题　contribution"贡献,捐助"。

第 **6** 题　share"共有,分享",如:They shared their joys and sorrows. 他们苦乐与共。

第 **7** 题　favorite"最喜爱的"。B 项 preferable"更可取的,更好的"。

第 **8** 题　make an effort to do sth. "努力去做某事",make every effort to do sth. 是"竭尽全力去做某事"。但是我们不说 make every attempt to do sth。

第 **9** 题　confirm"证实,确认"。全句意思是"来自前线记者的消息还没有得到证实。"如:The sad look on her face confirmed my suspicions that her husband had passed away. 她脸上悲伤的面容证实了我的猜疑:她丈夫过世了。A 项 affirm"断言,肯定地说"。C 项 reform"改革"。D

项 inform"通报,通知"。

第 **10** 题　value"价值,意义"。D 项 taste"味道,欣赏力",如:They don't show much taste in music. 他们在音乐方面没有欣赏力。

第 **11** 题　assist"帮助,援助",如:I assist him in compiling a dictionary. 我帮助他编字典。B 项 resist"抵制,抵抗",resist temptation 抵抗诱惑。C 项 insist"坚持(认为)",与 on 搭配。D 项 persist"坚持(做),执着",与 in 搭配。

第 **12** 题　profit"得益,利润",make a profit"获利",如:We can make a profit on everything we sell. 我们能从卖出的每样东西中获利。B 项 benefit"利益,恩惠",如:My trip to the south was of much benefit to my health. 我去南部旅行对我的健康很有益。

第 **13** 题　sense"意义",make sense"合理,能理解,有道理",如:To send troops abroad when we need them here simply does not make sense. 在国内需要军队的时候把他们派往国外,简直毫无道理。A 项 make sure"确信无疑,获得证实"。

第 **14** 题　spoil"惯坏,宠坏",如:Children who are over-protected by their parents may become spoiled. 受到父母过分保护的孩子易被宠坏。C 项 ruined"毁坏,毁灭",如:Heavy smoking ruined his health. 过度吸烟毁了他的健康。

第 **15** 题　hold back"抑制,阻止",如:Shortage of capital was a factor holding back economic development. 缺乏资金是阻碍经济发展的一个因素。C 项 hold up"延误",如:But since your train's leaving so soon, I'd better not hold you up here any longer. 既然你搭乘的火车快要开了,我就不多留你在此了。A 项 hold on"继续某事,坚持",如:How much longer can you hold on? 你们还能坚持多久?D 项 hold on to (sth),"握住……不放",如:Hold on to the rail or you'll slip. 抓住栏杆,不然你会滑倒的。

第 **16** 题　regualr"正规的、有规律的",如:Everything was regular when the fire broke out. 火灾发生时一切井然有序。D 项 normal"正常的,按照通常的情况",如:We took the infant's temperature and it was normal. 我们测了婴儿的体温,体温正常。

第 **17** 题　extremely"极端地,过分地",如:We welcome rain, but an extremely large amount of rainfall will cause floods. 我们希望下雨,但是降雨过多会造成水灾。D 项 extensively"广泛地,全面地"。

第 **18** 题　warn"警告,预告"。B 项 charge"指控,控告"。D 项 instruct"通知,告知"。

第 **19** 题　on the contrary"正相反"。B 项 by contrast"(与……)对照之下"。如:The rooms in the new flats were bright and spacious;by contrast their old houses looked dark and small. 新公寓的房间明亮、宽敞,对照之下他们的老屋则显得阴暗狭小。A 项 on the whole"整体看起来,就全体而论",如:On the whole the composition is well-written, although there's much room for improvement. 尽管仍有不少改进的余地,但就整体而言这篇作文写得不错。D 项 by comparison "同……相比较而言",如:This house is very expensive but it is really cheap by comparison. 这套房子非常昂贵,但比较而言它真是价格低廉的。

第 **20** 题　necessarily"必然地"。

第 **21** 题　in return"作为回报,以为报答",如:My friend sent me a present in return (for the help I had given to him). 我的朋友寄给我一件礼物作为(我给予他帮助的)报答。A 项 in reply "作为答复",后面与介词 to 搭配,如:in reply to your letter 为答复你的信。B 项 in turn"反过来"或"依次,轮流",如:Theory is based on practice and in turn serves practice. 理论的基础是实

践,又转过来为实践服务。D 项 in answer,后面也与介词 to 搭配,构成 in answer to"作为对……的回应",如:The doctor came at once in answer to my telephone call. 医生一接到我的电话立刻就来了。

第22题　A 项 someone else 和 C 项 somebody 一般用于肯定句。B 项 anyone else 和 D 项 anybody 用于否定句或疑问句。

第23题　as to 中的 to 是句尾动词不定式的标志,as 与前面的 not so much 构成固定搭配,表示"与其说……不如说……",如:It wasn't so much the clothes as the man himself who impressed immediately. 给人以深刻印象的与其说是衣服,还不如说是这个人本身。本题的意思是学校教育的重要效用与其说是传授知识,还不如说是教授学习方法。C 项 rather than"(是……)而不是……",通常强调 rather than 前面表达的意思,否定 rather than 后面表达的意思,如:He would beg in the streets,rather than get money in such a dishonest way. 他宁愿在街头乞讨,也不愿以这种欺诈手段骗钱。

第24题　略。

第25题　that 是引导同位语从句的连接词。全句意思是"已发现许多证据,表明这起交通事故是粗心的司机造成的。"在 idea,fact,rumour,thought,belief,order,doubt,concept,evidence 这类名词之后可以用 that 引导一个起解释说明作用的同位语从句。有时这个从句会离开它解释或说明的名词;特别是当这个名词在句中作主语的时候,句子的谓语部分就会把两者隔离开,本题的句子就是这样。

第26题　with 可以与复合结构"名词(人称代词) + 现在分词(过去分词)"搭配构成介词短语,作句中的状语,如:What is the family income with so many people working? 全家有这么多人干活有多少收入呢?

第27题　expected me to 的后面省略了前半句中的 pass the exam. 全句意思是"尽管我那位令人尊敬的老师期望我能通过这次考试,但我还是没有通过。"B 项 expect sth. of(from) sb. 是正确的英语搭配,如:Don't expect sudden improvements from this class. 不要指望这个班会有突然的改进。Parents often expect too muich of their children. 家长常常会对子女期望过高。

第28题　whatever"不管是什么"可以充当连词,引导状语从句,如:Whatever happens,I'll fulfil the task as planned. 不管发生什么事,我都要去按计划完成这项任务。

第29题　understood 作它前面 make himself 词组中宾语 himself 的补语。

第30题　参见"综合提高训练 1"第 1 题. C 项 despite"不管,尽管",等同于 in spite of,这种含义决定了它们不能和虚拟语气形式的谓语动词出现在同一个句子中。